The Warden's Daughter

Also by Jerry Spinelli

Stargirl

Love, Stargirl

Milkweed

Crash

Knots in My Yo-Yo String: The Autobiography of a Kid

Hokey Pokey

With Eileen Spinelli

Today I Will

Jerry Spinelli

The Warden's Daughter

A Yearling Book

Text copyright © 2017 by Jerry Spinelli
Cover art copyright © 2018 by Pascal Campion

All rights reserved. Published in the United States by Yearling, an imprint of Random House Children's Books, a division of Penguin Random House LLC, New York. Originally published in hardcover in the United States by Alfred A. Knopf, an imprint of Random House Children's Books, a division of Penguin Random House LLC, New York, in 2017.

Yearling and the jumping horse design are registered trademarks of Penguin Random House LLC.

Visit us on the Web! rhcbooks.com

Educators and librarians, for a variety of teaching tools, visit us at RHTeachersLibrarians.com

Library of Congress Cataloging-in-Publication Data is available upon request.

ISBN 978-0-375-83199-7 (trade) — ISBN 978-0-375-93199-4 (lib. bdg.) — ISBN 978-0-553-49463-1 (ebook) — ISBN 978-1-5247-1924-1 (intl. ed.)

ISBN 978-0-375-83202-4 (pbk.)

Printed in the United States of America
10 9 8 7 6 5 4 3
First Yearling Edition 2018

To Springton Lake Village

— and —

Anthony Greco
(Chubs)

CAMMIE

2017

It's a birdhouse now.

It used to be a jailhouse. The Hancock County Prison.

Cellblocks once rang with beanboppers on iron bars and bad words flying day and night. Now finches and warblers and scarlet tanagers sing and flutter behind walls of glass.

The old Quiet Room, with its glass roof and tin wheelbarrow pouring water into a tiny pool, was designed to keep the prisoners calm. Almost no one went there but the trustees who tended the plants and flowers. Now children squeal as butterflies land on their heads and shoulders.

Where there used to be two exercise yards—men's and women's—there is now a single garden, a paradise where turtles and peacocks roam. It has a second waterfall—high as the wall! Pebbled paths. Ponds. Water lilies. Foot-long goldfish.

An occasional turkey buzzard lands wherever it likes.

Except for the sign, it looks the same as always from the front: like a fortress from the Middle Ages. Massive, sooty stone walls. Arched oaken doors. A sky-piercing tower with narrow bow-and-arrow slots should the castle ever need defending.

The prison was one city block long. It was home to over two hundred inmates, men and women, from shoplifters to murderers.

And one family.

Mine.

I was the warden's daughter.

CAMMIE

1959

1

BREAKFAST TIME IN THE PRISON. THE SMELL OF FRIED scrapple filled the apartment. It happened every morning.

"I could teach you how to do it yourself," she said. "It's simple."

"I want *you* to do it," I said.

"You'll be a teenager soon. You'll have to learn someday."

"You're doing it," I told her. "Case closed."

Her name was Eloda Pupko. She was a prison trustee. She took care of our apartment above the prison entrance. Washed. Ironed. Dusted. And kept me company. Housekeeper. Cammie-keeper.

At the moment, she was braiding my hair.

"Okay," she said. "Done."

I squawked. "Already?" I didn't want her to be done.

"This little bit?" She gave it a tug.

She was right. I'd wanted a pigtail down the middle, but all my short hair allowed was barely a one-knotter. A pig*stub*.

I felt her leaving me. I whirled. "No!"

She stopped, turned, eyebrows arching. "No?"

I blurted the first thing that came to mind. "I want a ribbon."

Her eyes went wide. And then she laughed. And kept laughing.

She knew what I knew: I was anything *but* a hair-ribbon kind of girl. I sat on the counter stool dressed in dungarees, black-and-white high-top Keds and a striped T-shirt. My baseball glove lay on the other stool.

When she had laughed herself out, she said, "Ribbon? On a cannonball firebug?"

She had a point on both counts.

Cannonball was my nickname. As for "firebug" . . .

In school two months earlier we had been learning about the Unami, the Native Americans from our area. This inspired me to make a fire the old-fashioned Unami way. For reasons knowable only to the brain of a sixth grader, I decided to do so in our bathtub.

On the way home from school one day, I detoured to the railroad tracks and creek and collected my supplies:

a quartz stone, a rusty iron track-bed spike and a handful of dry, mossy stuff from the ground under a bunch of pine trees. I laid it all in the bathtub. And climbed in.

Over the mossy nest I smashed and scratched the stone and spike into each other. My arms were ready to fall off when a thin curl of smoke rose out of the nest. I blew on it. A spark appeared. "What are you *doing?*" said Eloda from the doorway. I glanced up at her—and screamed, because the spark had flamed and burned my thumb. Stone and spike clanked on porcelain. Eloda turned on the shower, putting out the fire and drenching me. When I dried off and changed my clothes, she put Vaseline and a Band-Aid on the burn and told me to tell people I had cut myself slicing tomatoes.

Eloda tapped my hand. "Lemme see."

I showed her. The burn was just a pale pink trace by now. She took my hand in both of hers. She seemed to hold it longer than necessary.

"Number one law," she said.

"No more fires," I said. She had made me recite the words every time she changed the Band-Aid. She still made me say it.

Then her hands were off me, but I was still feeling her. It was her eyes. She was staring at me in a way that seemed to mean something, but I would not find out what till years later.

"Tell you what," she said, breaking the spell. "If you make it to three knots, I'll get you a ribbon."

Again she started to leave.

Again I blurted, "You're so lucky."

Again she stopped. "That's me. Miss Lucky."

"I mean it," I said. "You get to have scrapple every day."

"You're right," she said. "That's why I decided to live here. I love the scrapple." She walked away.

"Stop!"

She stopped. She waited, her back to me.

"You can't go," I told her.

"I have work to do." She stepped into the dining room.

"I'm your boss!" I called—and instantly wished I could take it back. I added lamely, "When my dad's not here."

Her shoulders turned just enough so she could look back at me. Surprisingly, she did not seem angry. She sighed. "Miss O'Reilly—"

I stopped her: "My name is Cammie."

"Miss Cammie—"

"No!" I snapped. "No *Miss*. Just Cammie." She stared. "Say it." She kept staring. "Please!"

Now she was angry. My name, barely audible, came out with a blown breath: "Cammie."

She walked away.

This was in mid-June, the fourth day of summer vacation when I was twelve, and I had decided that Eloda Pupko must become my mother.

2

THOUGH I DID NOT KNOW IT AT THE TIME, MY DECISION had begun to form about a month earlier. On a Sunday. Mother's Day.

As always, that holiday began with my father and me driving to Riverside Cemetery, just west of town. As always, he parked on the grass and we walked up the hill. We stopped at the right of the big tree. We looked down at the headstone and once again read the words we knew by heart:

ANNE VICTORIA O'REILLY
APRIL 16, 1921
FEBRUARY 3, 1947
LOVING WIFE
LOVING MOTHER

As always, I put a vase of daffodils in front of the headstone. As always, we stood there, saying nothing, staring at the stone.

I did not remember my mother. She died when I was a baby. She was hit by a milk truck a moment after saving me.

It was the most famous accident in Two Mills that year. Maybe ever. It made me famous. The Baby Girl Whose Mother Saved Her from the Milk Truck. When my father became warden of the county prison, I became even more famous.

As always, I knew it was time to leave the grave when my father said, "Okay." We returned to the car and rode off.

We always went somewhere then. Philadelphia Zoo. Boat ride on the Delaware. Lancaster County and the Amish buggies. This year we went to a Phillies game. We went to three or four games every year, always on a Sunday. But never before on Mother's Day.

At the ballpark they gave pink carnations to the mothers. We sat along the right-field line, in a spot where a lot of foul balls came down. As always, I had my glove. I loved baseball. Since I was a girl and could not join Little League, my next best dream was to catch a major-league foul ball.

Halfway through the seventh inning everyone stood up, but no one faster than me. I took great pride in being the first one to stand for the seventh-inning stretch. I always made sure to flex my shoulders and arch my back, which by then, sure enough, were stiff from sitting for so long.

Then something unexpected happened.

The organ stopped playing "Take Me Out to the Ball Game." The PA announcer said, "Ladies and gentlemen, please be seated." Thirty thousand people sat. Then he said, "As you know, this is the day we honor our mothers." A faint tremor went through me. "If you will direct your attention to the box seats on the first-base side, you will see mothers and wives of many of our Phillies ballplayers. Ladies, will you please stand."

Several rows of women stood and turned to the crowd. Every one of them was smiling and waving. Every one wore a pink carnation. The stadium clapped and cheered and whistled. You might have thought someone had hit a home run.

Then the PA voice said, "And now we ask that *every* mother in the ballpark please stand and receive our love and thanks for all you do. Ladies . . ." And there was a great wave of movement throughout the masses, and hundreds, thousands of women came to their feet—young, old, a pink blizzard of carnations—all of them bathing in the cheers and whistles of the multitude.

If I had to write my first thought at that moment, it might have been something like this: *Wow, all these mothers and not one of them mine.* It was just a flat calculation. There was no feeling to it.

And then there was.

For right beside me, inches from my shoulder, a presence

13

that until then I had barely been aware of abruptly snapped to her feet. Her low-heeled shoes were gleaming white as Chiclets, with gold-trimmed white bows and quarter-size holes in the front for her big toes to peek through. Her dress was mint green. Her snowy white gloves had little slits at the wrists.

I dared to look up at her face. I was surprised she was not smiling. Instead she looked proud. And then laughter suddenly burst from her and she was looking down to the other side as a little voice piped: "Yay, Mommy!"

And then they were all sitting back down, thousands of mothers, and the game was resuming—and I didn't realize that I had never stopped staring at her until she turned and cast on me the most dazzling smile I had ever seen, and for a moment it seemed as if this perfect stranger had known me all my life.

And then I was bawling. Suddenly. No warning. No reason. Out, as they say, of left field. I couldn't stop myself. Her smile changed instantly to something like horror. A white-gloved hand went to her bright red lips. "Oh dear," she said. And then my father's arm was around me, squeezing, and he was asking me what was the matter and did I want to go, and I blubbered "No!" and I pounded my fist into my glove until the last of the tears went away.

We stayed until the last out. I did not look at the mint-green lady again, and no foul ball came anywhere near us.

3

How do you be a child to a mother you never knew?

For twelve years my father had been enough. Family photos and a yellowing newspaper story had been enough.

Sure, from the time I'd first heard the story, I'd thought about my mother. Anne O'Reilly. The lady who saved me from the milk truck. I cried for her. For myself. Sometimes. And that was it. That's how the world was. Other kids had mothers. Cammie O'Reilly didn't. End of story.

Now, in the weeks after Mother's Day, something was changing. Enough was no longer enough. Dormant feelings stirred by a smile at a ballpark moved and shifted until they shaped a thought: I was sick and tired of being motherless.

I wanted one. And a second thought: If I couldn't have my first-string mother, I'd bring one in off the bench.

But who?

A teacher?

The next lady who smiled at me?

The flash point came in five words.

4

"PUT THEM IN THE SINK."

Okay, back up. . . .

The last day of school had been a half day. I ran all the way home, burst through Reception, up the long stairway and into our jailhouse apartment. I sat myself down at the kitchen table, where my lunch was waiting. Peanut butter and jelly sandwich. Tastykake chocolate cupcakes. Empty glass—but not for long. A hand appeared, pouring chocolate milk from a Supplee Dairy glass bottle.

A hand—that's how I thought of it. There had always been a hand, serving me this, cleaning up that. In the absence of a mother, I had grown up with a parade of hands serving and taking care of me. The hands of women inmates—Cammie-keepers—whom my father trusted to be with me during the day while he was working. The hands came with faces and names, but to me they were mostly hands. Hands that did my bidding, more often than not before I even asked. Handmaids.

The hand that poured my chocolate milk that day was simply the latest in the long parade. It did differ from the others in one way: the name attached to it. Eloda Pupko. It sounded like it belonged in a comic book. I asked my father if it was her real name. He said it was.

So the hand of Eloda Pupko poured my milk, and I ate my lunch and got up from the table and was almost out of the dining room . . .

When it happened.

"Put them in the sink."

I stopped, out of sheer surprise. I recognized the voice as the trustee's but could not determine whom she was talking to.

I heard it again: "Put them in the sink."

I turned. She was standing by the table. She was looking straight, unmistakably at me.

"What?" I said.

She said it for the third time: "Put them in the sink."

I heard the words. I understood them one by one. But what they added up to made no sense.

"Put *what* in the sink?" I said. In my mind I was doing her a favor just by asking the question, by not turning my back on her and walking out.

"Your lunch things," she said. "They go in the sink."

What she was saying was utterly foreign to me, unprecedented. My job was to sit down, eat lunch, get up and walk away. Her job was to take care of whatever I left behind.

"Right," I said. "So do it."

I walked away.

I rode my bike that first afternoon of summer vacation. East End. North End. West End. The park. The zoo. Celebrating my freedom from books and tests. I imagined I hit a hundred miles an hour flashing down Monkey Hill.

When I returned home, Eloda was vacuuming the living room rug. As I passed through the dining room, I tried not to look, but I couldn't help it. My lunch stuff—plate, glass, napkin—was still on the table.

At five o'clock I took another peek: still there. My father usually came home around six.

Any minute now Eloda Pupko would head for the kitchen to get our dinner ready. Was she going to leave my lunch mess on the table for my father to see? Would she dare?

I snatched the things from the table and dumped them in the kitchen sink, as noisily as I could. And heard her voice: "Better wash them while you're at it. I don't want to be cooking with dirty dishes in the sink. Let 'em dry on the rack."

I just stood there, staring into the sink. But I wasn't

seeing the sink. I was seeing myself smashing the glass and dish into a thousand pieces on the kitchen floor. And saying in my best mistress-of-the-house voice: "Try putting that on the rack, *maid*."

That satisfying scene never made it out of my head. I washed the dishes, set them on the rack and stormed off to my room.

The next day, I didn't take any chances. I took my allowance to the Blue Jay on Main Street and ate my breakfast there. Scrapple. Lunch, too. More scrapple.

But the day after that, I had my breakfast at the kitchen counter as usual. I left the dishes there. As I walked away, I waited for her to say something. She didn't.

Same thing at lunch: I left my mess on the table. Walked away. And heard it. Just one word, singsongy: "Dishes."

I knew at once why I had stayed home for my meals that second day. I was not only waiting to hear her say it. I *wanted* to hear it.

I took the dishes to the sink, washed them and put them on the rack. I even swiped a wet rag over the table.

On the third day—breakfast and lunch—I cleaned up without being told.

Why?

Because in that voice—"Put them in the sink"—I recognized something I had been waiting to hear for twelve years. It did not come from my father but from a lady who was already taking up mother space in my house. Well, yes, other housekeepers had done that, too. But this one . . . this one was doing something new. This one was saying mother words. To *me*. And suddenly, with more than half my childhood gone, it seemed I was being offered a chance to become something I never thought I could be: a mother's daughter.

I jumped at it.

That's how I did things. Fast. If you were in my way, watch out. My schoolmates had figured it out early. I was only halfway through first grade when they started calling me Cannonball.

And so the very next morning the housemaid had a new duty. "I want a pigtail," I told her.

Which sounded crazy even to me because a pigtail was a girl thing and I was a tomboy. But I'd decided that doing hair was a great mother-daughter bonding moment. I wasn't discouraged by Eloda Pupko's resistance. I would work on her. I would wear her down. I would *make* a mother out of her. When she told Cannonball Cammie to do the dishes, she had no idea what she started.

5

I COULD HEAR THE FEET ON THE STEPS BEFORE THE POUNDING began. I ran for the door, flung it open—only it didn't open. Once again I had forgotten about the colossal bar lock that was supposed to protect us from crazed, invading prisoners, not to mention King Kong. I shoved the bar aside and opened the door for Reggie Weinstein, my best friend.

Reggie had everything I did not. Beauty. Makeup. Breasts. Which was scary enough. But when she aimed her lipstick-framed thousand-watt smile at you, you flinched as if a Mack truck had backfired. She jabbed a 45-rpm record in my face. She screamed: "Dig it!"

I read the label:

Now we were both screaming and jumping . . . and now the record was spinning on my 45 player . . . and now we were waltzing around the dining room table, around dusting Eloda, puckering and cooing at each other: "I want you! I need you! I-huh-huh love you! With all my"—stretching out the last word with every one of Elvis's seven ever-lovin' syllables—"huh-huh-huh-huh-huh-huh-heart!"

We collapsed, howling, onto the rug as Eloda veered around us and shut and locked the massive oak door. We lay on our backs, winding down to whimpering giggles.

Reggie sniffed, made a face. "I hate that smell. *That's* the punishment around here. I sentence you to three years of scrapple."

I drew in a long, dreamy breath. "And soon as I'm eighteen I'm going to eat scrapple every day of my life."

"Not around me, you won't." She poked me. "So let me see. Turn."

I faced away. She tugged at the pigstub. "One twist," she said. "Pathetic. Who did it? The warden?"

"Eloda."

"The maid." I could feel her fingers inspecting. "Not bad. But it looks dumb this short. A ribbon might help."

23

"I'm getting one when it gets three knots long," I said.

She sighed dramatically. "Tragic." She tapped me on the back. "Turn. Face."

I turned. No doctor or dentist had ever studied my face so intently. Reggie had a mission: to girlify me before we entered Stewart Junior High School. She blew a breath through her nose and wagged her head in despair. "Your eyes are a disaster. Which doesn't mean your lips and complexion are anything to brag about. And you know what the really tragic thing is?"

"What?" I said.

"Even if we get all that fixed—hair, eyes, lips—even *if*—there's still the nose." She pushed it with her finger. Hard.

"Ow!" I whined.

She released. "See? It bounces right back. Not a thing I can do."

"You could powder it," I said, trying to lighten the tragedy.

She didn't laugh. She pointed to my bandaged thumb. "That doesn't help. Makes you look like a scruffy tomboy."

"I *am* a scruffy tomboy," I reminded her.

Her eyes implored the sky. "Help me."

She scanned me from the bottom up, wagging her head. She was in pain. I felt bad for being the cause.

When her eyes reached my chest, they stopped. They

stayed there for a full minute while she sighed and wagged. Finally she said, "When do we go back to school?"

"Day after Labor Day," I said.

She nodded. "Okay. You have till then. If there's nothing poking out by Labor Day, I'm stuffing a pair of socks in there." She threw up her hands. "I have to have *something* to work with."

I wanted to help. I really did. But all I could come up with was silliness. "Maybe if I hold my breath long enough," I suggested, "they'll pop out."

"Maybe," she countered, "if you stop going to the bathroom."

"Eew!" I screeched, and kicked her, and we were howling on the floor once more.

We played "I Want You, I Need You, I Love You" ten or twenty times more before Reggie flicked off the record player and said, "Okay, I'm ready to meet a murderer."

6

"You won't meet a murderer," I told her as I opened the back door.

"I'll settle for manslaughter," she said, hope in her voice.

"We're going to the women's yard," I said.

"I want men. Murderers."

"Forget it. We're not allowed near them."

"Says who?"

"Who do you think?"

"I hate the warden." She pouted. "He takes all the fun out of prison."

"You're lucky he's letting you do this," I told her.

Until this day, my visitors had been confined to the apartment. The night before, my father had, surprisingly, agreed to let Reggie come along on my daily through-the-fence talk with the inmates. I led her down the outside stairway and through the backyard.

Reggie stood at the chain-link fence that separated our backyard from the women's exercise yard. She looked like a kid at a zoo. She boggled. "Wow!"

The prison never had more than thirty or so female inmates. (None of whom were murderers, which could not be said of the men.) The women were mostly just lolling about the dirt-packed yard, chatting, strolling. A few sat in the shade, their backs against the interior stone wall separating them from the men's exercise yard. At the far end two women batted a badminton bird back and forth. There was no net between them.

They were all dressed identically: shapeless denim dresses. Sacks, really. No pockets.

Everywhere you looked, cigarettes were kissing. My father knew how much his people—that's what he called them, "my people"—craved smoking. But he was afraid to let them have matches. His solution: As the inmates, men and women, filed out to their respective yards each day, a trustee was allowed to light one person's cigarette. From then on, the only way to get a light was to kiss the end of your cigarette to the end of one already lit. Almost everybody had a cigarette in her mouth and a pack in her hand, even the badminton batters. Almost everyone smoked Salems.

Most of the women were white, with pallid skin the

color of vanilla Bonomo's Turkish Taffy. Although one person was aiming to change that.

Deena, who was in for stealing archdiocese funds for retired priests, lay on her back on a shower towel by the yard's west wall. Her dress was hiked up over her pasty knees. Egg-shaped black plastic cups covered her eyes. She occupied the same spot every day.

The loudest and largest inmate of all was Boo Boo. Boo Boo was one of a half dozen black women. Boo Boo was a shoplifter, but I always found this hard to figure, as she was anything but quiet and sneaky. Her bellow rang out—"Hey, Miss Cammie!"—as she came bounding and laughing across the yard like a huge denim beach ball. Her hair erupted from her head in wild, woolen gushers that must have added a foot to her already imposing height.

It was all this that Reggie took in and that brought forth her "Wow!"

The fence bellied toward me with the force of Boo Boo's arrival. Ten long red fingernails poked through the chain links.

"Hi, Boo Boo," I said.

"And who is this, Miss Cammie?" she asked.

"This is my friend Reggie. Reggie—Boo Boo."

"*Best* friend," Reggie corrected.

Boo Boo beamed. "Please to meet you. Call me Boo for short." She laughed and stuck her finger through the fence. "I'm a shoplifter."

Reggie hesitated, then shook the finger. Boo Boo laughed again. Boo Boo was the jolliest person I'd ever known.

Boo Boo turned thoughtful. "Reggie . . . ain't that a boy's name? I got a cousin Reggie."

She waved at the tower guard. "Jim! This look like a boy to you?"

Aqua short shorts. Silver sandals. Aqua toenails. Silky charcoal blouse. Everything about Reggie broadcast: *seventeen!* Except her eyes, gaga over Boo Boo's attention, which said: *little girl. Christmas.*

Jim Carilla, the weekday tower guard, waved from afar but didn't reply.

A voice came from the other black women clustered behind Boo Boo. "Good thing the men can't see her."

A constant volley of shouts flew over the interior wall. The men were playing baseball.

Boo Boo shook a cigarette from her pack of Salems. She poked it through the fence at Reggie. "Smoke?"

Reggie stared for a beat, then took it. "Thanks."

I slapped it from her hand. "Not in my jail," I said, and Boo Boo was laughing again.

Suddenly there was a commotion at the far end of the yard. The badminton players, Helen and Tessa, were yelling:

"Wha'd you do?"

"What's it look like I did?"

"That's the only one we had!"

"So go get it, then!"

Tessa had swatted the badminton bird over the back wall.

"You stupid criminal!"

"Stupid, huh?"

Tessa wound up and sent her racket cartwheeling over the high wall. Now Helen was advancing, holding her racket like a club.

Tessa tapped a nostril and shot a snot into the dust. She balled her fists. "Come on—come on—"

Nothing else in the yard moved.

"Jeez," I growled to myself. I yelled: "Hey! Stop, you two! *I'll* get it!" I yanked Reggie's hand. "C'mon."

7

We dashed up the back stairs, through the apartment, out the barred door, down the front stairs, out the prison door to Airy Street, where Reggie barked, "Halt!" She pulled her hand free. She waved me onward. "Go. I'm walking."

I wasn't surprised. Since she'd become glamorous, Reggie no longer did running. Or sweating.

I ran down the alley between the prison and city hall—the full length of the long, high stone wall. Before I rounded the corner onto Marshall Street, I could hear ecstatic yelps. Kids were stampeding into the parking lot between the eye doctor's office and the Hancock County SPCA.

A minute later, after shrieks of battle, one of the kids came out, waving high a gray, coverless ball as if he had just caught it in the left-field bleachers at Connie Mack Stadium.

Many of the men in the prison had jobs making woven rugs. With leftover yarn they made their own baseballs, or stringballs. And whenever school was out, neighborhood boys squatted like vultures across Marshall Street, waiting for jailbird home runs.

A littler kid was holding Tessa's badminton racket.

I pointed at the racket. "Could I have that, please?"

The kid's face went scrunchy. He was only six or seven. "It's mine," he said.

"It's the prison's," I said.

He put it behind his back. "It came over."

Somebody said, "Don't give it to her, Mookie."

Mookie stuck his tongue out at me.

Then a voice from behind me: "Here, Mook. Trade ya."

It was a boy on a green-and-cream Roadmaster bike. His eyes were shadowed by the brim of the red Phillies cap he wore. He was holding a baseball card.

A big kid piped, "Whose card?"

"Mantle," said the Roadmaster kid. An infielder's glove dangled from his handlebars.

"Yer lyin'," someone said.

The kid showed the card for all to see. It was Mickey Mantle, all right. Somebody gasped. Somebody whistled.

Another kid piped, "I'll give ya . . . wait"—he fished in his pocket, counted change—"eighty-four cents."

"It's Mookie's," said Roadmaster. "If he trades the racket."

Reggie was just arriving.

The kid with the stringball snatched the racket from Mookie and held it out to Roadmaster. "He'll trade." He looked like an older version of Mookie. Mookie howled.

Roadmaster grinned, took the racket and handed over the Mickey Mantle. It was in Mookie's hand for an instant before Big Brother snatched it. He kissed it and stuffed it into his pocket. "I'll save it for him," he said. Mookie bawled and kicked his brother, and the other kids laughed.

"So I guess you want this, too, huh?" Roadmaster was speaking to me. He was holding the badminton bird in front of my face.

I took the bird. I took the racket. "Thanks," I said, and ran off.

I got a cheer from the women when I returned with the racket and bird.

Tessa came to the backyard fence. "Heave it over, Miss Cammie," she said.

"What?" I said. "So you can do it again?"

Tessa gave a snorty chuckle. "That wasn't nothing, Miss Cammie. We're all buddy-buddy now." She pulled Helen to the fence, draped an arm over her. "Ain't we, Helen?"

Helen gave a reluctant "Uh-huh."

"You'll get them back tomorrow," I said.

Tessa whined, "Aw, man—"

I held up a finger. Tessa went silent. She knew what everyone knew: warden's authority flowed through the warden's daughter. It wasn't written down anywhere. It was never spoken of. But that's how it was in the women's exercise yard. "Tessa," I said, "you got a temper."

The yard cracked up. Boo Boo howled. "You got that right, Miss Cammie!"

Even Tessa couldn't suppress a grin. But still she couldn't keep her mouth shut. "But, Miss Cammie—"

Up went my finger. Silence.

"Tessa, the warden already took your net away. Do you want him to take the rackets, too? So you can bat this thing back and forth with your hands?"

She cocked a hip and glared at me. She wasn't going to give me satisfaction. I liked Tessa. She reminded me of me.

I sniffed. "I'll take that as a no. So here's what I'm going to do. I'm going to lay them down right here"—I put the racket and bird on the ground; I was speaking calmly and slowly, something I had learned from my father—"so you can see them and you can think about it till tomorrow." I looked at her. Her mousy brown hair drooped over a fox-thin, pale face. "Okay?"

I didn't wait for an answer. As I turned and made my dramatic exit, the yard broke into cheers and applause behind me.

I had run all the way back from Marshall Street. Reggie

had finally caught up. She stood halfway down the back steps. As I approached her, she gaped at me in wonder. "Wow. You."

"Welcome to my world," I said.

"You don't mess around, do you?"

"Know what they call me behind my back?" I said.

"What?"

"Little Warden."

She stopped at the top step. "So is that—what—good?"

I laughed. "Oh yeah. It's sort of . . . an honor. They like me."

In the apartment, where hints of scrapple smell still hovered, she wet a fingertip and traced over my eyebrows. "Well, I think somebody else likes you, too."

"Huh?" I said, swatting her hand away.

"That boy on the bike? He kept looking at you."

"Big deal," I said, and hoped the heat rising to my face wasn't showing. "He was *talking* to me. Where's he *s'posed* to look?"

"At *me*," she sniffed. "But he never once did."

8

Carl brought me a pie every Monday, before Eloda served supper. Carl was the prison baker. He had once been a master sergeant baker in the army. He was in jail for breaking and entering, but I saw him as my personal pie maker. He named his masterpieces. Peachy Geachy. Very Cherry. Lemon Boommeringue. Chocolate Cream Dream. I was never disappointed.

I set to my Monday pre-supper ritual. I lovingly sliced my pie—it was Blueberry Crumbbum—into seven identical slices. I put six in the refrigerator and one by my dinner plate. God help anyone who touched them. Thankfully, my father was a cake man.

Dinner this day was Swiss steak, mashed potatoes and peas. I spoon-pressed a hollow into the mashed potatoes and made a little brown pond with Swiss-steak gravy. I had been thinking of something for days, and now I just blurted it out: "I want the key to the exercise yard."

My father stared at me, blinking. I loved catching him off guard. "Really? Why would you want that?"

"Dad, you're always saying they're not dangerous. Or you wouldn't let me in the backyard with just the fence between us."

He nodded. "True. But that doesn't mean I want you in there. It's their yard."

"Dad—" I jumped up, ran to my room and returned with the latest copy of *Corrections*, a monthly journal for prison administrators. I opened it. I slapped it down in front of him. "Look."

It was a two-page spread showing pictures of prisoners with dogs. The headline read:

PETS: KEEPING THE PEACE

My father looked it over.

"They help keep inmates calm. Less stress. Less problems for you. You're always talking about that."

He closed the magazine. "You want me to bring in puppies."

I thumped my chest. (I could be dramatic.) "I want you to bring in *me*."

He smiled, made a sniffy noise and went back to his Swiss steak. "I don't think so."

I hovered over him. "Da-ad. If dogs can help keep prisoners happy—"

"Peaceful."

"Right, peaceful. If *dogs* can do it, imagine what a *person* could do. Especially the *right* person."

"You're a kid."

Ha—he had just blundered into my trap. "*Exactly!* I'm a *kid*. Inmates think kids are cute, little, harmless—like *pets*."

"You want to be the prison puppy. My daughter Fido."

I couldn't help it; I laughed. I hated when he did that. He was always turning my serious arguments into jokes.

I corked my giggles. "No! I just want to help."

He looked up at me. "I know," he said. And I could see it in his eyes—he *did* know. More than I was willing to admit.

"They *like* me," I told him. "I'd be a good influence. Something to look forward to each day. And it's summer. Heat means stress. Problems."

"Stop looming over me," he said. "Go sit and eat."

I sat.

He put down his fork, looked at me. "Why do you think I added an hour to yard time? Why do I feed them so well? Or create a Quiet Room?"

The Quiet Room. My father considered it his masterpiece. It had a glass ceiling, like a greenhouse. There were plants and even small trees. The highlight was a mini-waterfall that fell three feet from a tin wheelbarrow into a plant-circled pool. It was supposed be a sanctuary for the inmates. A healing place.

Even I would not have said the following if I hadn't already known that he knew: "Dad—nobody *goes* there."

He didn't argue. "Give it time."

"No," I said, "give *me* time."

He pointed his fork at me. "Eat your dinner."

I pointed my fork at his fork. "You haven't heard the last of this."

His eyes grinned. "Eat your dinner."

In those days, at dinner with the warden, I had two modes of operation: verbal combat and sullen silence. On this occasion I was too charged up to be silent. So I changed the subject. "Okay, then," I snipped, "what did she do?"

Predictably, he pretended he didn't know what I was talking about. "Who? What?"

"Stop it, Dad," I sneered. "Your acting stinks. You know what and you know who."

He did know. Perfectly. The *who* was Eloda Pupko. The *what* was: What did she do to get herself in prison? I had been asking my father forever.

He said, "Her record is none of your business."

"Dad—I know everybody *else's* business. Boo Boo is a shoplifter. Carl's a burglar. Tessa's a drunk."

He picked at his teeth. "They *were*. They're recovering."

39

I laughed. "Dad—Boo Boo? *Recovering?* From a cold, maybe."

He almost grinned. "Okay, maybe not Boo Boo."

"So—see? I know about them all."

"Because they blab."

"They blab to *me*. They tell me everything through the fence."

"Fine." He nodded. "So ask her yourself."

"I did. She won't say."

He shrugged. "Then neither will I."

I warned him. "I'm gonna pester you every day for the rest of my life. Is that what you want?"

He seemed barely interested. "Suit yourself."

Exercise-yard key? *Strike one.*

Eloda's crime? *Strike two.*

I went for the strikeout. With my father it was all or nothing.

"I want scrapple," I said.

"Pig snouts," he said.

"Scrapple."

"Pig snouts."

It was all he needed to say. A hundred times during the past few years I had demanded more scrapple. A hundred times he had told me that scrapple was made of pig snouts (it was—still is—but there's lots of other stuff in it, too) and that no daughter of his was going to start out the day with pig snouts in her stomach instead of cereal.

"I'm not saying seven days a week," I said reasonably. "Only three."

"Pig snouts," he said.

"It's torture!" I whined. "Smelling it every day."

"Put a clothespin on your nose."

"I can go to the Blue Jay and get it there with my own money. They have breakfast all day. I can do that. Any time I want."

"Go for it," he said.

"I will," I said. In fact, I already had. But it used up a lot of my allowance.

And then he did something unforgivable: he made me laugh. He said, "At least I'll know it wasn't my fault when you start growing a snout."

I gave one of those sudden laughs that blow a booger bubble from a nostril. I quick used my napkin. I turned away so he wouldn't see my face. Didn't he know that making me laugh was the worst thing he could do? Not to mention: *Strike three!*

I slammed down my fork. "I'm leaving." I got up and walked off. I got as far as the old RCA Victor floor-model radio.

"Camille."

I stopped.

"Finish your dinner."

I came back. I finished my dinner in less than two minutes. I didn't look at him. I didn't speak.

He pretended not to notice. He drank his coffee and flipped through the pages of *Corrections*. He wasn't fooling me. He hated the silent treatment.

And that wasn't my only weapon.

I cleaned my plate. And I mean *cleaned*. I held it up to my face and licked every speck off it. He pretended not to notice. I got up and walked off for the second time. He called, as I knew he would: "You forgot your pie."

I would not give him the satisfaction. "You eat it," I snapped over my shoulder.

I stormed out the big door and up the stairs of the Tower of Death.

9

SOME KIDS HAD TREE HOUSES. SOME KIDS HAD HIDEOUTS. I had the Tower of Death.

I had been calling it that since I was little. How lucky was I! I lived in a hundred-year-old house—the prison had been built in 1851—that resembled a Norman fortress. The tower was the best part of it. Dark. Gloomy. A single lightbulb threw frightful shadows.

When I was younger, I climbed the creaking stairs with delicious apprehension into the Middle Ages. The room at the top was circular. From the battlement slots that served as windows, I pretended to zing flaming arrows into the hearts of attacking enemies. They screamed magnificently as I poured cauldrons of boiling tar upon their heads.

It was easy to imagine that the smoky, meat-house smell in my nose was that of battlefield slaughter. Above my head, hanging from the ceiling, were dozens of imported salamis. They were hard and black and long and evilly twisted and they made me think of lopped-off toes of hellish monsters. They came from Italy. The owner of DiRenzo's Market paid the county an annual fee to store them here, in what I came to call the Salami Room.

As I got older, the tower became a different kind of place. The hangman's noose, flopped in the corner, had become more than merely fascinating. Questions rose like dust from its moldy fibers. Was it ever used? If so, whose neck did the honors? Was death fast? Slow? Was his family there to see? His child?

Over the decades many other relics had washed on an upward tide into this jailers' attic: wooden cabinets with a century's worth of prison files, gas-lamp sconces, an old porcelain sink, a sign that said NO SPITTING, a zinc-clad washtub full of prisoner-made rag dolls, all with hair of yarn, the same yarn from which the inmates made rugs and stringballs.

I looked out the south-facing slot window. The invading hordes had vanished with my little-kidhood. Now it was the dusky rooftops of Two Mills that I saw, sloping down to the shopper's feast of Main Street. And below that the long, red-tiled roof of the train station, where a Pennsy electric of matching red was pulling out for Philadelphia. Beyond came the river and, spanning it, the bridge and P&W trolley trestle: twin stitches sewing my town to Bridgeport across the water.

The slot window to my right faced west and the setting sun. As always, I was drawn to it. For from this vantage I could see The Corner. Well, more sense than see, really: gaps in the checkerboard of rooftops meant *streets*. Oak Street. Cherry Street. Oak and Cherry.

The Corner.

Where my mother had gently nudged my carriage—baby me throned like a potentate (or so I've always pictured it)—off the curb and into the street . . .

Where my mother stepped off the curb after me at approximately ten-fifteen on the morning of Monday, February 3, 1947 . . .

Where the Supplee milk truck turned the corner . . .

Where the truck hit and instantly killed my mother, but not before she sent my carriage racing across the street so fast that when it hit the curb I popped out and went flying to a landing on the sidewalk in front of 203 West Oak Street—without a scratch, so abundantly bundled was I . . .

Where milk from broken bottles spilled across sidewalks and over curbstones and down the guttered hill: a thin white stream to meet the waters of Stony Creek.

Though I stood at the westward window, I resisted the

temptation to look out. I could never do so without crying, and on this night I did not want to cry. I wanted to fume. At my father. At the world.

So I stalked about the Salami Room. I grabbed the hangman's noose and pulled it over my head and mock-hanged myself, just to show him.

I punched hanging salamis. I grabbed stupid rag dolls by their yarny hair and hurled them against the wall.

I heard music. Little Richard screaming "Long Tall Sally."

I returned to the south-side slot. The windows were sealed to protect the hanging salamis, but sounds from Airy Street came through easily. A long red convertible was cruising below. It looked like half a high school class was packed into it. Having a great old time. Not a care in the world. Radio full blast. When it came to the best line, everybody screamed along with Little Richard and threw their hands in the air, including the driver: ". . . he duck back in the alley!"

Over the red convertible, over the town and the river and Bridgeport and all the way to the Gulf of Mexico, I sent back a wordless scream of my own.

And then, even though I wasn't at the westward window, I cried, kicking the wall because, once again, sad had displaced mad, and I had tried so hard to stay mad.

I retreated to the wooden file cabinets.

While other kids read Nancy Drew and the Hardy Boys, I lost myself in the jailhouse histories of felons. The oldest file was for an inmate named Ebert Haverstack. It was dated September 1853. According to his record, Ebert Haverstack was in the pokey for "chronic and habitual theft of cow's milk," the cow being Ethel, owned by farmer A. Bechtold.

But on this day I wasn't interested in Ebert Haverstack or any of the others, except one: Thomas Browne. I pulled his file. I sat on the floor, my back against the wall. The Salami Room, like me, was free of cosmetics. The circular wall was nothing but the inner surfaces of the stones one saw from the outside. Even in summer it was cool in the Salami Room.

Thomas Browne's record dated from 1870. His crime was listed as "uncomplicated mayhem." It was those two words that had first caught my attention. I had looked up "mayhem." Basically it seemed to mean going bananas. I pictured Thomas Browne marauding down Main Street, his boots—no, bare feet, and he's in long johns—careening through wagon ruts in the dust. Maybe he was waving a bottle of whiskey and insulting ladies with parasols. Or slashing the reins of hitched horses and sending them off to Philadelphia with mad whoops and slaps on the rump. But it was the word "uncomplicated" that most beguiled me. My father had no idea what it had meant as a legal term in 1870. To me it came to suggest mayhem in its purest, rarest form. Perhaps only one such perpetrator per generation came along. Somehow I found that admirable—noble, even.

And all the more so when I read The Letter.

10

IT WAS THE LAST THING IN THE FOLDER. THE PAPER WAS yellow and thin and crazed like shed snakeskin. Thomas Browne had beautiful handwriting. He would have gotten an A in my Palmer Method class.

The Letter began: *To My Dearest Loved One.* That was it. No name. Was he writing to his wife? Sweetheart? Mother? I'll never know.

The Letter went on: *Many of my fellows here crowd the common windows by day, conversing through the bars with passers-by on the street. I find no need to occupy myself thus. I am content to mind my cell or stroll the yard with none but my memories for company. And what wonderful memories! I can not more strongly advise you—the bad time is over. Do not allow your future to be plundered by the past—neither the*

*bad nor even the good of it. Leave the memories to me. I shall
keep them warm for the both of us. As to your own dear self,
you must*

That was it.

As I sat cross-legged on the floor of the Salami Room,
I asked for the hundredth time: *Thomas Browne, why does
your letter end so abruptly? Did the hangman come for you?
(For mayhem so rare?) Did you get word just then that you
were pardoned, and so tossed the letter aside for the embrace
that awaited you outside the bars?*

I lowered myself into the familiar words as into a warm
bath. They rose about my shoulders, steeping me in a love
so uncomplicated that it demanded nothing. *Leave the
memories to me.*

I returned The Letter to the folder, the folder to its
drawer. I pulled open another drawer, the bottom one. I
pulled it all the way, so I could reach into the space behind
the files. I took out the shoe.

It was my mother's. A light brown, low-heeled oxford.
A plain and simple shoe. The kind of shoe a mother might
have worn when taking a baby out for a stroll. It was on
her foot when it happened. No one had ever told me so.
No one had to. I simply knew it when I found it a couple
of years before. I was snooping in my father's bedroom
closet and there it was, wrapped in a towel in the corner. I
transferred it at once to the Salami Room. In the following

years I never felt a moment's guilt, only a dim surprise that my father never mentioned it.

I went to the westward window. In the dying light my eyes found the intersection of rooftop gaps that marked The Corner. Again I heard the rattle of the milk truck. I held the shoe to my heart and I whispered her name— "Anne O'Reilly . . . Anne O'Reilly"—and I cried.

Night had fallen by the time I came down from the Tower of Death. I went straight to the fridge. There it was, the same slice of Blueberry Crumbbum, on the same plate, covered in wax paper. I had known all along that he would not eat it. I didn't bother with a fork.

11

We were in Charming. Where else? It was the only place Reggie shopped for clothes.

She was flipping through tops. Each one provoked a sneering remark:

"Groaty."

"Nowheresville."

"Barf."

"Ugh."

She wore her usual short shorts, white this time. White sandals. Black, collared shirt, tail out and knotted in front at the waist.

The rest of her was pink.

"Did you notice," I inquired as I watched her flip through tops, "you're pink?"

She glared at me and went back to flipping. "Not for long, Hopalong."

"What do you mean?"

"You'll see."

Reggie Weinstein was cursed with the worst affliction (according to her) that a person could have. She was white. I mean milk white. Snow white. This was okay—barely—in December. In June, unforgivable.

She had never even noticed her whiteness until she turned twelve. That's when she discovered *tan*.

From the first day of the previous summer vacation, her backyard became a beach. She lay on her "Earth Angel" towel and basted herself with Coppertone and soaked up the rays. But the tan wasn't coming fast enough to suit her. So she stopped the Coppertone—and got burned. Blisters! Pain! No sun for a week! Torture! Whiter than ever from slathers of Noxzema, she smelled like a cough drop.

It wasn't until August that the last signs of white and pink and red were gone. By the time we entered sixth grade, she was brown as a caramel apple. By January she was snow white again.

And here she was the following June: pink.

She pulled a top from the rack, draped it over herself. "What do you think?"

It was a slit-sleeve jersey with wide horizontal black-and-white stripes.

"You look like an escaped prisoner," I said.

She held it out, studied it, nodded. "You're right. I'll take it."

She gave it to me and went to the next rack. Then she snatched it back. "Hey, you—go," she commanded. She waved at the aisles. "Shop."

I could have told her that the allure of Charming was lost on me. I was perfectly happy with my T-shirt and dungarees. And—hey—my dungarees were rolled up to pedal-pusher length. Who said I wasn't fashionable?

But I gave her my other reason: "I need my money for Eloda's present. Her birthday's tomorrow."

She shoved her shirt back to me. "Okay. But I'm warning you. Your days in the kiddie section of Chatlin's are over. Don't *ever* let me catch you shopping anywhere but here."

I saluted. "Yes, ma'am."

She bought two more tops and an ankle chain and we went cruising down Main Street. Pretty soon I became aware that Reggie wasn't simply walking beside me. Something else was going on.

My first clue was the car horns.

Voices came with the beeps. Some I could make out:

"Va-voom!"

"Hee-yah!"

It was coming from summer-free high school boys cruising Main: car windows open, convertible tops down.

My attention turned on a whistle. A crew-cut boy was

standing shotgun in a baby-blue convertible, directing his shrill, two-fingered blast at . . . *us?* Then it hit me. All these noises I'd been hearing were aimed at the thirteen-looks-seventeen girl at my side.

For the first time, I noticed the other sidewalkers: boys, men, even females. Almost no one passed us without casting an eye her way, from quick glances to bold stares. It seemed everyone on Main Street, even the traffic lights, was looking at Reggie Weinstein.

And she knew it.

One peek at her face was all I needed. She seemed to be looking straight ahead, to be merely strolling. But *that* was the giveaway. Normally she'd be stopping and gawking into every storefront we passed. Normally she'd be chattering away at me. But she was silent, her Passion Pink lips appearing to pout and faintly smile at the same time. Heck, Reggie Weinstein wasn't walking down Main Street. She was walking down the runway. I could almost hear Bert Parks crooning: "There she is . . . Miss America . . ."

Good grief, I thought, *she's pink. What's gonna happen when she's tan?*

And then she was reaching into her little silver mesh purse and pulling out a pair of cat-eye sunglasses. The frames were white. And then she put them on.

And then I heard a sharp squeal of car brakes.

"That's it," I said out loud. I grabbed her and yanked her into the nearest store.

12

THE STORE WAS WOOLWORTH'S, WHICH WAS WHERE SHE wanted to be anyway.

She headed straight for Records, where she bought Lloyd Price's "Stagger Lee."

We spun each other on chrome-trimmed stools at the soda fountain. We both had Cokes: Reggie, cherry; me, lemon. As the soda jerk took our empty glasses, Reggie cut loose a ferocious belch that almost blew the jerk's white cap off. He went boggle-eyed and cracked up. I pounded the counter. "That's the Reggie I know and love!"

Reggie just sniffed and got up from her stool, like, *That wasn't me,* and headed off to Cosmetics.

She stood before a display of chocolate-brown plastic

jars in the shape of hockey pucks. The product was called Tan-er-Ree.

"I thought you use Coppertone," I said.

"It's not sun lotion," she said. "I'll never need that junk again."

"So what is it?"

"It's tanning butter. I read about it in *Seventeen*."

I wasn't sure I'd heard right. "You put it on *toast?*"

She ignored my question. She pulled a jar from the display. She sounded like a salesman: "You put it on before you go to bed. When you wake up, you're"—she threw out her arms—"*tan!*"

Her beautiful wide eyes invited me to join her in the wonderment of it all, but I could only reply with blunt sarcasm: "A miracle."

She didn't get it. She nodded with vigor. She turned to the jar. She kissed it. "A miracle."

I was hoping she would just buy it so we could get out of there. Cosmetics departments made me nervous. But she kept fussing over everything she saw: eye stuff, lip stuff, skin stuff, feet stuff.

I tried to distract myself by thinking of Boo Boo let loose in Woolworth's. I pictured her snatching whole rows of eyelash curlers and lotions and creams.

Suddenly there was a bullet of lipstick in front of my face and Reggie was saying, "I'm buying this for *you*."

It was Passion Pink. The tip of it touched my upper lip. I flinched back. The pink bullet came after me. I slapped it away. I yelled: "Stop it!" I ran from the store. Outside in the bright sun, my eyes hit the sign across the street, and I knew what I was going to get Eloda for her birthday.

13

She stared at it mutely so long I finally said, "It's a diary."

She kept staring. "I see that."

The cover was red. The letters saying MY DIARY were gold.

"You're welcome," I said.

She cleared her throat. "Thank you."

We were sitting at the dining room table.

When I had seen Verlane's Stationery the day before, the idea had hit me. It had seemed brilliant then. Now I wasn't so sure.

"You're supposed to write in it every day," I explained. "But you don't *have* to. Maybe every other day. That'd be okay, I bet."

Her finger traced the gold letters. She opened it, moved a few pages. One hand still clutched a dustrag. "Or whenever I feel like it."

I yipped, "Yes! Absolutely. Whenever you feel like it." I touched the tiny golden key. "And see—it locks. It's private. You can write anything. What you did that day. Your thoughts. Your feelings. *Anything.*" A submerged thought bobbed to the surface like a cork on water: *Me, for instance.*

She seemed entranced. She kept staring at the diary, as if waiting for it to speak or dance. I kept staring at her, waiting for a sign.

As with Boo Boo, the most striking aspect of Eloda's appearance was her hair. It was short and wiry. But the color was the thing. On her reception sheet (I had sneaked a peek) it said *Hair: red.* But really it was more orange than red. And that's how I thought of it: orange. Almost carroty.

At last she snapped out of her trance. "Well"—she pushed herself up from the table—"back to work."

She fingered the wrapping paper and ribbon but didn't seem to know what to do with them. "Gimme," I said. She handed them to me and headed for the hutch, where I had interrupted her. In her wake she left a quick "Thank you."

I crumpled the paper and ribbon till they were the size of a golf ball. She kept her back to me as she dusted the hutch. I squeezed the paper and ribbon and willed her to turn around and look at me—at *me*—for she had been looking only at the gift the whole time. *Look at me, Eloda,* I silently implored. *Say my name. Say, Thank you, Cammie. . . . Thank you, Cammie. . . .*

But she only said, not even turning, "Aren't you going out?"

14

I HAD FOUR FAVORITE THINGS TO DO WHEN I WAS MAD: ride my bike, eat junk, spit in the spittoon in the back of the prison lobby, known as Reception, and punch the imported lunch meat in the Salami Room. On this day I did the first three.

I slammed out of the apartment and down the stairs to Reception. I hawked up a lunger and fired it into the spittoon. I grabbed my bike (which I kept parked just inside the door) and stormed outside and down the concrete steps and onto the sidewalk. I rode down Airy Street to city hall at the corner, turned left and rode down Hector to the end of the block.

The tail end of the city hall building—like the prison, a full block long—was a merchants' bazaar. There was a fish guy, a vegetable guy, a picture-frame guy. I went to the candy guy. I still had money after the unappreciated birthday gift, so I got a handful of Milky Ways, five candy cigarettes and a Bonomo's Turkish Taffy.

Then I headed for the North End, where the rich people lived. Houses in the North End stood alone and often had yards in front as well as back, not to mention driveways and even garages. More to the point, the North End was bicycle-friendly. Little commerce—only the occasional corner grocery. Little traffic. No hills.

I tore around the streets, my baseball glove swinging on the handlebars. I gritted into the wind: *Who needs her . . . Who needs her . . .* I pictured her beside flashy, loud, interesting Boo Boo. Eloda was so plain and dull. Except, of course, for the orange hair, which clearly belonged on a more flamboyant person. On Boo Boo orange hair would have been perfect.

I ignored stop signs. I raced up and down driveways, even across a few front yards, daring somebody to call the cops, somebody to yell, "Hey!" Nobody did. I pulled up, took a candy cigarette from my stuffed pocket and pretended to strike a match. I cupped my hands and pretended to light the cigarette, tilted my head back and pretended to inhale deeply and blow out the smoke as I listened for a grown-up voice to call, "Hey!" There was only silence. Not surprising, as there were no people in sight. The rich kids were off at summer camp. The rich fathers were at work making more money. The rich mothers were locked behind their curtains and venetian blinds, sipping tea. The North End was a ghost town. And then, suddenly, my heart froze. I caught the sound of rattling bottles—a milk truck was going by.

This had been happening for a couple of years. I felt an electrified jolt whenever I heard the rattle of a milk truck. I crushed the cigarette in my teeth and rode on.

The East End was a better match for my roiling emotions: traffic jams, disorder, noise, people. I had to ride more slowly through the East End traffic and hills, but that made it easier to stuff myself with Milky Ways.

Who needs her . . .

I rode down Main Street. I rode through red lights. I cut in front of a Schuylkill Valley bus. I tossed candy wrappers over my shoulder. I stopped on the Airy Street bridge and spit on cars passing below. I dared somebody to yell. Stop me. Arrest me.

Nobody did.

I saw a little kid screaming at his mother: "I don't want to! I don't want to!" He was clinging to her leg as she dragged him along the sidewalk. Then he started kicking. I veered to the curb. "Yo!" I yelled. "Knock it off! That's your *mother*!" The kid and the mother both froze, gaping at me as I rode off.

I pedaled to the far west end of town, Forrest Avenue. Past the brickyard and the pigeon farm. Right turn and the long coast past the cornfields and the crumbling tunnels of the State Hospital and on to the park.

They were there, at the Little League field. The baseball guys. On this day there were four. Two white: Romig and Ears DelFina. And two black: Mug Williams and Benny House. Benny House was there only because he was Mug's cousin. He was eight and threw like a girl.

I didn't. I had been playing catch and chasing fly balls with my dad for years. Every April since I was nine I had showed up at Little League tryouts, only to be told, "No girls." But they couldn't stop me from playing sandlot. They couldn't stop me from dreaming of becoming the first female major leaguer.

We got up a game. Batter. Pitcher. Infielder. Outfielder. And Benny House, exiled to the wastelands of right field. I was about to feed the first pitch to Romig when someone called, "Hey!" and came sliding up to the backstop on a green-and-cream Roadmaster. It was the kid from outside the prison wall. "Too late to get in?" he said.

Romig and I looked at each other. What kind of kid was this? Didn't he know you don't ask questions? You don't ask permission. You just do it.

I should have said, *Yeah, too late.* But I remembered how he had recovered the badminton racket and bird for me. So I flipped my head toward the outfield. You might have thought I'd just given him free movie tickets. He beamed and piped, "Thanks!" He pulled his glove from the handlebars and let his bike fall like it was trash and lit out for center. Everything this kid did was annoying me.

But he could play. Each time he came to the plate, he ripped a line drive. He was the only player on the field as good as me.

"How do we know who's winning?" Mister Question said at one point.

"It's too complicated," I told him. Which was true. We had our own system that could never be explained to an outsider. We kept track by scratching lines in the dirt in the first-base coach's box.

Everything was going along hunky-dory, but Mister Question couldn't keep his mouth shut. "Hey," he said, "when does Benny get to bat?"

Dead silence from me, Romig and Mug Williams. The whole plan had been to park the eight-year-old in right field (which nobody hit to) and let the dummy think he was in the game. We prayed the kid hadn't heard. But he did. "I wanna bat!" he cried out.

"Wait your turn," Mug told him. "We'll tell ya."

Each time somebody picked up a bat, the whine came from right field: "I wanna bat!"

Finally he slams his mitt to the ground and says, "I quit!" Which was great, except then he adds: "I'm goin' home." And starts walking off.

Mug looked stricken. "Oh no. I gotta stick with him. My mother said. If he goes, I gotta go."

So Mug runs after his cousin and drags him back. He tells the kid okay, he can bat, but first he has to be catcher. Usually the wire-mesh backstop did the catching.

So I step up to the plate with Benny the catcher pounding his mitt behind me and yelling, "Okay, Mug, zip it in here!" and Mug lobs it in and I belt a screamer to left center. I'm rounding second, and when I see Romig is having trouble digging the ball out of the picket fence, I know I'm heading home. My cap flies off, I'm rounding third full-speed, and when I look up, who's standing on home plate but the runt, yelling, "Peg it here!"

I don't see the ball. All I see is somebody blocking home plate. I cannonball him. Kid goes one way, glove another, ball another. The kid is screaming. Something is bleeding. Mug is on me. "Whaddaya doin'? Ya tryin' to kill 'im?" Spit flecks hit me in the face.

"The catcher was blocking the plate," I say calmly. "It's my job to score." I spit in the dust. "It's called baseball." I go for my glove. I climb on my bike.

Mug follows me. "He's a little kid!"

"He's a catcher," I say, and pedal off.

Mug fires: "And get a girl's bike!" As if that's going to hurt me. I laugh. My bike is a Columbia Jet Rider. And yes, it's a boy bike, with the bar from front to seat.

As I pass the right-field fence, I don't look back. But I know the Roadmaster kid is standing at shortstop, watching.

15

I COULDN'T CARE LESS THAT THEY WERE TICKED OFF AT ME. I was used to it.

Because I was the Little Girl Whose Mother Was Hit by a Milk Truck, adults in Two Mills were mostly nice to me. But it didn't make *me* nice. I once overheard a woman on a sidewalk whisper, "She's such a little curmudgeon." I looked it up. It meant grouch. So that's who I was. Cool.

I was especially not-nice to other kids, who cut me no slack for having a dead mother.

I headed for Ned's on the park boulevard above the baseball fields. Ned's was the home of the foot-long hot dog. Perfect. I used up the last of my money on two foot-longs and a black-and-white ice cream soda. With every bite, I threw a punch at the world.

I was halfway through the second foot-long when Ned's doorbell tinkled and an old man stuck his head in and called: "They got him!"

"You're kidding," Ned called back. He was washing glasses. "When?"

"This morning," the old man called. "Just heard it."

"Where?"

"Bridgeport."

"You're kidding."

There was no reply. The screen door slapped shut. The old man was gone.

Ned looked at me. "Hear that?"

"Yeah," I said.

He plunged a sponge into a glass. An ugly sneer curled his lip. "Good . . . good . . . that son of a—" He cut himself off in mid-curse, the way grown-ups did when a kid was around.

I knew what they were talking about. Everybody did. A week before, a boy fishing at the river had made a gruesome discovery. The body of a girl was floating in the shallows—beside a dead sunny, the newspaper said. She had been visible from the P&W trestle over the river, if any trolley-rider had bothered to look down.

Her name was Annamarie Pinto. She was sixteen. She stood five foot one inch and had long black hair and she listened to "Lavender Blue Dilly Dilly" every day because her favorite color was lavender. She was going to be a high school senior next year. She planned to attend Peirce Business School to become a secretary. Her mother was a checkout lady at Fiore's Market on East Main Street. I knew her from stopping in to get sodas and Tastykakes.

Annamarie Pinto had been strangled. But that accounted for only half the town's uproar. The other half was about this: the killer had used Annamarie's own lipstick to draw something on her stomach. It was a star surrounded by a circle. For the first day or two, most people were baffled. Did the star mean something? Or did the killer just like stars?

And then the pastor of the First Baptist Church said, "The point of the star goes down, not up."

"So?" the town said.

"A downward star points to Satan," the pastor said. "This is a pentagram."

No one had ever heard of a "pentagram," but within hours it was on everyone's lips. Phrases like "devil worship" and "satanic cult" flew from house to house. A madman was out there. Was he a thousand miles away by now? Or living next door?

So when the old man called "They got him!" Ned knew—and I knew—exactly what he meant.

But my juices didn't start to boil until I was rolling away from Ned's, licking mustard from my mouth. That's when I heard the sirens. I knew the difference between police, ambulance, and fire-truck sirens. This was police. A lot of them. Front doors were opening. Kids were running.

I flew to the end of the boulevard, pedaled furiously up the Elm Street hill, veered right on Cherry. I was so excited I didn't realize I had fired right through The Corner. People screaming. Sirens screaming. When I saw the mob on Airy Street, I detoured to Marshall, then flew to the back of the prison and down the high-walled alley to the front.

That whole block of Airy Street was packed with people. I could see only the police cars' red flashers, inching through the crowd. The sirens' scream pinched itself into pulsing balls of warning: *Make way!*

I ditched my bike. I'd worry about it later. I hoisted myself up the side wall of the jail's tiny front yard, which was packed. I fought my way through the crowd to the main walkway. Unlike everywhere else, the walkway was perfectly clear of people, from the sidewalk to the massive, ironclad front door. And in front of the door, magnificent in the navy-blue uniform he used only for special occasions, stood my father.

He wore the billed, cop-like hat with the silver badge that said WARDEN. My mother had given him the badge for his birthday. She'd had it made special at Keystone Jewelers.

He hadn't even been warden at the time—he was captain of the guard and was taking courses in criminology—

but she knew he would make it. Two years after she died, he did.

His face was all business. He stood at attention. He gave no hint that he was aware of the tumult around him. Suddenly I felt proud—proud that it was my father standing there. The warden. The monster's master. My dad. And then his eyes moved, a tiny movement I doubt anyone else noticed. They landed on me, and one of them—the left eye—winked. Winked at me! For an instant I found myself both surprised and grateful that he even knew me.

And then the squad car was at the curb. The mob was wild and loud as the back door was opening and then . . . sudden . . . dead . . . silence. The silence of a classroom when the principal walks in.

He was dressed in gray pants with the cuffs rolled up. An olive-green T-shirt. Cigarette pocket. White socks. Black shoes. Policemen helped him onto the sidewalk—he was shackled, wrists and ankles—but even after they stepped back to give him room, he remained hunched over, as if by standing up he would have to face the fact that he had arrived at his destiny. A voice from the mob cried out: "Killer!"

Still bent over, he took a step. Then another. The car door swung shut behind him.

Step by step he began to unbend. His face came into view. I stared, fascinated: the face of a murderer. A homicidal maniac. Within the hour I would learn his name:

Marvin Edward Baker. He worked for a company that installed windows. That surprised me. I must have thought that "murderer" was a full-time job, like milkman or teacher.

His face was pasty and bristled with black whiskers. In fact, whatever skin was visible was pale, as if he had been living in a hole or under a rock . . . or in a prison. His hair was stringy and long and so obviously packed with oil that I imagined a glassful could have been squeezed out of it.

His eyes were last to come up. They were pale, gray, blinking in a daylight that seemed foreign to him. They glanced about briefly, then settled straight ahead. I found them disappointing, empty. They were aimed in the direction of my father but seemed to have no focus on him or anything else. The only sounds were the footfalls of himself and his uniformed escorts—and the sound of ankle shackles, which was not unlike the rattle of milk bottles.

As he shuffled past me, I think I half expected him to glance my way, as my father had, to single me out. He did not. But his sheer presence, the nearness—I could have reached out and touched him—chilled the skin on my shoulders. I happened to look up. I saw a face—Eloda's—in the window of my bedroom.

As Marvin Edward Baker approached my father, the crowd began to spill over the perp walk. They stopped in their tracks, however, as I chose that moment to vomit up my morning's angry binge of junk onto half a dozen shoe tops and pant legs.

16

THE APARTMENT DOOR WAS OPEN. ELODA WAS WAITING AT the top of the stairs. Her eyes were wide with alarm.

"You all right?" she called down.

"Wonderful," I growled, dragging myself up the endless steps.

She whipped off my baseball cap and flung it to the sofa. She took me into the kitchen. She gave me ginger ale. "Gargle. Spit," she said. She reached into a drawer and produced a Life Saver. "Crush it in your teeth. Chew." She wet a clean dishrag and wiped my face, hard. I yelped, "Ow!" She sat with me at the kitchen table. She felt my forehead. She felt the glands in my neck. "No fever," she said. "No swelling." She stared at me. "How you feeling?"

"I told you," I said. "Hunky-dory."

"Maybe all the excitement," she said.

"Yeah, maybe," I said. I was dying to tell her *she* was the reason I got sick, but with her staring at me like that, I just couldn't.

"You want some Alka-Seltzer?" she said. "Settle your stomach?"

I told her no.

She wet the tip of her finger with her tongue and rubbed a spot on my cheek that she must have missed . . . and suddenly there was yelling on the stairs outside the apartment and the door flew open and Reggie was bursting in: "Is he gone? I missed him, didn't I? I missed him! Oh farts, I missed him!"

And then she was sprinting past us into my father's bedroom. There was a little square window in the back wall. It looked down onto Murderers' Row. "I can't see him! I can't see him!"

She came back, flopped onto a chair. No lipstick. Bare feet. Huffing. *Sweating*. ". . . heard too late . . . ran all the way . . ." Then she was gushing at me. "What did he look like? Was he skinny? Did he say—" Suddenly, horror struck her face. She turned up the bottom of a foot, stared at it. "Eewww!" She hopped over to the sink, grabbed a dishrag, scrubbed vigorously at the foot. "Somebody barfed on the walk. I ran right into it."

I said nothing.

"Well," she said, tossing the dishrag away, "at least I heard something."

I perked up. "What?"

She sat back down. "I heard somebody say that he said, 'I ain't never goin' to Rockview.'" She popped back up. She was too worked up to sit. "What do you think that meant?"

Among kids in town, I was considered the expert on crime and prisons. "Sounds like he's going to either escape or kill himself," I said. "Or go down in a hail of gunfire."

She was impressed. "Wow! So what's Rockview?"

"State prison," I told her.

"So? Is that so bad?" She waved her hand in a circle. "Worse than this?"

"In one way," I said. "Rockview's where the electric chair is."

Reggie boggled. Her awestruck eyes stared down through the floor. The name came to her lips like a whispered prayer: "Marvin Edward Baker . . . the chair . . ." She turned to Eloda, whose hand, I just then realized, was resting on my shoulder. "He's even *more* famous than I thought."

Eloda usually made herself scarce when Reggie came to visit. This was her longest exposure to my melodramatic friend.

Reggie was pacing, holding her arms as if receiving the ovations of adoring audiences. Her dream was to become a star in musicals. First Broadway, then the movies. Her plan was to get on the TV teen dance show *American Bandstand* and be discovered by a talent scout.

"Can you dig it?" she said. "His name is on a thousand lips. *This minute*. Tomorrow it'll be millions."

"He's a killer," said Eloda, her boldness surprising me.

"A famous killer," said Reggie.

"A child killer," said Eloda.

Reggie turned to Eloda with a look of hurt, as if our housemaid was spoiling her fun. Then the hurt look gave way to something else: blinking, quizzical. "So . . . Eloda . . . why did he do it?"

Beneath her spoken words was a pointed undervoice: *So . . . Eloda . . . you're a criminal. You know how the criminal mind works. Why did he do it?*

I felt Eloda's fingers tighten on my shoulder. An awkward silence followed. Then her hand was gone and she was out of the room.

Reggie shrugged. "Big help she is." She looked me over. As usual, she failed to find anything to her liking. She poked me between the eyes. "Next time, I'm bringing my pluckers. I will *not* have a friend with one eyebrow." Then she, too, was gone, flying down the long stairway, screaming about feeling naked without mascara.

My father must have seen the big barf, but he did not mention it at dinnertime. Neither did he speak of the new prisoner.

It wasn't until I lay down to sleep that the grandest moment of the day came back to me: Eloda wetting her finger and cleaning the spot on my cheek. Something sweet spilled inside me. I had been mothered!

17

It DIDN'T LAST.

By next morning, Eloda was back to her stony-face self, and I was once again mad that she didn't like the diary. But my mad lasted only until I saw what was lying at my place at the breakfast counter. It was a key.

My father, as usual, was already off to work. But no matter—I didn't have to ask what the key was for. I knew instantly. It was for the gate to the women's exercise yard.

I had won!

Yard time began at ten in the morning. I looked down from the kitchen window. By ten-fifteen Helen and Tessa were playing netless badminton. (I had returned the racket and bird to them as promised.) Deena was sunning on her shower towel. Boo Boo was holding court, laughing, smoking.

I went down. I acted all casual, as if I were just coming for my usual other-side-of-the-fence visit. "Greetings, female people," I said. I held up the key. I grinned. The yard was suddenly all silence and eyes. I inserted the key in the padlock. Opened the gate. Stepped in.

Pandemonium.

"MISS CAMMIE!"

I was mobbed. Everyone came running but Deena, who removed her eye cups. An unidentified voice flew from the crowd: "Little Warden!"

In truth there were two mobbings. First I was mobbed by Boo Boo. Or maybe "swallowed" is the word. I found myself engulfed in her massive arms and struggling to breathe in the pillowy depths of her bosom. I might have died there had not hands pulled me away for the second mobbing. Thirty-some women—fingers pecking at me like chickens, as if they couldn't believe I was real, as if they'd never touched a person before.

I managed to look up. Atop the far wall Jim Carilla was out of the guardhouse with his rifle, staring. I waved. "It's okay, Jim!"

And then the squeals turned to questions. Everyone wanted to know about the new celebrity inmate.

"Does he look like a killer?"

"Did he look at you?"

"Does he smell bad?"

When one of the women said, "They gonna fry that boy," the hubbub came to a sudden stop. Eyes shifted to the great wall separating the women's yard from the men's.

Our inmates—inmates everywhere, I suppose—practiced the art of forgetting where they were. Those with long sentences in particular kept no calendars in their cells to remind them of the endless jail time remaining. They tried to not look ahead, as those afraid of heights are told not to look down. Another way to forget was to busy oneself with reminders of life on the outside: cigarettes, reading, radio ("The Shadow knows!"), candy. Simple things like daydreaming and sleep were vital in this regard.

But there were intrusions that made forgetting impossible. The clack of the guard's beanbopper as he made the count at lights-out. Sitting down on a toilet with no door or walls for privacy. And the grimmest reality check of all: knowing there was among them an inmate headed for death row. It was not the crime he'd committed, but the likelihood that Marvin Edward Baker had a date with the electric chair at Rockview that was the source of the women's fearful fascination with their new jail mate. I understood the fascination. I myself could never climb the Tower of Death and not stare at—not touch—the hangman's noose.

The questions and the commotion went on for a while, but in the end thirty women were no match for Boo Boo.

"Okay—enough!" she declared, her red-nailed fingers flapping. "Let the little girl be!" Suddenly I was slung over her shoulder.

Jim's voice barked from the high wall: "Hey!"

I craned up, waved, called: "It's okay, Jim! I'm okay!"

And she hauled me away.

18

Boo Boo deposited me onto the concrete bench in the Quiet Room. As usual, the place was empty. The only sound was the mini-waterfall pouring eternally from the tin wheelbarrow into the plant-ringed pool. Boo Boo kept squeezing my hands and shoulders as if making sure I was still in one piece. She smelled like strawberries. She fussed at my hair and clothes. I issued a feeble protest: "Boo Boo, I'm all right. They weren't hurting me."

Sudden anger flared in her eyes, as if I'd just put the thought in her head. "They better not," she snarled.

I was getting more mothering from Boo Boo in one minute than I ever had from Eloda. In that moment, I wished Boo Boo was our housemaid.

And now Boo Boo was showing me a side I'd never

seen. Her voice was soft, confidential. Her eyes kept flicking toward the yard, as if someone might discover her not being loud and jolly.

She paraded her fingers before my eyes. She smiled hugely. "Like my nails?"

Long, bold-red fingernails on Boo Boo seemed as out of place as lipstick on a hippo. It might have been comical or pointless, but the effect on me was somehow endearing. I nodded. "Cool."

"You can touch."

I touched one.

Her voice went whispery. "Cosmetics ain't allowed. But your daddy lets *me*." She leaned in. "Your daddy likes me."

"I know," I said. And for some reason I noticed for the first time that several strands of her wild hair were white.

It occurred to me that I had never asked Boo Boo my Big Question. "Do you know Eloda Pupko?" I said.

"Arnge hair. Hell on wheels outside, I heard," she said. "Why?"

"Do you know why she's in?"

Her answer came at once. "Firebug. Tried to set the town on fire."

She saw the shock on my face, laughed. "Maybe. Maybe not. Don't believe ever'thing you hear down here. But I'll tell you right out what that girl's crime is now."

"What?" I said.

"Snootin'."

"Snootin'? What's that?"

"Snooty. She used to snoot away from the resta us. Spend alla her yard time in here, you b'lieve it."

"Here? The Quiet Room? Eloda Pupko?"

She smacked the seat. "On this here bench."

Maybe, I speculated, it was the Quiet Room that had made her silent and grumpy. Not exactly my father's intention.

"Now," Boo Boo went on, "she be up there"—she gestured toward the apartment—"snootin' around with y'all. Like she *live* there. Come back down here to sleep, then right back up. No time for us common folk. The *high* life." She reached down between her bosoms and pulled out a huge red bandanna. She dusted my face with it, made me laugh. "Y'all tell your daddy, fire that arnge hair and hire on Boo Boo. Boo Boo'll do him some dustin' like he ain't *never* seen!"

We laughed.

She poked me. "Pies? You like pies?"

"Love them," I said. "Carl makes me a pie every week."

She sneered. "Shoot, I'll make you a pie ever' *day*. Soon's I get out. What's your favorite kind?"

Some questions are impossible to answer. "All of them," I said.

"Carl never made you sweet potato pie, did he? Marshmallow on top? Did he now?"

"No," I conceded.

"*That's* gonna be your favorite. Boo Boo's sweet potato pie. Day after I get out . . . the *day*"—she poked me—"I'm walking right into 'ception with that pie in my hands. . . . It's still warm. . . ." She took a deep breath that seemed to double her already enormous bulk. "Can you smell it? . . . Can you?"

"I think so," I said. I wasn't kidding.

"And the guard'll say, he goes, 'Mm-mm. 'Chu got there, Miss Boo Boo?' He calls me Miss 'cause I'm *out* now. And I say, 'Never mind, this's Miss Cammie O'Reilly's.' 'Oh, well then,' he says, 'you go right on up them stairs there.' And that's what I do. I go on *up* the stairs and—now listen—here's the best part. When I get to the top of them stairs, I *won't* have to knock on your door." She grinned. She poked me. "You know why?"

I was barely breathing. "Why?"

"Because you *know* it's coming, girl! You know Boo Boo's sweet potato pie is coming, and so you're *already outside* your door; you're sitting on the top step waitin' and waitin' like you do for Santy Claus." She was up now and pacing about the Quiet Room, waving her arms. "And I give you the pie and I start to go back down the stairs and you call me back and you say, 'Boo Boo—wait! Come in. I can't eat this pie all by myself.' And that's what we do. We go into the kitchen and we slice up the pie and we just sit there and eat and talk and laugh and talk and eat. . . ." I could taste it. She was facing the waterfall. She reached out. The water splashed over her hand. She turned. Her face was serious. "Soon's I get out."

"How long, Boo Boo?" I said.

She gazed up through the glass ceiling. "Any day now," she said. "My 'torney's workin' it. I'm s'prised I didn't get a phone call already."

Her dreamy mood abruptly shifted to instructor, as she gave me a lesson in shoplifting. She said there were two rules: (1) wear a loose skirt or pants, not a dress; (2) get fat. When you shoplift something, you stick it in your underwear (easier and quicker to do going down pants than up a dress). The fatter you are, the bigger your underwear, and hence the more stuff your underwear can hold—and the less likely anyone will notice a few extra pounds on you.

She grabbed a roll of herself in each hand. "Where you think I got all this?"

"I don't know," I said.

She crowed: "Scooper Dooper!"

Scooper Dooper was on West Marshall Street. It was the best ice cream place in the world. "Really?" I said.

She jiggled the fat rolls in front of my face. She seemed to be inviting me to take a bite. "Sundaes . . . cones . . . triple dip! . . . Black-and-white milkshakes . . . But you know what I like the most?"

"What?"

She released her belly rolls. She took a deep breath. "*Banana. Splits.*" She said it like other people said "Amen."

"If I ate one of them things, I ate five hundred." She jabbed a glamorous fingertip at me. "And every one the same. All three scoops chocolate—nunna this chocolate *and* vanilla *and* strawberry stuff. And wet walnuts. *Wet*. And extra whip cream. And hot fudge. And *no* pineapple." She poked my knee. "*And*"—she held up four fingers—"four cherries. One for each scoop plus one."

"Wow," I said. She had a way of talking about food. I was getting hungry.

She regrabbed her belly rolls, looked down at them. "Scooper Dooper. Banana splits." She looked at me. She took my arm, squeezed it. "Gimme two years—maybe three—you, me, Scooper Dooper . . . girl, I'll get two hundred more pounds on you, and you and me'll be walking out of that Woolworth with enough stuff to start our own store!"

We were both laughing so hard that at first we didn't hear the whistle. Then we did: the long, breathy toot from Scheidt's Brewery, squatting massively on the eastern slope of Stony Creek. Wherever you were—hanging wash in the East End, removing an appendix at Sacred Heart Hospital, fishing at Rohm's Quarry in the far west, counting the days and years in Hancock County Prison—if you were alive and awake, you heard it. Grown-ups set their watches by it. At precisely noon every day, the brewery whistle cried out to all of Two Mills: *Lunchtime!*

Boo Boo and I said goodbye and she joined the rest of

the women heading inside. I paused in the empty yard before heading back out. I felt myself smiling as I recalled their shock and delight when they saw I was coming in to join them. Such a difference it had made, being on the same side of the fence. I entered my backyard. I locked the gate behind me and climbed the stairs to the apartment. In my mind I rewrote a certain headline from the *Corrections* journal:

WARDENS' DAUGHTERS:
BETTER THAN PETS?

19

I DID NOT RETURN TO THE YARD NEXT DAY. I WAS PRE-
occupied with thoughts of Eloda and what I'd heard from
Boo Boo.

I watched Eloda as I ate my breakfast. I watched her
empty the wastebaskets and Hoover the rugs. I tried to fit
the word "firebug" on her. The more I watched her, the
more mysterious she became.

Pretty soon I couldn't take it any longer.

She was in the laundry room. She was at the ironing
board, pressing one of my father's dress shirts. A heap of
wrinkled clothes sat on the washing machine. I pushed
them to one side and hoisted myself up. I didn't waste words.

"So," I said, "I hear you're a firebug."

I was disappointed. Her face did not show a trace of the shock I'd hoped for. But her hand did come to a standstill, the iron poised above a snow-white sleeve. For the first time I noticed her fingernails. They were short and plain as a man's, nothing like Boo Boo's. There was not a hint of glamour about Eloda Pupko. Eventually the iron came down and resumed pressing the sleeve.

"You're not speaking?" I said.

Her eyes never left the sleeve. "What is there to speak of?"

"I asked you a question."

"You made a statement."

I groaned. "Okay . . . is it true? *Are* you a firebug? Is that why you're in here? Did you try to burn the town down?"

She gave an indifferent shrug. "If you say so."

"I'm *not* saying so. I'm asking *you*."

"Who said?"

"Boo Boo."

"Must be true, then."

"Eloda, will you please look at me?"

She lifted the iron. She looked at me. For two seconds. And went back to work.

Infuriating woman. "Why are you being such a poop?"

She stopped again. Spoke to the iron: "I'm a poop." Went back to work.

I corked a laugh ball. "I'm *trying* to have a conversation."

She hung up the finished shirt. "Congratulations." She started in on another, first squirting it with the mister.

I wasn't giving up. "Boo Boo says you're snooty."

No reaction. Iron, iron.

"She says you think you're special because you're up here all day. You think you're better than the other inmates."

She shrugged. "I'm snooty."

"Yeah," I said. "You forget you're just a jailbird."

She nodded. "That's me."

Would it kill her to take me seriously?

I slammed my heels into the washer. Reckless words were coming and I could not stop them. "You think you *live* here. You think you're part of the *family*."

No movement except two raised eyebrows. "Do I?"

"Yeah." I jabbed my finger at her; I couldn't stop myself. "Who do you think you *are*? My *mother*?"

The reaction didn't come at once. While my words hung in the air, she continued to iron for another ten full seconds. Then she set the iron on its end and looked up, into my eyes. "Don't worry," she answered with devastating assurance. "I'm not your mother." And returned to the iron. And added: "And never will be."

It took a moment for her words to sink in. When they did, I screamed at her: "Well, good!" I jumped down from the washer. I swatted the misting bottle. It smashed against the wall. Glass and water all over. "Great!" I yelled. "I'm glad we got that straightened out! And you wanna know what else? Huh? I'll tell you what else! I'm telling my father to send you back down where you belong! You'll be making rugs and stringballs with everybody else!"

Unfazed as ever—except for a flinch when the mister hit the wall—she stood amid the water and pieces of glass and said, "That so?"

My fury leaped off the charts. "Yeah, that's so!" I yelled. "You can kiss the high life goodbye!"

She lifted the iron from the shirt and gave me her eyes. But that was all. I found no emotion, no satisfying response in her face. Who knows how long the stalemate of eyes might have gone on. As it was, a sudden commotion came from outside the jail. I seized the chance to escape a showdown I didn't really want. I ran to the front window. Below me a mob was surging over the sidewalk and into the street.

Even before I spotted the murderer Marvin Edward Baker, I knew what was happening. The prisoner was returning from his arraignment.

The Sixth Amendment to the Constitution of the United States of America says an accused person has the right to be told exactly why he or she has been arrested. Not only that, but it needs to happen fast, so the prisoner isn't left sitting in a cell for months, wondering what's going on. That's why the arraignment happens within forty-eight hours after the arrest. The accused is informed of the charges and offered the chance to plead guilty or not guilty.

Wanting to avoid another mob scene, my father had sneaked Marvin Edward Baker out a side door and down the short block to the courthouse at four-thirty in the morning. But he couldn't control the whole course of events. By the time the judge said the words "willfully and with premeditation did cause the death of one Annamarie Grace Pinto," a river of people was flowing from the courthouse to the county prison. The citizens of Two Mills knew their Sixth Amendment.

The multitude parted reluctantly as the flashing squad cars inched down Airy Street. This time it was not silence that greeted Marvin Edward Baker when he emerged from the car. A storm of the ugliest words I had ever heard flew through the screen of the apartment's open window. This time the celebrity felon was visible for only a few seconds before vanishing into the ironclad maw beneath my living room.

For minutes afterward howls of damnation raged against our dark fortress, drowning out the rushing footsteps that on an ordinary day I would have heard. Sudden thumps on the apartment door along with cries of "Cammie! Open up!" announced the arrival of Reggie Weinstein. The wide-eyed wonderment, the excitement bursting from her every perfect pore, told me that she had just made up for missing the murderer's perp walk the first time around.

I was wrong.

She grabbed me by the shoulders and shook me like a pom-pom and screamed into my face: "I'm going to *Bandstand!*"

20

SCREAMING FILLED THE NEXT TWENTY MINUTES. MOSTLY Reggie. ("I can't believe it!" "I'm really going!" "Pinch me!") Though I did my share, as I really was happy for her. ("Wow!" "Oh my God!" "Cool!")

When actual conversation became possible, I learned that Reggie's father had finally caved in. She had been begging him for the past year. His big objection was that she was too young. *Bandstand* age range was fourteen to eighteen. Reggie argued that you didn't have to prove your age: you just lied and they believed you, especially if you looked old enough.

The big moment had come that morning. Her father was in the bathroom, shaving. Reggie was planted outside, whining and begging. Suddenly the door flew open and her father was standing there with a face full of shaving cream, raging: "Okay—go! Go! I hope you get arrested!"

As for Reggie's mother, she had never been a problem. One look at her and you knew where Reggie got her looks and style. Reggie's mom called her daughter's friends "hon" and jitterbugged with Reggie to *Bandstand* in their living room.

"So," I said, "are you gonna dance?" This might seem like a dumb question, but the *Bandstand* dance floor was small and usually monopolized by the regulars from South Philly. Just watching them, either in-studio or on TV, was practically a national sport. They had their own fan clubs.

She sneered. "Does a bear poop in the woods?"

"So what about Tommy D?" I said.

Ah. Tommy D.

That was all the name you needed. Tommy DeBennedetto was the cutest guy on the show. Black hair curling over his forehead. Midnight killer eyes. Every girl in the Delaware Valley was in love with him, including Reggie. Including Tommy's girlfriend and co-*Bandstand* regular, Arlene Holtz.

"What about him?" said Reggie.

I hadn't thought this through. "I don't know. . . . I never saw him dance with anybody but Arlene."

"So?" she snipped. "Who needs Tommy D?"

And I thought: Bandstand—*look out*.

Reggie had brought the *Bandstand* tote that held her

records. Shapewise it looked like either a large coffee can or a small hat box. It had a picture of Dick Clark, the host of *Bandstand*. We sang while we danced:

> *You cheated*
> *You lied*
> *You said that you love me*

Despite Reggie's endless labors to girly me up, when we danced, the boy was always me.

> *Splish splash, I was takin' a bath*
> *'Long about a Saturday night*

We did slow. We did fast. We did the jitterbug (with the new push step), the hand jive and the stroll and the birdland and the cha-cha and the chalypso.

We only stopped dancing to sing—more shout, really— our personal national anthem, by the Cookies:

> *Don't say nothin'*
> *Bad about my baby*
> *(Don't you know)*
> *Don't say nothin'*
> *Bad about my baby*
> *He's true*
> *He's true to me*

We jabbed our fingers into each other's face and snarled the last line over and over:

So, girl, you better shut yer mouth!

Eloda made the mistake of appearing in the dining room. "Eloda!" Reggie cried. "I'm going to *Bandstand*!"

Eloda looked up from her dustrag long enough to flatly reply, "You don't say."

If Eloda had been smart, she'd have run downstairs and locked herself in her cell. Reggie birdlanded over to her, flung the dustrag away and danced her around the dining room table. She even let Eloda be the girl.

Eloda tried to be a good sport, but she couldn't disguise the pain on her face. I felt bad that she had to endure my friend's exuberance—and felt all the worse for having made her endure me in the laundry room. I had to rescue her. I called out the first thing that came to mind: "Eloda, my room smells. Would you please open the window and air it out?"

Eloda broke from Reggie and fled.

Reggie raided the fridge for a black cherry, her favorite soda. We always kept bottles on hand for her.

"Must be great," she said, flopping onto the sofa, "having a maid."

Reggie had always called my Cammie-keepers that. It had never bothered me before.

"She's not a maid," I said. "She's a trustee. This is her job."

"You must trust her a lot. What if she steals stuff?"

I shushed her. "Quiet. She'll hear. And she doesn't steal."

"But what *if*?"

"She *doesn't*."

She took a long swig of black cherry. She leaned forward. "All I'm saying is, she's behind bars for a reason. Trustee or not."

Eloda was under attack. My defenses were bristling.

"There's a reason they're called trustees," I countered. "You can *trust* them."

"And there's a reason they're in jail. They're criminals."

"She loves me!" I shot back.

To this day I don't know who was more surprised at my words, Reggie or myself. Why did I say it? I knew it wasn't true. But I wanted it to be. Reggie and I just gawked at each other.

Then her face changed, softened. She put down her soda and came to sit on the arm of my easy chair. She smiled. "Cammie, I'm only trying to—"

Whatever it was, I didn't want to hear it. I blurted: "Sometimes I pretend she's my mother."

She blinked. She didn't believe me. And then she did. She glanced around to make sure Eloda wasn't nearby. She whispered, "She's in *jail*."

Defend. Lie.

"Not for long," I said.

That slowed her down. "No?" she said. "When does she get out?"

Lie. "Any day now. Her old job is waiting for her."

"Really?" She looked interested. "And what job is that?"

"It's a cleaning business. She cleans people's houses. They give her a key and let her in the house even when they're not there." I couldn't stop myself.

"Really?" she said.

"Yeah," I said.

"So what was her crime?"

"Shoplifting."

"Really?"

"Yeah."

"Shoplifting what?"

"A pack of cigarettes."

"A pack of cigarettes. They threw her in jail for stealing a pack of cigarettes?"

"She didn't even steal them. She just forgot to pay. And she had a bad lawyer."

Reggie wagged her head. She smiled down on me. It was a smile of enormous pity, the pity of the righteous for an unfortunate, misguided soul. She hadn't believed a word I'd said. "Cammie, Cammie . . . life isn't a comic book." She squeezed my hand. "Bad people don't get good just like that."

"Tell that to *Corrections* magazine," I told her. "And my father." I thought of the Quiet Room. The forever-empty Quiet Room.

"Most people that get out of jail, they do something else and come right back in."

"That's bullpoop," I said. "What do you know about prisons?"

She squeezed my hand. "Bad is bad. I know that."

I was out of arguments. "I don't care," I said, hoping she would drop it.

She didn't.

She came down from the armrest. She knelt on the floor before me. The shock and condescension were gone. She was simply dead serious, as if she were studying the cosmetics rack at Woolworth's. "Cammie . . . ," she said. She laid her hand on mine. "I just don't want to see you get hurt."

I stared over her head. "What do you care?"

"You're my best friend."

"Big deal."

She squeezed my hand again. "Cammie, she's in *jail*. She *can't* be your mother. She's tricking you."

I snatched my hand away. "Says you."

She gestured at the apartment. "Cammie—look." I didn't. "Just look at this nice place you live in. If *you* were stuck in a jail cell, wouldn't *you* love to have a nice, cushy job up here?" She squeezed my hand for the third time. Suddenly I couldn't stand her touching me. "Wouldn't *you* be all peachy to the warden's daughter so you could keep this nice, cushy job?"

I heard Boo Boo's voice: *snootin'* . . . *high life.*

I smacked her hand away. I shouted into her face. "She's *not* peachy!" And thought: *I wish she was.*

"Fine," she said: calm, reasonable, Reggie the grown-up. "Not peachy. So let her be your maid. Your friend, even. Invite her to your *wedding.*" Animated now, tossing up her hands. "But for Pete's sake, just don't make her your *mother*! She's a *criminal*!"

I shoved her. Hard. She toppled backward. Her head bounced off the floor. I raged down at her: "You don't know nothin'!"

Shock. Disbelief. Tears. She was so anxious to reach the door she crawled halfway before picking herself up. She struggled with the bar lock, screaming curses, heaving with sobs. Finally the door flew open. She wheeled. Her cheeks were black with eyeliner. She thrust a finger at me and shrieked: "Just because you lost your mother doesn't mean . . . doesn't mean . . ." She choked on her own sobs and went clattering down the stairs and, I assumed, out of my life forever.

21

THE DOOR WAS STILL OPEN FROM REGGIE'S DEPARTURE. I climbed the Tower of Death to the Salami Room. I peered out the narrow window. Reggie was passing the courthouse. Her hand was going back and forth to her mouth. It was hard to tell for sure at that distance, but I thought: *She's smoking a cigarette!* She turned left on Swede Street and was out of sight, heading for Main, downtown.

I went back down the tower stairway to the door I was not allowed to open. It was a curiously little door, no higher than my nose. It led to the battlement, a notched, narrow walkway around the base of the tower. The battlement was off-limits to me. I didn't care. I opened the door, ducked my head and stepped out.

The outer wall came up to my waist. I walked back and

forth. Or at least my feet did. The rest of me was in my head, the morning's debris sloshing around like so much laundry in Eloda's washing machine: *glass on the laundry room floor . . . I'm going to* Bandstand! *. . . Marvin Edward Baker . . . mob on Airy Street . . . she's in jail . . . Tommy D . . . bad is bad . . . she loves me . . . she doesn't . . . sometimes I pretend . . . so, girl, you better . . . hell on wheels . . . firebug . . . she doesn't . . . shut your mouth . . . she doesn't . . . she doesn't . . .*

Was Reggie right? Was that all I was to Eloda—a way out of the cellblock? A nice, cushy job?

And of course, compared to an inmate's usual routine, it *was* a cushy job. Or, as Boo Boo would say, "the high life." So why *didn't* Eloda try harder to stay on my good side? Didn't she know the warden's daughter had some clout around here?

And why, of all people, had I confided to Reggie Weinstein in the first place? Yes, she was beautiful. She was fun. She was cool. But did she wear the crown of Miss Sensitivity? Hardly.

How long had I been fitfully pacing the battlement? Suddenly a face was poking through the little doorway. It was Tony, the day guard from Reception, the first person people saw when they entered the prison. He always had a big smile for me. Not this time. "Miss Cammie, you need to come in off there. Right now."

I didn't argue. Tony explained that people were calling

the prison switchboard. They saw someone moving outside the tower. They thought an inmate was escaping. Now I knew why I wasn't allowed on the battlement.

I returned to the Salami Room. The brewery whistle flung its lunchtime bulletin over the town. I wasn't hungry. Even if I had been, I would not have gone down. I needed to be alone in the one place in the world I could call my own. My attic. Where my feelings and memories and questions were stored. Where I could safely take them from their drawers and trunks and blow the dust off them and turn them over in my hands. Where I could grope for and occasionally touch the feathery outermost fringes of peace.

Why Eloda Pupko?

What is there about her?

What if one day she shocks me and says, Okay, call me Mom?

What then?

Will I be happy?

Me?

Happy?

Reggie . . . Eloda . . . my father . . . Is there anyone I get along with?

Ah—Boo Boo.

I sat on the flagstone floor, my back against the curving wall. I held my mother's shoe in my lap. I read and read again the thin, yellowed letter of Thomas Browne to his Dearest Loved One. I closed my eyes and recited it to myself like a memorized poem. I fondled the phrases. *Leave the memories to me. . . . Do not allow your future to be plundered . . . the bad time is over. . . . you must . . .*

You must . . .

Why did it have to end there, leaving me alone with what was missing? What if Thomas Browne had finished the sentence? What would it have said? I could not banish the notion that it would have said something to me, something that would have left me standing gloriously clear and free atop a hill, all the burrs and prickles finally fallen from my skin.

Dust drifted lazily in shafts of sunlight. Through the sealed windows, from below, came the eternal din of traffic, the occasional human shout. Beyond . . . to the west . . . always there . . . The Corner . . . The Corner.

I lay down on the stones, a rainbow-haired rag doll for a pillow. I must have slept, for I know I dreamed, of a quiet room where milk fell silently from a wheelbarrow.

22

NEXT DAY EVERYTHING SEEMED BACK TO NORMAL.

I awoke to the smell of scrapple.

I ate my usual breakfast. In the summer of 1959 that meant Cocoa Puffs.

When I finished my cereal, Eloda, as usual, was there to do my pigstub. We chatted as if the laundry-room mess had never happened. I even made her chuckle when I asked, "Is it ready for a ribbon yet?" If she had heard Reggie and me the day before, she didn't let on.

I went down to the yard. I plunged into the mob. All the fuss, the touching, the lips and eyes of excitement—I let it wash over me, wash away the discord of the previous day. I was their tranquility pet. And the rope in a tug-of-war: Boo Boo wanted me for herself, and so did the others.

This time they won. They had me till the brewery whistle sent them back inside.

After lunch I went to the movies. *Attack of the Giant Leeches* was playing at the Grand. That sounded pretty good.

It was. Monster leeches were dragging unsuspecting people down into their cave in the Everglades, where they slowly sucked the blood out of them. I was revolted and spellbound at the same time. Movies didn't get much better than that.

Then came Sunday.

23

Except for the occasional Phillies game, I hated Sundays.

In my house Sunday did not mean church. My father had forsaken church after my mother's death, so I never went to Sunday school. I first heard the name "God" in curses on the sidewalks and alleys where I played in my preschool days. I dimly recall once asking a playmate, Regina Shaffer, who this God guy was. I don't recall her answer.

In the years that followed, from streets and school I gleaned impressions of God. He seemed at first to be a man, a really important big-shot man, kind of like a president but even bigger. God was like a coach, directing everything that happened on earth. Whenever I came across God's name in print, the pronouns "He" and "His" came with a capital H. Not even George Washington could say that.

Another Sunday thing was angels. Angels seemed to be part human (they looked like us) and part bird (big white wings). They lived with God in the sky beyond the clouds, in a place called Heaven. They wore white nightshirts and no shoes or socks. That was about all I knew of angels until one day in third grade, when I was nine.

If you stood facing the front of Hancock County Prison, to the right you would see city hall, to the left St. John's Church. Running alongside the block-long length of the prison's west wall was the church cemetery.

On my way home from school I always took a shortcut through the graveyard. Sometimes I ran, weaving and dodging among the tombstones, pretending they were defenders in a football game. On this particular day in late spring, I came to a sudden stop on my way to a touchdown. A new gravestone had caught my eye. Unlike all the other worn gray monuments, this one was a smart, rounded tablet of pure white marble, like some front steps in town. I wandered over. I read the name on the stone:

MARGARET BIRD

I read the epitaph. When I came to the last two words—

OUR ANGEL

—the breath went out of me. Death? Angels? Heaven? Answers to questions I didn't know I'd had were snapping into place.

Angels are dead people.

Who don't stay dead.

Light from the radiant headstone blinded me, bathed me in a staggering thought: *Maybe my mother did not come to an end at The Corner.*

Maybe.

Oh, what a wonderful word!

I ran.

I raced from the cemetery, burst into Reception, blurted at Tony: "Where's my dad?"

"Cellblock," he said.

"I have to see him!" I was gasping.

"He'll be out soon," he said, much too calmly.

"Tony," I screeched, "I *have* to see him! Now!"

He knew he shouldn't do it, but I was the warden's daughter. He picked up the intra-prison phone. A minute later another guard was opening the door. I dashed past him, through the anterooms (which he should have locked behind himself) and into the cellblock.

"Daddy! Daddy!" I flew past barred, gaping faces to my father at the other end. "Daddy, guess what—" I gushed, and stopped when his finger pressed my lips. He pulled me into an empty cell. He sat me on the lower bunk. He was not happy with me. We both knew I was violating the rule about not interrupting him at work. "Keep your voice down," he said. "Now where's the fire?"

"Huh?" I said. "What fire?"

"What can't wait?"

I told him. It all came pouring out. Death. Angels. Heaven. Margaret Bird and the dazzling tombstone. The annoyance on his face changed to a flatness I could not read. But his eyes never left me. I had his attention. I took my best swing. "So *maybe*," I said, "she's in Heaven now. She's still alive up there. You think?"

For a moment there was no reaction. The guard, as I was gushing, had backed off into the cellblock gloom. Then my father smiled at me. I had not known a smile could be so sad. He touched me. "Sure, Cammie," he said. Just that. Then he waved for the guard to take me out.

Sure, Cammie.

The words followed me as the guard led me out of the cellblock.

Sure, Cammie.

I had never heard my name said so sadly. He was a terrible actor. He was lying. With those two words he knocked my barely hatched belief out of the nest. Angels were no match for my father. His "Sure" easily canceled my "Maybe." If my father didn't believe in angels, neither, at age nine, could I. I would not be meeting my mother in Heaven after all.

24

AND SO ON THIS SUNDAY THREE YEARS LATER, WHILE other kids went to church and got in touch with angels and Heaven, I grabbed my bike and went for a ride. I think I did it to escape the mads. It seemed I spent half my life being mad at somebody. My father. Mothered-up little kids. Boys. Friends. Reggie. Eloda. The milk-truck driver. Even my mother. Had I spent all those Sundays in church, no doubt I'd have aimed my mads at the whole host of Heaven. An unhatched egg of knowledge deep inside me understood that mad is a monster that chews itself. But at age twelve, all I knew was that I needed to get out of town, put some distance between me and Sunday.

Despite Eloda's forgiving demeanor and the adoration in the women's yard and the movie's giant leeches, I still felt rotten about Friday's carnage. In the space of an hour I had attacked both Eloda and Reggie. Count the daily infliction of my sour temper on my father, and I'd abused the three most important people in my life.

I rode west through the traffic of town . . . Airy Street into Jeffersonville . . . the endless asphalt of Egypt Road . . . Trooper Road . . . onto the Singing Bridge, the river visible below the steel grating . . . on into the hills and history of Valley Forge.

I rode without stopping. I pedaled to the top of Valley Forge Mountain, circled the observation tower at the peak and coasted back down. I lost myself among the hills and endless meadows, riding roads whose names I did not know. In the distance I faintly heard the brewery's lunch whistle, which never took Sunday off.

I rode and rode. Something in me wanted to keep going all the way to California. But I could not. I could never travel more than a bike ride from the nexus of my life, the seed from which I sprang: The Corner—the place that I could neither seem to leave nor visit. If I had any destination that day, it was oblivion. For in fact it was much more than the events of the past few days that had left me hanging from the hooks of guilt.

Accident investigation in 1947 was not very fancy. All that was known of the event came from the milk-truck driver himself, a man named Kirby, and a pedestrian half a block away. Their accounts were identical. Both told police that as the truck was upon her, my mother shoved the carriage across the street. Both agreed that the truck seemed to strike my mother at the same moment that my carriage struck the opposite curb. There the carriage stopped, but I went flying, presumably indicating the force of my mother's push. I lay on the brick sidewalk, utterly unharmed, saved by my mother in every way—the push, the pink snowsuit that had protected me against winter cold and sidewalk landings, and most of all the unimaginable love that had hurled me clear of her last moment on earth.

When I became old enough to be told about the accident and to think about it, the question of blame crept into view. Such a tragedy had to be the fault of someone, something.

Was the driver to blame?

Until then the driver, Kirby, had had a spotless record with Supplee Dairy. There was no suggestion that he was speeding or careless. He wasn't drunk. He was driving south on Cherry and turning west onto Oak. In those days not every intersection was a four-way stop. The stop signs were on Oak, not Cherry. So no, it wasn't his fault. He did nothing wrong. Which apparently was no comfort to him. Before the day was over, he quit his job.

The truck was not to blame. The brakes were checked and were found to be working perfectly.

My mother? Was she to blame? Of course not. Like the brakes, my mother was perfect.

How about God? It seemed possible, until I pleaded my case to my father in the cellblock that day. When he dismissed the whole God/Heaven/angels thing with a shrug and the "Sure" he didn't really mean, he deprived me of both relief and scapegoat. I could not blame Him.

That left me.

Was it my fault? Was I acting up, crying and fussing and distracting my mother's attention from the oncoming milk truck? Or was it a more positive sort of distraction? Was I doing something adorable, tempting my mother to take her eyes from the street and to lean into the carriage and nuzzle me as the truck barreled onward? I did not know. I still don't know. I never will.

Milk trucks rested in parking lots that Sunday as I pedaled to exhaustion over the hills of Valley Forge. In time I found myself, stunned and heaving, leaning from my bike seat on one foot. I was off the road, in the middle of a meadow, the bike wheels sunk in wild rye. I looked up. Hawks were circling lazily above me like winged kites, like black angels. In my Sunday state, I imagined for a moment that they had followed me from The Corner. I bolted from the meadow.

The hills were spilling shadows as I coasted down and out of Valley Forge, through Bridgeport, over the Hector

Street bridge and back into town. As I held for a red light at Main Street, I heard something to my right: the sharp snap of a cap pistol, accompanied by "Pow! Pow! Pow!" A little boy, skin the color of a Milky Way, was terrorizing storefronts with a toy silver gun. He was alone, heading east. "Pow! Pow! Pow!"

The light turned green. I forgot about heading home. I followed the boy instead.

25

Why?

I didn't know then. Don't know now.

I footed my bike along, staying well behind. I didn't want to spook him. Except for us, Main Street was empty. In those days stores were closed on Sunday.

He was tiny, maybe five. He wore a white belt and a holster that came down to his knee. Red bullets hung in loops along the belt. The red ribbon of the spent caps stuttered up out of the silver chamber and fell over his little fingers.

I found myself afraid that he might turn around, spot me, shoot me. But he didn't. He was furiously intent on wiping out East Main Street. Philly Tobacco. Zummo's Hardware. Linfante's Zeps. The ramshackle sprawl of Chatlin's Department Store. "Pow! Pow! Pow!"

He turned right on Mill. He was heading into Mogins Dip.

Mogins Dip was the black-only section of town. It sloped down from East Main to the railroad tracks, which in turn paralleled the river.

When I reached the corner, he was halfway down the block, firing along the row-house canyon of two- and three-story brick fronts. He pulled up before a house with a sky-blue door. For a full ten seconds he fired at the blue door. Satisfied at last, he holstered the silver gun and swaggered up the steps. And suddenly turned, spotting me five houses up. His eyes boggled. He went for the gun, aimed between my eyes. "Pow! Pow! Pow!" He waited. It took me a moment to catch my cue. I produced an unconvincing groan. I flopped—shoulders, hands, head—in my bike seat. Dead. I even closed my eyes. I heard the blue door open and close. When I peeked, he was gone.

26

THE NEXT COUPLE OF DAYS WERE ROUTINE. AT TEN EACH morning I visited the women's yard.

Now that I had the key and could go inside with them, I took my self-appointed role as tranquility pet even more seriously. In my most deluded moments I imagined that the only thing standing between my father the warden and an epic prison uprising was little ol' me.

Ha! Tranquility was nowhere in sight when I opened the gate each morning. I was mobbed. It was my first taste of mass popularity. They peppered me with questions: "Are saddle shoes still cool?" "What happened on *Perry Mason* this week?" "Tell us about Marvin Edward Baker!"

One day on a whim I took my hula hoop with me. They

went wild. Someone different was hooping with it every minute. At the end of the two-hour yard time I didn't have the heart to take it back with me. I left it there, a yellow toy on the packed gray earth.

I tried to give attention to everyone. I strolled about the yard, my retinue in tow. I said hi to the shy and the sullen. I stopped by Deena, sunning on her shower towel, and chatted for a moment at her black plastic eye cups, careful not to block her rays. I took a turn at badminton swats with Helen and Tessa. I was doing everything the Quiet Room did not.

I must have returned home each day reeking of cigarettes. There was no danger of smoking myself. Boo Boo had proclaimed to all: "Don't let me catch *nobody* off'rin' this here girl no cig'rette." Nobody ever did.

Of course Boo Boo would have loved to have me all to herself, but even she understood there would be mutiny if she tried to enforce it. We settled on a deal: the last half hour of yard time was hers. "Boo Boo Time" she called it. Inmates were not permitted to have watches, so how she knew when eleven-forty-five arrived each day I could never figure out. She would flick her cigarette away and take me by the hand into the Quiet Room. We sat on the concrete bench and her fingernails flashed red and the words flew nonstop from her through the strawberry haze of her scent.

She spoke of yesterday and tomorrow, never today. She

was born in Mississippi, she told me, the seventh daughter of a cotton sharecropper. She arrived in Two Mills at the age of ten. She worked as a dancer, a secretary, a hairdresser, a drive-in waitress. "Shakey's?" I said, referring to the drive-in west of town. *"Roller skates? You?"* She poked me. "B'lieve it." She knew I was trying to picture massive Boo Boo on skates. She laughed. "Girl, I was one hundred and seven pound in them days."

I was enthralled. So packed was her pre-prison life, I marveled that she'd had time for shoplifting.

I hated to hear the lunch whistle. As she was going back in, she always pointed her red-tipped finger at me and said, "Day I'm out, what I'm bringin'?" And I snap-pointed back: "Sweet potato pie!"

It was Thursday noon of that week, as I was climbing the back stairs to our apartment, when I heard thumping on the front door and the familiar voice: "Cammie! Open up!"

I grinned. Reggie was back.

I had long since collected her scattered 45s and stacked them in her *Bandstand* tote. It had occurred to me that I might bike the tote up to her house, leave it on the doorstep. But then I figured: *Shove or no shove, even if she hates me now, she can't live without her records. She'll come for them any minute.*

I took a deep breath and opened the door. It wasn't what I expected.

27

Yes, there was Reggie's ever-gorgeous, big-eyed face—with not a hint that it remembered the shove—but there were other faces, too, all screaming at me: "Hi, Cammie!"

Classmates. We were friendly, but I thought of them more as Reggie's friends than mine. I grinned at a funny thought: maybe Reggie had brought a group along to feel safer.

They poured into the apartment. I had had friends other than Reggie over before, but never so many at once. They practically ran over me and within seconds were swarming into every room.

"Where are they?" called Glenda Schmoyer.

"Here! Here! Look! It's the yard!" shrieked Gussie Kornichek from the kitchen.

Rosanna Scotti was in my face, breathless: "When can we do it?"

"Huh?" I said. "Do what?"

"Take the tour!"

I looked at Reggie.

She gave me her pearly smile. "I told them you'd give them a tour of the prison."

"Maybe even see Marvin Edward Baker!" Rosanna Scotti gushed. By now they were all crowded around me, panting exclamation points. I was afraid one or two might get sick from excitement.

"There's no *tour*," I told them. "You don't do *tours* in prison. This isn't Independence Hall." I turned to Reggie. "Why did you tell them that?"

Reggie gave a *what's the big deal* shrug. "You're the warden's daughter. You can do things. You took me down to the yard."

The calls came:

"She met the prisoners!"

"She talked to Boo Boo!"

"Boo Boo gave her a cigarette!"

"We wanna see Boo Boo!"

I glared at Reggie. "Boo Boo did *not* give her a cigarette. And that was *not* a tour. We were on the other side of the fence." I resolved to never tell Reggie that I could enter the yard now and mix freely with the women.

Donna Holloway looked ready to cry. "Not even a *little* tour?"

"A *teeny* tour?" peeped Gussie Kornichek.

"I'm sorry," I said. "I don't make the rules."

"Can't we just see *one* little ol' prisoner?" begged Rosanna Scotti. "What harm would that do?"

"Yeah," piped Glenda Schmoyer. "Just Marvin Edward Baker."

"Marvin Edward Baker!" chanted Donna Holloway.

And then they were all doing it: "Marvin! Edward! Baker! Marvin! Edward! Baker!"

I had to swallow a smile. It was pathetic and funny at the same time. I tried to look regretful. "I'm really sorry. He's in solitary. Only the guard and my father are allowed to see him."

Still, I wished I could give them something. But what?

"Okay . . . ," I said. "Maybe . . . if I can find the key to the gate . . . *maybe* I can at least let you into the yard for a minute. Only because it's empty now." You'd think I'd just announced a snow day. "For a *minute*!" I yelled over the cheers.

That's when Eloda made her mistake. Until that moment there had been no sign of her. She must have ducked into a bedroom when the mob charged in. Now she could be seen moving through the dining room and into the kitchen. She was visible for no more than two or three seconds, but that's all it took. The girls weren't stupid. They knew—or thought they knew—what someone in a denim dress in a prison was. Whispers pelted me:

"Who's *that*?"

"Is she a *prisoner*?"

"What's she doing *here*?"

"Is she *escaping*?"

I snapped at them. "Button it. She's a trustee. She helps in the house."

Rosanna Scotti's words came out wide-eyed: "You have a *maid*?"

"A *trustee*," I repeated. I pointed to the floor—"Stay here"—and left them in the living room. I was momentarily surprised that Reggie had not told them about the third person in our apartment.

Eloda was in the kitchen, about to make my lunch. I tapped her on the shoulder. I whispered, "Forget my lunch. Get outta sight."

She didn't have to be told twice.

The key was always in the bottom drawer with the dishrags. I made a noisy show of opening and closing drawers and doors. After a minute I called out: "Okay—I found it!"

They came running.

"Okay . . . ," I said. "I'm not supposed to do this. . . ." I opened the kitchen door and turned back to them. "No noise. Anybody talks—"

A giggling squeal came from the mob: "You'll put us in jail!"

I allowed myself to laugh with them. I waited for silence. I led them down the back steps and across our measly patch of dirt. A solitary dandelion, which had been a cheery yellow flower on the first day of vacation, was now a dusty gray puff. I unlocked the gate and turned to them. "Stay here."

I stepped into the yard. I called: "Jim! I'm letting them into the yard! Five minutes!"

He sent a thumbs-up from the tower.

Behind me I heard Reggie whisper: "That's the guard. He'll shoot anybody who tries to escape."

I glared at Reggie and waved them on. They filed in with intimidated silence. At first they just stood inside the gate, gawking. They weren't just loving it; they were wonderstruck. Inmates weren't necessary. They were standing on the same hallowed ground trod daily by felons. I was giving them the day of their lifetimes. I congratulated myself.

They began to fan out across the yard, tentatively at first and then more boldly. They touched the great walls, feeling the stones. Donna Holloway scooped up a small handful of dirt. She looked at me. I didn't say no. She put it in the pocket of her jeans.

They must have seen the cigarette butts from the start. You couldn't miss them. They littered the ground. It was an inmate's job to scoop them up twice a week. After a while

I heard a voice whisper-calling me: "Cammie!" Rosanna Scotti was standing in the center of the yard, holding up an inch-long butt. She mimicked putting it in her pocket. *Okay?* she mouthed. I nodded. And then they were swarming, all of them, racing from butt to butt, snatching them, stuffing them in their pockets with stifled squeals as if they were little kids at an Easter egg hunt.

We were well past five minutes. I clapped my hands twice. They came running. I herded them back through the gate. "Thanks, Jim!" I called.

"Thanks, Jim!" they called.

After I'd locked up, they were waiting for me in the kitchen, clustered. Gussie Kornichek gushed: "Cammie, we have a name!"

"Huh?" I said.

She hopped, squeezing her fists. "The Jailbirds! We're the Jailbirds!"

Five happy faces, thrilled to death at their clever notion. What could I say? "Nice," I said.

Gussie put her hand out. Other hands piled onto hers, like a team before a game. Mine was last. "One—two—three!" said Gussie.

And a shrill chorus of girly voices filled the apartment: "Jailbirds!"

28

THAT AFTERNOON WAS THE SORT OF GABATHON THAT only young girls can sustain. Every second, every gesture of the Yard Time, as it quickly became known, was rehashed. We giggled and howled and shopped and ate and jitter-bugged our way from one end of downtown Main Street to the other. And then back again. Twice. They compared and counted cigarette butts. Gussie Kornichek had the most—seventeen! They laid the butts out along the lunch counter at Woolworth's, which got us kicked out.

The questions about the prison never stopped. I must have been asked a dozen times: "What's it like?" I gave my answers to a breathless audience any teacher would die for. This was different from my popularity in the women's yard. There were no walls here. We were outside. They could aim their attention anywhere, but they were aiming it at me.

And the transistor.

From the moment they entered the apartment, I had seen it in Reggie's hand. It was rectangular and plastic and pink and not much bigger than a deck of cards. I had heard Reggie go on about a new kind of radio. "Transistor," she called it. "You can hold it in your hand!" "It doesn't need a cord!" "You can listen to music *anywhere*!"

And that's what we did, all day. We danced up and down Main Street to songs coming from the pink pocket radio—"Dream Lover" and "So Fine" and "Kissin' Time." How Reggie loved that transistor! It never left her hand. I knew now why she had not bothered to return for her record tote.

Of course, the word *"Bandstand!"* was uttered a thousand times over. Questions rained on Reggie:

"What're you gonna wear?"

"How old you gonna say you are?"

"You gonna dance with Tommy D?"

We would all be celebrating *Bandstand* Day, as it was now called, on Friday of the next week.

We rolled on across the Stony Creek bridge and up Marshall Street into the West End shopping district. You couldn't enter the West End without visiting Scooper Dooper. We all got double-dip cones. It was a hot day, almost July, so we had to lick fast or the ice cream would wind up on our hands instead of in our stomachs. I thought of Boo Boo, getting fat on banana splits.

As we stood in line to order our ice creams, I took Reggie aside and said the words that had choked me for a week: "I'm sorry I shoved you."

She looked at me with surprise and said, "Huh?" That was all—the word "huh?" and the look on her face—and I knew she had long since let it go. Reggie, I was beginning to learn, traveled light. She carried no grudges.

Of course, nobody ever credited *me* with letting anything go. Recalling what I'd seen from the Salami Room that day as she was passing the courthouse, I said, "Did you start smoking?"

This time there was no look of surprise, no "Huh?" Just that thousand-watt Reggie grin as she gave me the finger-point that signaled our personal national anthem, "*So, girl . . .*" she sang and then waited for me to fire back my own finger-point, and right there in Scooper Dooper we belted it out:

You better shut yer mouth!

"Tears on My Pillow" was playing on the pink transistor as we dispersed to our homes. I weathered a final flurry of attention. They seemed reluctant to leave me. Glenda Schmoyer hesitated, then practically knocked me over with a hug and ran off.

They all lived in the West End. Only I was left with a long walk home. Heading back down Marshall Street, I was aglow with the wonder of my newfound popularity, which I had believed I didn't care about.

By the time I reached the West-Mar movie theater, the glow was fading. It always did. There was no glow I could not darken, no sweet I could not sour. A question loomed above me as boldly as the West-Mar's marquee: *Do your friends like you just because you live in a prison?* I couldn't think of anything else I'd done to deserve their affection. I could be prickly. I was a cranky kid. Day in and day out, I was probably nicer to the prison inmates than I was to the kids I knew.

Do your friends like you just because you live in a prison?

By the time I got home, I figured I knew the answer: *Yes*.

29

My campaign to recruit Eloda Pupko as my mother was stalled. The touch on my cheek. The daily pigtailing. They were nice, gentle gestures. They made me feel good—but only for a little while. I needed more. I needed her to want me as I wanted her. I needed her to shower me with constant attention that said: *Reggie was wrong. You're more than a job to me. You're my kid.*

I tried a new strategy. I lifted it right out of the prison world: keep an inmate busy with respectable work (making rugs) and maybe he'll become a respectable citizen. In other words, play a role long enough and it becomes more than a role—it becomes *you.*

So I asked myself: What do mothers do? They comfort

you. They fix your hurts. They scold. They help. They tell you what to do and where to go and how to get there and what to do once you're there. They punish. They root for you. They tell you you're great even if you stink. They worry. They love. They save you.

Mother stuff.

I needed to coax more mother stuff out of her. Finagle her into the role.

I had an idea. Next time I saw her, I faked a cry. She looked up from her dusting. "Hurt yourself?"

"Yes," I said, sniffling.

"Where?"

Where? I hadn't thought this through. I pointed to my knee. She pulled up my pant leg. The knee was neither cut, bruised, or burned. She bent my leg twice. "You're okay," she said, and went back to her dusting.

Next time I was better prepared. It came to me as she was braiding my pigstub. Later that morning, when I visited the women in the yard, I picked up two cigarette butts. That night before going to bed, I put one of the butts in the wastebasket. I placed it so she couldn't miss it. The other butt I put under my bed.

Every morning Eloda made my bed and emptied my basket. Once a week she cleaned my room—officially, that is. Unofficially, she was constantly tidying up the place. It was practically half her job, because I was probably the sloppiest kid in Two Mills.

I hit the pillow that night almost too excited to sleep.
I kept imagining the next day's pigstub dialogue:

ELODA: Miss Cammie?

ME: Yes, Eloda? And call me Cammie. No *Miss*.

ELODA: I was cleaning up your room this morning.

ME: Yes?

ELODA: And I found something. Two somethings,
    actually.

ME: Oh really?

ELODA: Is there anything you want to tell me?

ME: I don't think so, Eloda. What would I want to tell
    you?

ELODA: I'm only asking because . . .

ME: Yes, Eloda?

ELODA: This is hard for me. It's none of my business.

ME (thinking): *Oh, Eloda, yes—yes—it is your business.*
    (Saying): You can ask me anything, Eloda.

ELODA: Well . . . then . . . are you . . . have you . . . do
    you . . . smoke cigarettes?

ME: Yes.

ELODA: Well, then . . .

ME: Yes, Eloda? Say it.

ELODA: I don't feel right questioning you like this. It's
    just that . . .

ME: Yes?

ELODA: I care about you. I know I don't always act like

it, but I really do care for you. You're more than a
job to me.

ME: Thank you, Eloda. You're more than a trustee to me.

At that point she would tell me about the evils of smoking, that I was way too young, that maybe Reggie was a bad influence on me, and so on. I played through several versions of the script in my head. They all ended the same way:

ELODA: I want you to stop.

ME: Okay.

ELODA: Immediately.

ME: Okay.

ELODA: If I ever catch you smoking again . . .

ME: Yes?

ELODA: *Ever* catch you smoking again . . .

ME: Yes?

ELODA: You'll be punished.

ME: Yes, ma'am.

ELODA: Are you paying attention?

ME: Yes, ma'am.

ELODA: Do you hear me, young lady?

ME: Yes, ma'am, I hear you.

ELODA: Look at me. *Look* at me. Are you going to
obey me?

ME: Yes, ma'am.

And the doors fly open to scenes from my future. I see Eloda released from jail. I see the two of us window-shopping on Main Street. I make her stop at Charming. "I want that," I tell her. "No," she says. "But I *want* it!" I whine. I beg and I pester. And I'm happy. Because that's all I really want: not the thing in the window, but a real, live mother to beg and pester like all the other kids.

Oh, how I wanted that scene to come true!

I could hardly sleep. In the morning I leaped out of bed. I forced myself to eat my Cocoa Puffs slowly, to give her plenty of time in my room to discover the cigarette butts. After breakfast, as always, I stayed on my counter stool. As always, moments after I put down my spoon, she appeared with comb and rubber band in hand. She took her place behind me. She began to comb back my hair. I tried to detect anger or disappointment in her touch. Was she pulling on my hair harder than usual? I was so nervous I could hardly breathe. There was still only one knot to do, so it was over way too quickly. She snapped the rubber band around my pigstub. "Okay," she said, giving the stub a little tug, my signal that pigtail time was over. That "okay" was the only word she said.

My legs felt like spaghetti as I wobbled into my bedroom.

I looked into the wastebasket. The butt was gone! So was the one under the bed.

She found them. She knew.

And said nothing?

Of course! How dumb was I! What made me think she would react immediately? She needed time to decide how she was going to handle me. This wasn't maid stuff. This wasn't her job. This was personal. Mother stuff.

I needed to make it easier on her. I needed to make myself as approachable as possible. I needed to hang around, be visible, friendly. I passed up my usual visit to the women's yard. I tried to lure her into conversation, warm her up. She was, after all, a quiet person, maybe even a chilly person.

I asked questions while she worked. She gave one-word answers.

Lunchtime came and went. Still no mention of cigarette butts.

I made up excuses to follow her from room to room. I said her name a lot. "Eloda, what do you think of—?" "Eloda, did you ever—?" I had learned this from my father. When detectives interrogate a suspect, they make a point to say his name a lot. It helps put the suspect at ease.

It didn't work. The scolding never came. All my jibber-jabber did was drive her to run the Hoover so she wouldn't have to hear me anymore.

I was fed up. What did a kid have to do to get punished around here? I stormed out of the apartment and down to Reception, spit in the spittoon, grabbed my bike and slammed out to the sidewalk. I went to the candy guy at the city-hall bazaar. I stuffed my mouth with two Milky Ways and I rode.

Somewhere along the way, as the chewing and pedaling dissipated my frustration, I remembered something I had seen when I'd sneaked my peek at Eloda Pupko's reception sheet. On the line for family there was one word: "sister."

30

THERE WAS A PHONE BOOTH AT HECTOR AND MARSHALL.
I leafed through the directory. Sure enough there was only
one listing in the phone book with that name: Pupko. 428
Swede Street. A three-minute ride.

I pulled up opposite the house. It was a twin. Porch
front. Gray siding. Narrow side yard with a black wrought-
iron fence. The front windows had venetian blinds. They
were closed.

Even as I steadied myself against the warm hood of a
parked car, I was beginning to lose my nerve. Minutes went
by with no sign of a sister-looking person, orange hair or
otherwise. I had pictured myself pounding on the door and
the door would open and I would say . . . what, exactly?

I'm the warden's daughter and Eloda Pupko cleans our house and I want to know what her crime was.

Why doesn't she care about finding cigarette butts in my room?

Is she really hell on wheels?

Why is she always so grouchy?

A closed blind on the second floor suddenly opened like a stack of shocked eyelids. My courage vanished. I took off.

I rode around town. I thought I was aimlessly cruising, but my bike knew better. It was bringing me turn by turn back to Mogins Dip. Mill Street. Since that Sunday I had not stopped thinking about the little kid who "shot" me.

I paused at the top of the hill. I could see the sky-blue door, halfway down on the left.

I coasted down the redbrick canyon of row houses. Parked cars lined both sides. No garages, no driveways, no front yards here. This was not the North End.

A few kids were playing, laughing. Hopscotch. Jump rope. Suddenly something hit me—or rather my bike. Smacked into the spokes. I looked down. An apple core lay on the ground.

"Bull's-eye!" A squealy voice came from somewhere. And out he popped from between two cars, the tiny brown gunslinger, charging and firing his cap pistol in my face: "Pow! Pow! Pow!"

Thrilled as I was to see him, Cannonball Cammie was

too combative to gracefully absorb an attack on her bike—
from anybody. My hair-trigger temper was about to com-
bust when he holstered his gun and shouted, "Gimme a
ride!"

He wasn't asking.

His lips were twisting as he tried to wrench my hand
from the handlebars. It took him both hands to pry up my
index finger. I released my hold. He was trying to climb on
in front of me but he was way too short. I hoisted him. My
hands almost went around his body. I could feel his ribs. I
sat him on the crossbar of my boy bike. His feet noogled
between the downbar and my leg. His arm shot out. "Go!"

From somewhere behind my heart, a voice whispered,
Not a good idea. But it had no chance, as the boy repeated:
"Go!"

We went.

From the start he wanted to take over. He clamped his
hands around the handlebars. He hunched forward till
his face was practically over the front tire. "Rmmm . . .
rmmm," he kept growling. "Faster . . . faster." He kept trying to aim the wheel, so I had to fight him on that. But it
was easy; he was so little.

"Turn here!" he called as we approached Washington
Street. I turned. Halfway up the block he called, "Stop!
Stop!" I stopped in front of yet another brick row house.
He cupped his hands to his mouth and yelled, "Yo, Herbie!"

Within seconds Herbie, another tiny brown kid, came out. "Herbie—look at me!" Herbie had barely begun looking when my rider's hand smacked me twice on the thigh, as if I were a horse. "Go! Go!" I went. "We gone to the park!" he called back. "Monkey Hill!" Leaving Herbie to stew in the green juices of envy.

Turning at the end of the block, I told him, "We are not going down Monkey Hill." It was dawning on me that I had this little kid's life on my crossbar. I had better start acting like it.

"Main Street!" he called.

"No," I said. "Too crowded."

"Ribber!"

So we went down to the river. It hadn't rained for a month, and the Schuylkill was showing its bones—tree limbs and rocks that in higher water were submerged. I pulled over. I taught him waterside skills. How to pop stones from fringe-water mud to expose pale, darting crawfish. What shore rocks to find salamanders under. How to skip flat stones across the water. When a dead sunny came floating by, I had to stop him from wading out to get it. We had a contest. Who could throw a stone the farthest? I let him win.

We rode some more, all the way down River Road to Conshohocken, to the steel mill. It was a bustling place in those days. Clanging diesels. Trucks. Smoke. Fire. Endless lines of coal cars. He became quiet. He gaped in wonder up at the brand-new basic oxygen facility, which towered above us like a squared-off, clay-red mountain.

My own attention was drawn mostly to the little brown head with the side-flap ears in front of me.

And then he gave me a moment that I treasure still. He let go of the handlebars, hung his arms out in the breeze and leaned back into me. I felt his head against my chest, and my heart sang. I tried to keep the ride as smooth as possible, to preserve the moment, but he flapped his arms twice and leaned forward again into the handlebars.

For some reason only then did it occur to me to ask the question: "What's your name?"

He said it so casually: "Andrew."

Andrew.

A *mother named him Andrew.*

He did not ask me my name.

We headed back to town.

We were on a weedy stretch of road when he cried out: "Stop!" I slammed the brakes, afraid he was hurt. Before I could stop him, he had jumped down from the crossbar and dashed across the road. He picked something out of the dust. It was an empty soda bottle. In those days kids often earned candy money by turning empty bottles in to stores for a two-cent deposit per bottle. *Little businessman*, I thought as he climbed back aboard the bike. Farther along, the road dipped under a railroad overpass. Without warning he yelled, "Wahoo!" and hurled the bottle straight up.

It shattered behind us against the concrete underside of the bridge.

I pulled over, braked to a stop, looked back. The shadow of the underpass was littered with glass. Already a car was coming. I grabbed him. My fingers overlapped his tiny upper arm. I shook him. I snapped: "Don't you *ever* do that again! You don't *do* that! What's the *matter* with you?"

Only when I saw the look of horror on his face did I realize how I must have appeared to him. I probably mistook his paralysis for obstinacy. I shook him again. "Do you hear me?"

A peep came out of him that might have been "Yes."

I mitted his chin in my hand as I would a baseball. "Do? You? Hear? Me?"

His face collapsed, and suddenly he was bawling into my chest. "I'm sorry . . . I won't do it. . . . I won't do it. . . ."

I held him, heaving, and turned to the door-blue sky. I took deep breaths. This was new territory for me. I had just met this kid an hour ago.

He was sobbing more quietly now, his little arms around me, clutching me. Gently I pulled him away. "All right now," I told him. "It's over." I wiped his tears with my shirt-tail. "Okay?"

He nodded. He looked up at me with eyes I had never seen before, eyes I'd have thought only mothers could see.

"Okay, then . . . ," I said, looking down the road. "So how about . . . a Marcy's?"

He threw up his arms, his face instantly transformed. "Yeah! Marcy's!"

"All right, turn around, then. Grab the handlebars; hold on tight."

He happily obeyed, and off we went to town to the beat of his chanting: "Marcy's . . . Marcy's . . ."

Marcy's, home of the world's best water ice. Andrew wanted root beer. Large, of course. I got it for him. And a medium lemon for me. I wasn't going to drive one-handed with him on the crossbar, so we sat on the curb in front of Holy Savior Church. Andrew finished his large before I was halfway through my medium.

Back on the bike. Turn onto Mill Street. Down the hill, the house with the blue door stood out. A woman sat on the front steps. She snapped to her feet when she saw us. The dream vanished.

I coasted down the hill. She waited at the curb. She wore a checkered apron over a pale yellow dress. Her hair was hidden in a bright lemon-yellow wrap. Her arms were folded. She was not happy.

Andrew called: "Mommy! Look at me!" Mommy's expression did not change.

I coasted to a stop. The woman's glare nailed both Andrew and me. Not that Andrew noticed. "Mommy, we rided!" he gushed. "All over! We went to the ribber! I won! We had Marcy's! I had a big!"

"Get down," she said. I helped him down. He ran to

her, wrapped his arms around her legs, buried his face in her apron.

But her eyes were only on me. "What's going on?" she said.

What could I say? I just stood there on one leg and two bike tires, staring. Not because there were no answers, but because there were too many.

"What are you doing with my child?"

"He wanted a ride," I replied lamely.

"He's a *baby*."

Andrew yanked her apron. "I'm *not* a baby. I'm five and a half."

"Who are you?" she said.

Who are you?

It was probably the first time I'd ever been asked that question. In my experience, everybody in Two Mills knew who I was. If not by name, then by label. The Girl Who Lives in Jail. The Girl Who Survived the Milk Truck That Killed Her Mother. The Crankiest Kid in Town. The Tomboy. Cannonball.

"Your name," she demanded.

Uh-oh. Dare I tell her my real name and reveal myself as top kid at the county prison?

I said, "Claire."

"Claire what?"

"Claire . . . Jones."

"Where you live?"

"Airy Street, ma'am."

She stepped forward till she was all I could see. "You don't just come along"—she was fighting to control herself; I thought she might hit me—"and take *my* child." Her lips were clenched to a thin line. Angry breaths came through her nose. "He know you?" Her eyes never left me. "Andrew. You know her?"

"Yeah, Mommy. She's my frenn. She buyed me a Marcy's."

"You don't *do* it. Unless you ask." She poked me in the chest. "Did you *ask?*"

"No, ma'am. I'm sorry."

I felt my lip quiver. I prayed: *Don't cry.*

"You *don't.*" Softer now: her voice, her eyes. "Take a boy off the streets. Not ask."

"I know, ma'am. I'm sorry."

"I seed crawfishes, Mommy!" He was tugging at her. She stepped back.

"How old are you?"

"Twelve, ma'am. I'll be thirteen."

She took another step back. I felt myself breathe. She seemed to be studying me, thinking. "Andrew, inside," she said sternly. Andrew flew up the marble steps and into the house. She followed him to the top step, but instead of going in, she just stood there, looking down at me. "You too," she said at last.

I didn't understand. I didn't move.

"Now," she said. "You're letting flies in. I'm not done with you."

I leaned my bike against the brick wall. I climbed the steps, imagining this was what a perp walker felt like. I entered the house. The blue door closed behind me.

31

THE SMELL HIT ME FIRST. LIKE A RESTAURANT, BUT NOT really. Like a flower shop, but not really. My daily smell of scrapple was just that: scrapple. This . . . this was . . . *a place*.

Then the colors. The room I entered was red, walls and ceiling. The next room was the same sky-blue as the front door. Fringed shawls draped the furniture like peacock tails.

Plants were everywhere, most with blossoms I couldn't name. In one corner, rising out of a terra cotta urn that came up to my waist, was either a huge plant or a small tree. Its great leaves were supple and buttery, as if they could be made into baseball gloves.

And baskets! Woven baskets in shapes I'd never seen, one so big I could have climbed in.

Two Mills had stopped at the blue door.

By now Andrew was seated at the table, chomping on an apple. At this point I was not even tempted to tell his mother what he did with cores. I was invited to join him at the table. Sunlight from a riverside window pooled golden on the back wall.

Between chomps Andrew was gabbing at a girl in shorts, telling her about his ride with me. She was at the stove. She might have been listening to him, but she was staring at me. She looked to me like an older teenager. Seventeen, maybe. Maybe Andrew's sister. Her skin was lighter than that of the others, closer to the nougat in a Milky Way than the chocolate jacket. Bare feet. Aqua nails.

"So," she said, "you kidnapped my little brother."

"No," I protested, "we were just—" and stopped because she was laughing.

"Hey, didn't my mother tell you? We been looking for somebody to kidnap him. Give us a break. Take him anytime." She tweaked Andrew's nose. Andrew squealed "Ow!" but didn't look hurt.

"Don't joke," said the mother, taking over at the stove. She was stirring something in a big pot with a wooden spoon.

"What's 'kidnap,' Missy?" piped Andrew.

Missy ignored him. "Ginger ale?" she said to me. "Milk? I can make it chocolate. Iced tea?"

"Ginger ale," I said. And remembered to add, "Please."

She poured me a glass while Andrew said, "I wanna ginger ale."

Missy pointed. "Eat your apple and be quiet. You had a Marcy's." She studied him for a moment. "You *made* her take you for a ride. *Didn't* you?"

Andrew squawked, "No!" He appealed to his mother. "Mommy, tell Missy I didn't make her do nothin'."

"Did he break a bottle?" Missy was staring dead-on at me.

I looked at her. I looked at Andrew. "Uh . . ."

Missy smacked a chair top. "I *knew* it." She turned to the stove. "Mama—"

Stirring the big pot, Mama uttered a single word: "Boot."

Andrew howled, spitting apple: "Nooo!"

Missy leaned into his face. Her lips puckered with the word: "Boot."

"No, Mama!" Andrew cried. "Not the boot! I didn't break no bottle! Did I?" He was yanking my thumb; my ginger ale was sloshing.

From the stove came a second word: "Now."

Andrew yowled and thrashed and cried out, "Noooo!" But he went. Flailing out of the kitchen and upstairs noisily. When he returned, one leg up to the knee was encased in a rain boot, a rubber galosh. It was so big on him he had to drag it across the floor as if a small animal were clamped to his leg. If I had ever seen anything funnier in my life, I couldn't think of it. A laugh-snort escaped from my nose before I could cut it off. I turned away. Missy slipped into the seat next to me. "He hates the boot," she whispered. "It's the only punishment that—" Her words spluttered into giggles. At the stove Andrew's mother kept her back to us. Her shoulders were hunched. She stirred faster and faster.

Glum-faced, Andrew clomped back to his seat and resumed eating his apple.

"You like chili?" Missy asked me.

"Yes, ma'am," I replied.

"I'm not a ma'am," she said. "You're staying for dinner."

Kidnapper to dinner guest. That was fast. Inside I was smiling.

Missy fascinated me. Like her mother, she wore silver hoop earrings a Ping-Pong ball could fit through. The aqua nails on her hands and feet complemented her beige skin perfectly. I wondered if she got her cosmetics at Woolworth's. I doubted even Reggie could find something wrong with her.

"Mama," she said, "turn Wibbage on."

Her mother reached above the stove and flicked on a white radio. Music poured into the kitchen from WIBG, the station all the kids listened to. I pictured Reggie and her pink transistor.

"So. Claire," said Missy.

I looked around. I wondered who Claire was. Then remembered. "Yes, ma'am . . . sorry . . . yes?"

"So what grade are you in?"

"I'm going into seventh."

"Ah." She nodded. She looked impressed. "Junior high."

"Yes."

"Gonna be thirteen."

"Yes."

"You can go back to ma'am. I kinda like it."

"Yes, ma'am."

"Hear that, Mama?"

Mama nodded smartly. "Yes, *ma'am*."

Missy studied me. "Thirteen." The sight of me seemed to tickle her. "Teenager."

"Get a Job" came on the radio. Missy started bopping her head to the beat. Having finished his apple, Andrew tried to thread the chewed-up core through the hoop of his sister's earring. It wouldn't fit. He chewed the core down some more. Tried again. Success!

"Thir-*teen*," said Missy.

"Teen-*ager*," said her mother.

"Well, almost," I said.

"You watch *Bandstand*?" Missy asked me.

"Sometimes," I said. "My friend Reggie is going to be on *Bandstand*."

"Dig it," said Missy. "She gonna"—she popped up, did a wiggle move I'd never seen before—"dance?" She sat back down.

"Yep," I said. And wondered if Reggie could do Missy's move.

The best part of "Get a Job" was coming. Missy called it out and rapped her knuckles on the table. Andrew climbed onto Missy's lap and did it, too. So did I. Their mother beat the pot with the wooden spoon.

Dip dip dip dip dip dip dip dip
Mum mum mum mum mum mum
Get a job

Before we could finish laughing, the Cookies came on. This time I was the only one singing along.

Don't say nothin'
Bad about my baby

I must have stood up, because suddenly I was looking down on Missy and Andrew. Their mother had turned around at the stove, wooden spoon in hand.

He's good.
He's good to me.
That's all I care about.

Their faces could barely contain their joy, and I understood why Reggie wanted to be a star. Stoking the finish, I poked my finger at each of them in turn.

He's true.
He's true to me.

And then suddenly Missy was standing beside me and we were belting it out together.

SO, GIRL, YOU BETTER SHUT YER MOUTH!

The house went wild.

We were too loud to hear the front door open, so the next thing we heard was a man's voice booming: "Home from the salt mines!"

I knew that voice. Into the kitchen came a short, stocky black man. He was dressed in the gray uniform of a Schuylkill Valley bus driver. Mr. Strong. My instructor at the park's baseball school every spring. He taught middle infielders.

When he saw me in his kitchen, he stopped dead. His eyes and mouth made a triangle of Os on his astonished face. Then the whole face went into smile overdrive. "Well, well, well—look who's in my house. Miss Shortstop. Cammie O'Reilly."

At the mention of my real name, everything in the kitchen stopped but the DJ's voice on Wibbage.

Eventually—hours later, it seemed to me—Perfect Missy said in a voice of wonder, "It's *her?*"

And Mrs. Strong, as if waking from a dream, chili dripping from her spoon onto the floor: "The warden's *daughter?*"

32

I PEDALED INTO THE SETTING SUN, WHICH HUNG LIKE A tangerine from the underside of the P&W bridge. I was mesmerized, dazed by the events of the day. I discovered I was smiling. I hadn't stopped smiling since my kitchen performance. Not even as I fumbled out an explanation about "Claire."

I was pumping up West Main before I realized I had gone a mile too far. I turned back for home.

My father was in the living room, watching Milton Berle on the black-and-white Emerson TV. I was hoping to sneak past. No luck.

"You're late."

"It's not dark," I pointed out. The rule was I had to be in

by dark. It was the same for most kids in town, even little ones.

"You missed dinner."

"I didn't. I ate somewhere else."

"Where?"

"Friends."

"Who?"

"You don't know them."

"Try me."

"Mr. Strong."

"Your baseball-school coach."

"Yeah." I was surprised he remembered.

Milton Berle came out dressed like a clown. His preposterous shoes practically overlapped the stage. The audience was cracking up.

"You have to call," he said.

"Okay," I said.

"If you're not going to be home for dinner."

"Okay."

He turned from the TV. "You hear?"

A surprising notion hit me: *He was worried*.

"I hear," I said.

He turned back to the TV. "And stay off the battlement."

Huh? "That was *ages* ago."

"Statute of limitations never expires on battlement violations."

More years would have to pass before I would begin to appreciate my father's sense of humor.

"Tony ratted me out."

"Could've been anybody."

On some level I understood what he was saying: *I love you. I worry for you. I have my people watching out for you.* But I didn't want to hear it. I did not appreciate that my father was giving me everything I wanted—the caring, the attention—because it wasn't from him that I wanted it. I wanted it from Eloda Pupko. I said nothing and walked away.

His voice stopped me. "You're welcome."

I turned. "What for?"

"The key."

Since the key to the women's yard had appeared on the breakfast counter, neither of us had mentioned it.

"Thanks," I said. "Can I go now?"

"Who's stopping you?"

I went.

Behind the closed door of my room I was free to reflect on my day. And what an amazing day it had been. In the end, a wonderful day. It had begun with Eloda's obstinate refusal to discipline me about the cigarette butts I'd planted in my room, or even to acknowledge that she'd found them. Then my ride to her house—just seeing it—at 428 Swede Street. And then the day's grand finale, the undeserved blessing of my hours with Andrew and the Strongs. As I'd often seen Eloda do with the wash, I sorted out my thoughts and feelings.

I was thrilled. For a million reasons I could not identify.

I was surprised. That a little kid could turn a Tuesday into such a beautiful day.

I was jealous. Of Andrew, for having such a mother.

I was happy. For Andrew, for having such a mother.

I was thankful beyond words. To the mother and the confrontation on the sidewalk. For in her ferocious eyes I had glimpsed a snapshot of my own mother twelve years before. Defenders of children. Sisters, of a kind. Would this Mogins Dip mama take a truck for her kid? In a second.

I was glowy. Warm. In the moment of moments. When Andrew had let go of the handlebars and hung his arms out to the breeze and leaned his little body back into mine, it had given me a taste of something I had not known to exist.

I was wishful. Chili and cornbread around the kitchen table with the family Strong, and thinking: *I want that*.

And regretful. That Eloda would not cooperate in my mother quest.

And hopeful. That maybe, after all, she already was co-operating. A little. Because I'd spotted the dinner setting— plate, glass, utensils, napkin—still on the table. Waiting. For me.

I fell asleep still smiling.

33

I AWOKE TO FAMILIAR POUNDING ON THE DOOR. "CAMMIE! Open up!"

Reggie had promised to show me the outfit she had chosen for *Bandstand*. Tomorrow was the big day.

Minutes later I was sitting on the sofa in my pajamas. Eloda sat beside me, only because I had made her. Historic moments had to be shared.

Reggie had rushed past me and into my bedroom. She was carrying a small suitcase. Now she came out of my room slinking like a model. She twirled. She vamped. She was perfect. She was seventeen. Heck, twenty-five.

Pink cotton sweater, buttoned up the back.

Silk neck scarf, a swirl of pink and charcoal, knotted at the side.

Hip-hugging charcoal straight skirt.

White socks.

Black-and-white saddle shoes.

It was as if the TV screen had delivered her into my living room.

"Wow" was all I could say. Eloda grunted and got up and returned to her dusting.

"And check this out," said Reggie. She hiked her skirt and put a saddle shoe up on the sofa. She removed her white shoelaces and replaced them with pink ones. She admired the new laces. "You gotta do something to stand out."

"But you can't see pink on TV," I reminded her. Television was black-and-white then.

She wagged a foot. "Dick Clark can tell."

I had seen Reggie excited before, but this was off the charts. Ball games at Connie Mack Stadium. Fireworks at the park. The entrance of Marvin Edward Baker. Those occasions had all had one thing in common: the excitement was generated by great numbers of people. But this . . . this excitement came from a single girl standing in front of me. It was the volume of a delirious stadium packed into a living room. The upholstery on the sofa seemed to crackle. In my memory she glows.

I knew it was a risky question, but I had to ask. "What if they make you prove your age? You sure they're going to let you in?"

Reggie's fist went to her cocked hip. She gave me her *I can't believe you just said that* look. "Would *you* let me in?"

My question slunk away.

I tried again. "So do you think a talent scout will be there?"

"Think, Cammie," she said. "It's Philadelphia. The place is swarming with talent scouts. Fabian. Frankie Avalon. All you have to do is get caught sitting on your front steps. I'll probably be discovered before I even get in the door."

Footsteps on the stairs.

Reggie bolted to my room. My father came in, went to his bedroom for something and went back out. When Reggie reappeared, she was once again dressed for Two Mills. Her *Bandstand* ensemble was back in the suitcase.

She swiped her brow dramatically. "That was close."

"Why did you run?" I asked her.

"Nobody can see me before the show," she said.

"What about me?" I said. "I'm somebody."

"You're not somebody. You're Cammie."

For some reason, that made me feel incredibly good.

"It's like, nobody can see the bride in her gown before the wedding," I suggested.

She kick-tapped my foot. "Exactly. Except the mother."

"How's that?" I asked her.

"The mother helps her get dressed. Get everything just right."

"So I'm the mother," I said.

"You're the mother," she said.

She went to the door. "When you see me next"—she flung out her arm—"I'll be on TV!"

From the landing I watched her go down the stairs. She stopped halfway, turned. "Keep watching me. When you see me tug my earlobe, that's for *you*." She clattered down the stairs and out the door.

34

THE SHOW DIDN'T START UNTIL THREE-THIRTY, BUT BY three o'clock we were all sitting on the floor, staring at some dumb soap opera on my TV screen. Donna Holloway was wearing a pale gray T-shirt. By three-fifteen her armpits were black from sweat. Glenda Schmoyer knocked over her glass of soda. Twice. Gussie Kornichek and Rosanna Scotti babbled hysterically. I looked at my hand and found a bead of blood. I had ripped a cuticle from my thumbnail.

In other words, we were excited. Not only for Reggie, but in a sense for ourselves. Reggie was an emissary into our own futures, which, even I conceded, would likely feature boys and dancing and romantic adventure. But for now we sat cross-legged in my living room, five girls-in-waiting.

Finally the soap opera was over. Gussie and Rosanna shut up. The between-shows commercials ended, and suddenly there they were, the notes of the *Bandstand* theme song pinballing into my living room: *ba-dopppa dop-dop* . . . There was the teenagery, perfectly groomed face of Dick Clark and the bleachers full of teenagers behind him. While he was talking, Gussie gasped: "Donna!"

We all turned.

Donna Holloway was lying on the floor, looking as if she was asleep. Which was impossible.

"I think she fainted," said Glenda.

At that point it got tricky. We had already taken our eyes from the TV for five seconds. More was intolerable. As one, we all turned back to the screen. Kids were pouring down from the bleachers onto the dance floor. "There's Justine!" screamed Rosanna, as Donna lay among us, her face the color of her pale gray T-shirt. I knew something should be done. A brilliant solution fell upon me.

"Eloda!" I called. "Eloda! Come here quick!"

From that moment on, my memory is confined to the fifteen-inch black-and-white TV screen. I assume Eloda must have arrived and ministered to Donna, because our fainted friend was soon up and sitting among us.

Whenever the camera showed the bleachers or dancing

kids, we strained forward. There were many false alarms. "There!" . . . "There!" Our hearts sank when we saw Tommy D dancing with his usual smooch, Arlene Holtz. When the camera closed in on other famous regulars, like Justine and Bob, we barely noticed.

Dick Clark poked the microphone into the bleachers, asking kids their names. None was Reggie.

Jackie Wilson came on and lip-synched "Lonely Tear-drops."

The Rate-A-Record poll came and went.

No Reggie.

The hour hand had long since passed four when we all jumped at Donna's shriek: *"There she is!"*

She wasn't in the bleachers. She wasn't dancing. It was better! She was filling up the screen. No Tommy D. No Jus-tine and Bob. Nobody but Reggie and Dick Clark. She was beaming. She was gorgeous. She looked just like a South Philly regular. Our Reggie.

"And we have with us today . . . ," Dick Clark said, and swung the mike to her. . . .

Many kids at this point said their name while gaping at the mike in Dick Clark's hand. Many mumbled. Some had to stop and think. Not Reggie. As the mike swung to her, her chin went up. She gave not a glance to the microphone. She turned not only her face but her whole bountiful body to the camera, and the camera, sensing the moment, edged out Dick Clark until Reggie's face alone filled the screen, and she said—no, she *proclaimed*—as boldly as a name had ever been proclaimed: "Reggie Weinstein!"

Pride paralyzed us, but only until Dick Clark's next question: "And tell our viewers what color your shoelaces are, Reggie Weinstein."

And Reggie giggled: "Pink."

"And where do you live, Reggie?"

And Reggie's right fist shot in the air, and she shouted to the world: "Two Mills!"

There was no audible reaction from the studio bleachers, but a certain living room above a certain jailhouse in Hancock County went off-the-charts bananas.

In our delirium we missed whatever Dick Clark said next and Reggie's energetic reply, and then he was gesturing to the bulletin board and Reggie was pinning up a pennant that said, even though none of us had yet set foot in the building: STEWART JUNIOR HIGH.

And then Dick Clark was sweeping his arm over the dance floor and music was rising in the background and Dick Clark was saying, "So now, m'lady, if you would be so kind, please lead us into Lloyd Price's coast-to-coast sensation . . . 'Personality!'" And there was Reggie, heading for the regulars standing around the floor, and . . .

"Oh my God!" shouted Gussie Kornichek . . .

"Oh my *God!*" screamed Rosanna Scotti . . .

. . . and there was Reggie walking right up to Tommy

DeBennedetto, plucking him out from the evil glare of Arlene Holtz and leading him by the hand onto the dance floor, into the heart of afternoon TV America, jitterbugging away, doing the push step she'd practiced with *me*—with none other than Tommy D himself.

35

THE SPOTLIGHT DANCE TURNED OUT TO BE HER ONLY ONE with Tommy D, but for the last half hour of the show she was never off the screen. Slow dances, fast dances— one cute, ducktailed boy after another claimed her as his partner.

Unlike the regulars, she didn't pretend she didn't know the camera was watching. She smiled right through it and into twenty million TV screens. It was during the final dance, a slow one—"Donna" by Ritchie Valens (Donna Holloway swooned but stopped short of fainting)—that Reggie caught the camera's attention one last time. She let go of her partner's hand for a second and, grinning straight into the eyes of the twenty million, tugged her earlobe. I could hear Ritchie Valens—"where can you be?"—but I could no longer see Reggie for the tears in my eyes.

She could have gone straight home after the show. Instead she took the subway and the P&W high-speed trolley back to town, ran from the terminal to the jail and came stampeding up the stairs into the apartment. Fortunately, I had left the door open or she would have crashed through it. I already had the record player going.

We cheered. We screamed. All five of us danced with her at once. She gave us the paper strip that certified her entry onto the show. We each tore off a postage stamp–size piece as a lifelong remembrance.

We stormed, screaming, down the stairs and into town. (My father dined alone that day.) We jittered down East Main to Linfante's, where we crammed into one booth and stuffed ourselves with zeps, Two Mills' distinctive type of hoagie. At one point during the onion-spiked gabble, Reggie winked across the table at me and tugged her earlobe. I winked back and silently mouthed, *Thank you.*

By nightfall we had scattered to our homes, but the phone calls continued till midnight. We could barely wait to reconvene the next day, the Fourth of July.

36

Cap pistols snapping in the streets. Cherry bombs booming in stairwells. Whistlers in the sky. Sparklers in the grass.

But inside the women's yard the Fourth seemed like just another day. Deena sunbathing. Helen and Tessa squabbling over badminton. Cigarette tips kissing.

In the Quiet Room, Boo Boo's story on this day was about the time she won the Fourth of July sack race at the park. She was ten at the time. Her partner was a little boy named Raymond. She snatched him from the crowd. "Raymond was about five," she said in a whisper, as if park officials were listening. "But even then he was small for his age. He looked three. And he weighed about as much as a peanut."

His size was the key to her brilliant plan. She dumped him into the burlap sack, one leg in, one leg out, told him to hang on and took off with the "Go!" Raymond was so tiny it was as if she was racing alone. He just hung on to the finish line. The officials conferred. They decided she'd done nothing against the rules and had no choice but to declare her—and Raymond—the winners. "Miss Boo Boo Dunbar!" came out of the loudspeakers, and that's how she replayed it to me on the concrete bench. The prize was a picnic basket full of Tastykake pies.

"I gave him the lemon," she said. "I hated lemon." She rubbed her massive stomach. "You *know* where the rest went."

The brewery whistle announced lunchtime. As the women headed back inside . . .

"Day I'm out, what I'm bringin'?"

"Sweet potato pie!"

Many of the women asked if I was going to the fireworks that night. The sound in their voices, the looks in their eyes, told me the Fourth was not after all just another day to them.

My band of Jailbirds headed for the park, where every grill and picnic table was occupied. Blankets and bare feet and deviled eggs wherever you looked. Face painting. Sack race. Baby-crawl race. Uncle Sam on stilts. Barbershop singers at the band shell. Talent show.

No doubt people thought they were celebrating the 183rd birthday of the USA. They were wrong. The parades across the country, the fireworks, the picnics, the speeches—it was all really a celebration of Reggie Weinstein's stupendous day at *Bandstand*. We roamed from band shell to zoo and everywhere heard the cries:

"Reggie!"

"I saw you yesterday!"

"Reggie!"

Thanks to our famous friend, we were all offered picnic food from a hundred blankets and tables. Every other minute another little kid asked for the celebrity's autograph.

We happened to stop by the talent show as some kid was playing the clarinet. Reggie jabbed me. "Hey—that's him."

"Huh?" I said. "Who?"

"*Him*. The guy that likes you. From outside the jail that day."

The boy was finishing his performance and taking the instrument away from his face, and—yes—it was the Roadmaster bike kid. He took a quick bow and waved and trotted off the stage as the audience applauded.

I jabbed her back. "You're crazy. He doesn't like me."

"He just waved at you," she crooned.

I corrected her. "He waved at everybody."

To my relief the focus quickly returned where it belonged:

"It's Reggie Weinstein!"

"Hi, Reggie!"

"Hi, Reggie!"

At least a hundred girls asked her what it had been like to dance with Tommy D. It got so routine, the rest of us began to answer for her, replying with her own dismissive shrug and her own words: "No big deal."

After the talent show a Philadelphia Mummers Parade string band came onto the stage. And then the Hancock County Memorial Band played into the dusk and the little kids started yelling, "Fireworks!"

Few waits in the world are as long as the wait for nightfall on the Fourth of July. The population of Two Mills gathered on the banks beyond the American Legion baseball field. On the sandy infield, pyro tubes stuck out like stubble on a giant's chin. An ambulance rolled in beyond the backstop. Then a fire truck. Screaming children ran amok while a thousand grown-up eyes measured the sky for the perfect pitch of darkness. Without warning came a deep, concussive thump and a whistling into the night, a plasticky crinkle above the trees—"There!" . . . "There!"— and red, white and blue pearls, pulpy as pomegranate seeds, canopied over the wonder-struck faces and spilled down over the park.

Thousands of eyes turned upward, marveling. I wondered if, somewhere in the multitude, two of them belonged to Eloda Pupko's sister.

As the night exploded, I thought of the inmates. I wondered if they could hear the thunder. I imagined leading them out of their cells and up a ladder to the top of the wall, where they would sit, their legs dangling over the side, their faces alit in wonder and joy.

The finale pounded the skies with the violence of a battleship bombardment. The end was sudden, unexpected. Dazed, the town waited for more. "Is that *it?*" In time the headlights of the ambulance went on. The cloud of cordite drifted up from the infield. Reluctantly we began to pick ourselves up from the ground and make our ways home.

I parted with the girls at the baby wading pool and headed for the railroad tracks. In those days it was not unusual for kids to take that route out of the park, even in the dark. I had done so many times.

I had just begun my trek along the tracks when I heard: "Cammie!"

37

IT WAS THE ROADMASTER KID, JOGGING UP BEHIND ME. HE carried what looked like a miniature black suitcase. Then I remembered: clarinet.

"Hi," he said.

"Hi," I said.

"Cool fireworks, huh?"

"Yeah."

After the way I had brutalized little Benny House at home plate the last time I'd seen this kid, I was surprised he wanted to talk to me. He wore his usual Phillies baseball cap.

Lately I'd been wanting to get one for myself. Now I decided I would not. We walked side by side on the railroad bed. We left the streetlights behind. Soon I could not see him.

"Better than the fireworks where I came from," he said.

Even unsociable me knew I was now supposed to ask him: *And where was that?* But I said nothing.

"I'm from Punxsutawney," he said.

Goofy name for a town, I thought.

Though darkness made my eyes useless, there was plenty to hear. Up and down the tracks voices of all ages filled the moonless night as families streamed home from their holiday at the park. A hundred footfalls on the railway cinders gave the sound of a cement truck's rolling crunch.

I could feel him staring at me, feel him wishing I would speak.

Finally he said, overpronouncing it: *"Punxsutawney?"* With a question mark.

"So?" I said.

"Groundhog?" he said.

"Huh?" I said.

And then he told me. About Punxsutawney Phil the groundhog and how the whole world turns to the coal country of Pennsylvania every February second to find out if Punxsutawney Phil will see his shadow or not so the world will know if there's going to be another six weeks of winter. *That* Punxsutawney. I had heard about the groundhog-and-his-shadow thing, but I'd thought it was a fable or some such.

He laughed, for no good reason that I could tell. "So since I came down here, when I tell people I'm from Punxsutawney, lots of times they say, 'You don't *look* like a groundhog.'" He laughed again. He was really cracking himself up. *Maybe you should've told jokes for your talent.* I thought of saying it, but didn't.

I figured his coming from another town explained a lot. Like why he was wasting his time with Cammie O'Reilly, the town curmudgeon.

"I'm Danny Lapella," he said.

As soon as I replied—"Congratulations"—I knew how mean it sounded, but he just laughed.

"Nice to meet you, Cammie," he said.

Something bumped my arm, went away, then came back and stayed. *He's touching me!* I thought, then realized he was going for a handshake. I decided to give him a break. Our hands fumbled in the darkness and did a quick shake.

"When I saw you outside the prison that day, I never knew you *lived* there." His voice had the same awestruck tone I'd heard a thousand times before. But something else annoyed me even more: he'd been asking around about me.

"Now you know," I said.

And just like everyone else, he said, "Do you know the prisoners?"

"No prison questions," I said.

"Okay," he said. If he knew I was rebuking him, he wasn't showing it. "So. Did you see me wave at you?"

Two reactions hit me at once. (1) Surprise: Reggie had been right. *He just waved at you.* (2) Resentment: this kid had a way of catching me off guard.

"No," I said, and decided to mess with him. "When was that?"

"At the talent show."

"You were in it?" I said, faking interest.

"I played the clarinet."

"That was you?"

"Sure. That was me. I waved to you afterward."

He was becoming visible. We were approaching the dead end of George Street and its last light pole. I looked straight at him. "Why would you do that?"

He stared at me. He was stumped. "I don't know. . . . I just . . ."

"There were lots of people there," I pointed out. "You could've been waving to anybody."

He protested: "Oh no. It was *you*. I saw you there. Standing near the flagpole with your friends."

I sniffed. "Sorry. Don't remember you."

It was fun seeing him squirm.

"Well," he said, "did you at least like the music?"

"What music?" I said.

"The *clarinet* music," he said, displaying the instrument case. Frustration was beginning to show in his voice. "Do you at least remember somebody playing the clarinet?"

"What's a clarinet?" I said.

Right *there*. If he'd had *any* sense he would have hauled off and hit me. But I guessed Punxsutawney kids were too dumb to know they were being messed with.

All he said, his voice deflating like an inner tube meeting a nail, was "It's a musical instrument."

It occurred to me to finish him off by asking, *Did you win?* and forcing him to say, *No*. And then to rub it in with *You mean you lost?* and forcing him to say, *Yes*. But I didn't. I just said, "Oh," and let it stand there by its unfriendly self.

At that point he should have taken the hint and gone slinking off into the night. Instead he promptly recovered and launched a monologue that lasted the rest of the way. He told me about his stamp collection. His dog, Bijou. His love of lowland gorillas and Swedish meatballs and his mixed feelings about the word "misanthrope." He told me he was going into seventh grade—"Just like you!"—and that he was nervous but excited, too.

He told me about what they did on the Fourth of July up in coal country. Kids poked holes in a tin can and attached it to a string and put glowing embers of coal in the can and then swirled the can in big circles in the night. "You should see it," he gushed. "A hundred kids doing it at once!"

And that's all I remember about the walk, Danny Lapella talking nonstop until suddenly he was saying, "Well—here we are." And I looked up, and indeed there it was, the fortress, my home, looming in the night. I was surprised. And then annoyed to realize why I was surprised: I had been paying much closer attention to his prattle than I had intended.

I snipped at him. "I don't *need* to be walked home, y'know. I can go anywhere I want by myself. I bike all the way to Valley Forge. I walk along the tracks at night all the time."

"Okay," he said, much too agreeably. "Bye." And with a wave he was gone.

In spite of myself I just stood there. Words fell from my brain to my mouth. All I had to do was let them out: *You don't* look *like a groundhog*. But I said nothing and went inside.

Two days later I heard he had won first prize in his talent-show age group.

A day after that I looked up the word "misanthrope."

38

THE RESONANCE OF MY TIME WITH ANDREW NEVER FADED. And yet, as the days before and after the Fourth went by, I did not ride my bike back to Mill Street. Why? I think I was afraid. Afraid of how much I cared. Afraid I might say or do the wrong thing—Cannonball Cammie!—and spoil the memory of that perfect day.

Then the coal came.

By 1959 all the houses in town were heated with oil or gas, not coal—except for the Big House. My father got most of the improvements he asked for from the county authorities. But oil-burning furnaces were not one of them.

Halfway down the alleyway side of the prison, before the exercise yards began, there was a pair of green wedge-shaped hatchways jutting out from the base of the stone

185

wall. The hatches were about twenty feet apart. They were secured with the biggest padlocks I had ever seen. This was how the coal got in, the coal that kept the prison so toasty in the winter that inmates often lay about their cells in underwear. (So I was told.) Like the Quiet Room and the Christmas party and steak once every two weeks, this was my father's doing: "It's a *penitentiary*. Shivering in the cold makes you bitter, not *penitent*."

So once in the summer and every month in winter, a convoy of J. Gresh coal trucks lined up down the alley from the hatchways to Marshall Street. The hatches were opened, a pair of sliding board–like chutes were lowered into the black maw and down came the coal, truckload after truckload. A guard stood by the hatches until they were padlocked once again.

On the morning in July when the coal was coming down the chutes, I opened the back door and let the full force of the noise hit me: thunder falling down a bottomless stairway. I closed the door. No yard today.

Eloda was cleaning the bathroom. I was on the living room floor playing Monopoly against myself. I didn't know someone was at the door until I heard the knock. The roar of the coal had muffled the sound of footsteps on the stairs.

I knew it wasn't Reggie. She never came this early. And she'd never asked to visit the women's yard again. Her interest in the prison was now focused on the person of Marvin Edward Baker.

With a chill I wondered if it might be Danny Lapella. I hadn't seen him since the Fourth of July night. I'd been trying not to wonder what it all meant. If I'd truly believed it was him on the other side of the door, I would have run and hidden under my bed and let Eloda answer. But the knock had the sound of a little kid's hand, not a big kid's.

I opened the door. It was Andrew.

He was beaming. He threw up his arms. "I'm not s'pose to come but I comed anyway!"

A shadow me left my body and scooped him up and squeezed and tickled while he howled with laughter. The skin-and-bones me said, "Hi." I was uneasy but I wasn't sure why. I was about to find out.

He frowned. "What's that noise?"

"Coal."

"We get coal," he said—then suddenly he was looking past me, wonder-struck. He pointed. "Is *that* a crimimal?"

I turned. Eloda was standing by the dining room table, gawking back.

"No," I told him. I cupped his little shoulder. "She's a trustee. Now what—"

He broke from me and started darting about the apartment. "I wanna see crimimals!"

Eloda had disappeared.

I caught up to Andrew in the kitchen. He was looking out the back window. He pointed. "What's that?" he said.

It was before ten. The women were not out yet. "It's the exercise yard," I told him.

He brightened. "Jumpin' jacks!" He did a few.

"Right," I said. "Keep everybody in good shape."

I pulled him away. He broke back to the window. "Where are they?"

"Too early," I told him, and suddenly he was out the back door. I caught him at the bottom of the steps. I hauled him back up, squirming and whining.

Eloda was waiting in the kitchen. "He goes," she said. She pointed to the front door. "Out." Her face, her voice said, *Don't mess with me.*

Andrew froze in mid-whine. Even then I didn't trust him to go on his own. I carried him to the door. I was on the landing watching him head down the stairs when suddenly he turned and raced back up. I slammed the door shut behind me and got set to block him, but it wasn't the exercise yard he wanted; it was me. He plowed into me and gave me the kind of wraparound squeeze I'd seen him give his mother that day. Before I could return the hug, he raced down to Reception and out to the street.

When I opened the door, Eloda was right there.

"Shut the door," she said.

I shut the door. I expected her to step back. She did not. For the first time, I could count the freckles under her eyes and across her nose. I could smell the dustrag in her hand. Lemony. Coal was roaring down the chutes.

"What do you think you're doing?" she said.

I didn't understand the question.

"You don't *do* that."

"Do what?" I said. And recalled my vague uneasiness when Andrew arrived.

"Bring little children in here. A place like this."

"Eloda," I said, "I didn't *bring* him. He just—"

"You don't talk back. You listen."

Not only was defense useless, it suddenly occurred to me that I didn't even want to defend myself. Circumstance had delivered to me the very thing I'd wished for. She was scolding me.

"Yes, ma'am," I said.

"Never again."

"No, ma'am."

"Expose a child to this."

"No, ma'am."

"And me"—she flapped her hand behind her, toward the yard—"us. We are not on display. We are not a freak show."

"No, ma'am."

She took my face in her hand.

"Do you *hear* me?"

I was shaking. "Yes, ma'am."

She squeezed my face till my mouth was fish-lipped. "You will straighten up and fly right. You hear?"

"Yes, ma'am."

She squeezed harder. The hurt both startled and thrilled me. She yelled in my face: "Camille?"

The coal was roaring. I yelled back: "Yes, Mother!"

We stood gaping at each other, both of us astonished at what I'd just said, petrified in a suddenly empty bucket of sound: the coal had stopped falling. I broke first. I left her there, facing the door as I ran to my room.

39

AFTER THAT WE AVOIDED EACH OTHER LIKE A PAIR OF house cats. If I was in the living room, Eloda was in the laundry room. When she was in the kitchen, I was anywhere else. Normally, when the great lunchtime whistle sounded, I ran up from the women's yard and met Eloda at the kitchen table. Out of habit I did so on the first day after Andrew's surprise visit. As I entered the back door, I glimpsed blue denim fleeing the kitchen. On the table were a half-drunk glass of ice water, crumbs, and an unused napkin—a household misdemeanor that would never happen with the Eloda I knew. From then on, at the whistle, I dawdled in the yard, kicking cigarette butts, before slowly—and noisily—mounting the outer stairs. I always found the kitchen empty and spotless.

The most painful minutes of our estrangement happened each morning. Normally, the moment I finished my cereal, she was behind me with comb and rubber band. It was then, feeling the artful tug of her hands on my hair, that I came closest to a daily dose of mothering. It was then that we talked.

This no longer happened. Because I was so terrified to face her, I now ate my cereal at the kitchen table instead of the breakfast bar. I meant this to be a signal to stay away from me. It worked. My hair went unbraided. I could barely believe there had been a time when she had laughed herself silly over my request for a ribbon. Our frosty, wordless estrangement hardened into ice.

Of course, the best way to avoid Eloda was to get outta town. So I rode my bike. Every day. To Valley Forge. East Norriton. West Norriton. Conshohocken. Anywhere but downtown. Anywhere but Mogins Dip. For no reason that made sense, I was still afraid to go anywhere near Andrew Strong.

Camille! . . . Camille! . . .

With every push of the pedals I replayed Eloda's voice. It didn't matter that she was mad at me, yelling at me. My name had come from her lips. The name Anne O'Reilly had given me. *Camille!* No, it wasn't the "Cammie" that I longed for. But neither was it the hated "Miss Cammie."

I rode past the porch house at 428 Swede Street. Three times. No sign of a sister.

There were eleven mulberry trees in town. I rode to them all, climbed them all, sat on their branches gorging myself, staining myself and the sidewalks black with juice.

I rode to the park. I explored the creek. I picked raspberries, red and black. I roamed the zoo. The baseball glove no longer hung from my handlebars. I did not go near the Little League field. I stopped for a foot-long hot dog at Ned's once, and from the steps I could see the guys at play. Danny Lapella was there in his red Phillies cap. I rode on.

In the mornings I continued to lose myself among the inmates in the women's yard. And Boo Boo. I attached myself to her more than ever. I thrilled to the stories of her incredible life. Dancer. Roller-derby blocker. Circus-animal handler. Only one person sat beside me on the concrete bench, but sometimes it seemed like ten.

Boo Boo had a special love of water. "Bright water," she called it. She said it came from her days growing up in the bayous of the Mississippi River delta. "I used to ride a alligator to school!" she told me with a flourish. And I was on my way to believing when her wink and sly grin warned me not to.

But grow up in gloomy swamplands she did, and through all the exotic turns of her life she never took her eyes from her dream of "bright water." And even though she often said, "I'm gonna live by the bright water," I took it to be just that, a dream. A cellblock soother. A mood-uplifting jailhouse pipe dream.

Until the day she confessed.

The imp was gone from her eye. Her voice went low, as if someone might overhear. She pulled me closer on the bench. "I'm gonna confess," she whispered.

She let the words sit there as she searched my face for a reaction. All I could guess was that she was about to violate the prisoner's classic claim: *I didn't do it.*

"Boo Boo," I said, keeping my voice whispery, too, "you don't have to confess. Everybody knows you did it. You're always bragging about your shoplifting career."

She made a sound like a soda popping open. "That's over."

"Over?" I recalled her shoplifting instructions. "I thought we were going to be partners."

She snarled, surprising me. "Where'd you get that?"

"Sorry." I snapped back onto her track, wherever it led. "So what's over?"

She waved at the air. "All that. Over." She looked down at me. "Know what I'm gonna do?"

"What?"

"Settle down."

I wasn't sure how this information qualified as a "confession," but I wasn't going to quibble over words. "That's nice," I said.

"Get married," she said.

"Great."

"Have kids."

"Great."

"Six."

"Wow."

She pulled back. "Too many? How 'bout five?"

"Hey, no," I said quickly, "they're *your* kids. Six is cool."

"I got the names. You wanna hear them?"

"Sure."

She recited them easily. She had obviously been thinking about this. "Audrey. Angela. Adele. Amos. Alan. And Alvin." She grinned. "Notice anything?"

"They all start with A," I said.

"What else?"

I wasn't seeing it. "What?"

"Three girls. Three boys."

I smacked the bench. "Ah! Right."

And then she told me about Delancy Worthington.

40

SHE MET HIM ONE SUMMER'S DAY.

She had just done some "shopping" up and down Main Street. Normally she would go straight home to unpack her underwear. But the day was too perfect to spend indoors, and there across the street was the pocket park between the back side of the massive courthouse and the sidewalk. She crossed over and sat herself down on a bench by the gray snub-nosed World War I cannon.

She had the park to herself for about a minute, and, to hear her tell, it was "the second-bestest minute of my life." She just sat there in the sunshine and watched the walkers and the cars go by on Main Street and the P&W trolley pull up to the high terminal and she couldn't stop smiling at the perfection of it all. If the bounty in her pants was causing her sitting discomfort, she never noticed.

The Scheidt's whistle went off, and half the courthouse, toting paper bags and lunch pails, seemed to empty out onto the park's benches.

One of them was a tall, handsome man who took a seat at the other end of Boo Boo's bench. When he unwrapped his sandwich and the smell hit her, she couldn't help herself. She laughed and said, "Liverwurst." He might have taken offense at her cheeky presumption. He might have ignored her. But what he did was meet her laugh for laugh, so she was emboldened to add, "And onion!"

"What a nose!" he exclaimed, and cracked up. By now the clock was already ticking on "the first-bestest minute of my life."

"We couldn't stop laughing," she kept repeating, as if she still didn't quite believe it. He broke off a piece of his liverwurst-and-onion and made her eat it. Then he rose and said, "What flavor?" and she said "cherry" and he hustled down to the curb at Main, where the hokey-pokey man parked his white cart every noontime, and back he came with a pair of red cherry water ices.

He worked as a clerk for the Recorder of Deeds, he told her. He was going to night school to become a lawyer. "Who knows?" he said. "Maybe DA someday." "Maybe," she said, "a *judge*." They laughed some more.

She told him then about her dream of living by the bright water, and he stood—he literally jumped up from his seat. "Me too!" he said with amazement.

Boo Boo squeezed my hand as she told me this. "It was like I just said the words he was waiting on all his life."

Well, "dreams don't need no preacher," she said, and hers and Delancy's were married by the time he tossed his wax paper into the trash can and headed back to the courthouse. She returned to her whisper. "Ever since then we been planning. He's looking for a place."

I loved the story. I must have been in its spell, as the words that followed would never have come from the real Cammie: "Maybe someday I can have a first-bestest minute like that."

Her eyes rose to the waterfall and beyond. "And that minute ain't over yet."

I was so happy for her. I felt honored that she'd told me. I felt as I often did in the Salami Room as I read Thomas Browne's letter to his Dearest Loved One.

"So does he come to visit you?" I asked her.

"Every weekend," she said. "Ain't nothin' can keep that man away."

"And does he want six kids, too?" I was half kidding.

"He wants ten!" she cried, and we both howled.

The noon whistle sounded then, and we had to go our separate ways. I turned and called, "But remember what comes first."

She swung about in the crowd exiting the yard and jabbed her finger at me and called for all the world to hear: "Sweet potato pie! *You!*"

Never had Boo Boo been so endearing, so compelling, so close to me. From the scarlet flash of her fingernails to her wild hair and booming laughter, she virtually demanded favorable comparison with the drab, sullen, silent maid in my apartment. With each step up the back stairway, I took the measure of one against the other. When I reached the kitchen door, I had come to a surprising conclusion: for all her virtues, Boo Boo was not mother material. Maybe for her own six or ten, but not for me. Until that moment I had not even known that the mother-seeking orphan in me had been auditioning her.

This insight had the effect of revoking all complaints against Eloda. It also emboldened me. Next day at cereal time I was back at the breakfast-bar high stool. I grew more and more nervous. I could hardly swallow the last bite. The spoon hovered above the bowl. I stopped breathing—and began again when I sensed her come up behind me. I felt the familiar tug on my hair. She couldn't see me smiling.

"Number one law," she said.

"No more fires," I said.

And the cold crust of our estrangement fell to the floor in a tinkle of ice.

41

THAT WAS THE DAY REGGIE SHOWED UP WAVING AN ENVE-lope in my face and screaming, "Fan mail!"

It was a handwritten note—pencil, printed letters, lined paper—from a boy in Minnesota named Gary. There were four sentences. One of them read, *I think you are the most beautiful female I ever saw!!!* The last one read, *I give you a 99!!!* The highest score on *Bandstand*'s Rate-A-Record was 98.

No homework assignment was ever more intensely scrutinized than those four sentences.

"I *think*? Why not *know*?"

"*Most* beautiful!"

"*Ever* saw!"

"Ninety-*nine*!"

"*Three* exclamation points!"

We must have read it in chorus ten times.

We even studied the envelope. It had been originally sent to the *Bandstand* studio address on Market Street in West Philly. They had forwarded it to Reggie.

"Now you're like Tommy D and Justine and Bob!" I gushed. Her muted "I know" told me she had long since thought of that.

"And maybe you'll get your own fan club!"

"I know."

I wound up and heaved the next one as far down the road as I could. "Maybe even a *magazine!*"

Bingo. Her eyes went wide. "Y'think?"

"Heck, yeah," I told her. "By this time next year they could be selling your magazine—"

"My *fan* magazine—"

"—selling your *fan* magazine at the newsstand across from the P&W."

"At Care's Drug Store!"

I gestured at the world. "Everywhere! Coast to coast!"

"Like *Seventeen!*"

We had to stop and catch our breath. Give the future a chance to catch up.

She clutched my arm. "What's it gonna be called?"

"What else?" I said. "*Reggie!* With an exclamation point."

She fished in my eyes for a moment until she saw the

cover. *"Reggie!"* she whispered solemnly. And then she was clutching my arm again, hard this time. "Oh my God . . . oh my God . . ."

"What?" I said.

"You know what this means, don't you?" She was looking through Gary's note to somewhere else.

"What?"

"Where it all leads."

I grabbed her arm. "Where?

She mouthed a word silently with her Passion Pink lips. I didn't understand it. I shook her. *"Say it!"*

She said it: "Broadway."

I joined her, looking through the penciled paper in her hand. And then I saw it, too: the long tunnel of time passing through mountains of fan mail, newsstands hawking *Reggie!*, screaming fans reaching for a touch—and there, at the end of the tunnel, velvety curtains swinging open to reveal . . . "Reggie Weinstein!" . . . in a gingham frontier dress belting out a song from *Oklahoma!*

I slept over at Reggie's most of that week. The mail arrived each day just before noon. Each day we sat on the curb in front of her West End duplex, breathlessly awaiting the mailman. When we spotted him turning the corner onto her block, we ran to him and babbled away until he reached her house.

The first day's haul was three letters. One . . . three . . .

we could feel the deluge mounting. I suggested framing them. Reggie sensibly pointed out that there wasn't wall space in the whole block of houses for what was coming. Meanwhile she retrieved from the backyard trash a tall cardboard box that had housed the family's new vacuum cleaner. With the swipe of a paintbrush she canceled out HOOVER and replaced it with FAN MAIL. It stood chest-high next to her bedroom dresser.

We were together morning, noon and night. If I had been Reggie's doll before, I was now her audience, her witness. "Maybe someday you'll write about this," she said to me one day at Scooper Dooper. She had found out where New York City was and had taken to gazing dreamily in that direction, to Broadway, as if to Mecca. She did so now over her vanilla fudge double-dip, whispering in prayerful wonder, "A star is born."

Two more fan letters arrived on the day after the three. Then none—well, it was Sunday. Then one. Then none. And none. And none. We were mystified. Too many were piling up at the Market Street studio, we theorized. They would bring them all at once, probably in a truck. We asked the mailman if there could be a mistake. Could he be delivering them to some other address from that leather pouch of his?

Ah, such rookies were we in the game of fame. In the space of that week Reggie Weinstein's world—and by best-friend extension, mine—went from a planet to a pea.

Somewhere along the line we stopped waiting at the curb. We staggered in a fog of disbelief. My last moment in her bedroom is with me still. I'm looking down into the FAN MAIL box, which seems much deeper than the length of a vacuum cleaner. The daylight barely reaches the depths. The envelopes—seven—don't even cover the bottom.

42

I RETURNED TO MY WORLD TO FIND THAT SOMETHING NEW was happening. Demonstrators were marching outside the prison with signs that said things like FRY BAKER and NO MERCY.

Inside, two new women had appeared in the yard. And three were gone—time served!—including Deena the sunbather. As a memorial, she had left her eye cups on the ground. The black, spoony surfaces faced the sun as always, as if she had merely dissolved away from beneath them and would at any moment rematerialize. No one moved them.

Boo Boo was mad at me. "Where you been?" she demanded.

I told her about Reggie and the whole *Bandstand* and fan letters thing, but she pouted till the lunch whistle that day and halfway through the next morning. She was silent and sullen. She answered my questions with grunts. I barely recognized her.

To show her displeasure, she refused to sit with me on the concrete bench. She paced about the Quiet Room. She lectured me on true friendship. She kept casting her eyes skyward, through the glass roof, as if seeking relief from having to look at me. She swept her hand through the waterfall, sending sun-spangled droplets to the dirt floor. She swung a red-pointed finger at me: "You never smile!" And said no more that day.

Her words stung. They went straight to the heart of my identity: I was not a happy person. This was something I seldom reflected on. It was simply my normal state, the only world I'd ever known: *The sky is blue. The grass is green. Cammie O'Reilly is not happy.* Oh sure, there were moments: a shared laugh with Boo Boo . . . Reggie's *Bandstand* Day . . . Eloda's wet fingertip on my cheek . . . Andrew. If you had spotted me at such a moment you might have called me happy. But such moments were brief. They seemed to occur only when I got caught in someone else's happy shower. When the shower was over, I was left damp and empty. Happiness had to happen to me. I could not make my own.

And now I felt responsible for the happiness of Boo Boo, who had come to rival Reggie as my best friend. It disturbed me to think that my long absence was all it had taken for her jolly disposition to disappear. Was I—was my smile—that important to her?

And then suddenly next day she was charging me. I froze, thinking she was attacking. But it wasn't anger in her eyes as she flopped beside me on the bench. It was fear. She squeezed my arm. "Did you hear about the Spootnik?"

She meant *Sputnik* and, yes, I had heard of it, barely. It was something called a satellite. In 1957, the Russians had shot it into space, and now it was circling the earth like a tiny, basketball-size moon. That was all I knew, I told her.

She told me more. She had heard it on the radio—the radio my father had directed be installed in the middle of the women's cellblock. Some people were getting nervous, she explained. They believed Sputnik was spying on America. "They up there," she said, gazing skyward. "Watchin' us." She stared into my eyes. "They can see ever'thing. Ever'thing!"

She was jittery. She kept glancing up through the glass roof and muttering "Spootnik . . ." As the lunch whistle blew, she grabbed my arms. "Miss Cammie . . . tell your daddy I'm ready for my release now. You hear?" And then, inside with the group and out of sight, her voice calling: "You tell him!" As I walked from the Quiet Room, it came to me that she no longer smelled of strawberries.

Perhaps I would have been more sympathetic to Boo Boo's sense of urgency if I had not been dealing with an urgency of my own. One morning I entered the kitchen to find a new page and a new word on the wall calendar: August.

The summer was flying. On August twenty-ninth my preteen years would come to an abrupt end. On September eighth I would enter the terrifying big-kid world of junior high school. The summer that had once seemed endless was threatening to run out before I could solve my biggest problem. My efforts to become an honorary daughter to Eloda Pupko were as fruitless now as they had been in June. I convinced myself that I had only these last few weeks of summer in which to succeed. Once school began, I'd be in classrooms all day. I'd no longer have the time and freedom to focus on my goal.

My urgency came from another source as well. When I'd seen the full load of love that Andrew got from his mother, I had not been jealous at all. Quite the opposite. What the experience had done was give me an up-close, eyewitness taste of what I was missing. I wanted it now more than ever.

But I'd been trying all summer. I'd tried being needy, to trick her into motherhood. I'd tried being adorable, lovable, grateful. I'd given her a diary. Called her Mother. If that didn't break her, what would? What else could I do?

Nothing, as it turned out. For life, not I, was writing my story. When you're *inside* your own story, you don't see things like a reader. You don't see your life in tidy paragraphs and chapters. What you see is a mishmash—no, scratch that. You don't even *see*. You simply *feel*. And even then, it's mostly a low-grade feeling, the flat doldrums of the routine, the everyday. And then, sooner or later, feeling spikes. The boring pool has become a raging torrent. Life is writing you in italics.

As I look back, that's what I see in the final weeks of that summer of '59: myself tumbling helplessly in a torrent. I cannot steer. I cannot control. I cannot resist.

But now, more than half a century later, it is I who holds the pen. I must decide where to begin the story's final pages—the climax, if you will. It could be any of a dozen days, for events did not always follow neatly or sensibly. It was, even in hindsight, a mishmash. So . . . let's say it began sometime after the day Boo Boo told me about "Spootnik" and called back to me in the Quiet Room, "You tell him!" Let's say it began the day I heard pounding on the front door and found a suddenly rejuvenated Reggie beaming and shoving a big, glossy black-and-white photograph in my face.

43

It was Marvin Edward Baker. From the shirt collar up, occupying all eight by ten inches. Unsmiling. Needing a shave. Not trying to look good. Just happening to be in the same room with a camera. His black hair more plastered than combed, as if it had been troweled onto the top of his head.

"Where'd you get it?" I said.

"*Times-Herald*," she said. "They make copies you can buy. I paid half a dollar. My father did it for a picture of me once."

I glared at her. "A murderer. You paid fifty cents for a picture of a murderer."

The look she was giving the picture was creepy-close to affection. "Not just *any* murderer."

"You're sick," I told her.

"I'm going to frame it!" she chirped, ignoring me.

I pictured her bedroom walls, with framed pictures, mostly cut out from magazines, of *Bandstand* regulars and Broadway and movie stars.

"I'm gonna say it again," I said. "Real slow. He's . . . a . . . murderer."

She smiled at me with great patience, as if I were a child. "Famous is famous," she breezed.

I suppose on some level I dimly understood what was happening. The focus of her dream had never really been *Bandstand* or Broadway or the movies. It was fame. Fame its own raw self. If fame would not attach itself to her, then she would attach herself to it. In this my friend Reggie was apparently not unique. I dared not tell her what my father had recently revealed to me: Hancock County's most famous criminal had begun to get fan mail of his own.

She was holding out the photo.

"Don't give it to *me*," I told her.

"I want it autographed," she said.

"Huh? Why do you want my—" And then it hit me. "Oh no." I swatted her hand away.

"Cam-*mee* . . . ," she squealed. "Just give it to him. Tell him to put 'To Reggie Weinstein, with best wishes.' That's all. Well, and his name, of course."

I started laughing, shaking my head. I couldn't think of a word. "What's *worse* than sick?"

She thought for a moment. "Grotesque?" she said helpfully.

"You're grotesque."

She flopped onto the sofa. She glanced about. She popped back up. She ran to the kitchen, returned with a saucer. From the waistband beneath her shirt, she pulled out a green pack of cigarettes. Kools. She produced a pack of matches and lit up right there in my living room. She dropped the spent match onto the saucer.

"I *knew* it," I said.

"Fine," she said. "I'm sick. *And* grotesque." She jabbed the picture at me. "Just get his autograph? One little teeny-weeny favor for your bestest-ever best friend?"

In truth, I was not shocked by her request. Because I lived inside the prison walls, people often assumed I had greater access to the inmates than I really did. People seemed to think I roamed everywhere at will and played cards with them in their cells.

"Reggie," I told her, "he's in *the hole*."

"What's the hole?"

"Solitary confinement. Even other inmates can't see him."

She took a drag on her Kool. Her cheeks puffed. She swished the smoke about like a grown-up tasting wine. Apparently she had not yet learned to inhale. When she opened her mouth with a faint "puhh," the smoke, with no push from its smoker, seemed to wander out reluctantly and loiter about her face. She steepled her hands in prayer. *"Pleease."*

That's when I noticed she was also carrying a ballpoint pen. But not her ever-present pink transistor. "Where's your radio?" I said, trying to change the subject.

It took a moment for my question to register. "Home," she said distractedly. Which proved how obsessed she was over the picture. "But you *know* people. Your father's the *warden*." She was whining.

I was fumbling for my next defense when Eloda came into the living room, pillowcase in hand. She had been changing my bed. She planted herself in front of the sofa. She ignored me. She glared at Reggie. "Put that out."

Reggie blew a cloud. She gave a snooty sniff. "I'm a big girl. I can smoke if I want to."

"Not in my house."

No doubt Reggie was as shocked as I was to hear a prison trustee refer to my apartment as her house. I was delighted. Reggie's point of view, predictably, was different.

Reggie casually tapped ashes onto the saucer. She stared pointedly at the pillowcase. "Well, I got news for you. It's not *your* house."

I saw Eloda's jaw clench. Her fist tightened on the pillowcase. I'll never know what might have happened next because I snatched the burning cigarette from Reggie and dashed it out on the saucer. "Yes it is," I said.

What exactly did I mean by that? Even I wasn't sure.

But the words were out, in the room, as real as the ribbon of smoke curling up from the saucer.

And then Eloda was turning abruptly and heading back to my room. I grabbed the saucer and took it into the kitchen. I cleaned the saucer and dried it and put it in the cupboard.

I should have gone right back to the living room then. But I didn't. That was my mistake. I went to my room. Why, I'm not sure. To put off returning to Reggie? To receive Eloda's gratitude for defending her? If that was my reason, I was disappointed. Eloda was her usual workaday self, all business. She ignored me. I grabbed the other side of the sheet she was fitting over the mattress, intending to help her. She stopped. She sent me a huff of displeasure. Her hand went to her hip. "Miss Cammie—now who's the housekeeper around here." It wasn't a question.

When I got back to the living room, Reggie was gone. I assumed she'd taken off. I was relieved. I hoped I'd heard the last of her Marvin Edward Baker infatuation. By now it was well after noon. I realized I was hungry. Even to this day I cringe to think what might have happened had I not walked into the kitchen.

44

Blame Gonzalez.

In 1909 a man named Gonzalez, an inmate at Folsom State Prison in California, was sent to the hole. After a week he couldn't take it anymore. No human contact. No sunlight. But plenty of rats. It was driving him crazy. So he went on a hunger strike. Fifteen days later the prison agreed to his demands. Gonzalez was returned to his cell. By then he was famous.

Newspapers had spread the story about the Folsom hole dweller whose legs were covered in rat bites and who never heard another human voice. CRUEL AND UNUSUAL PUNISHMENT crowed the headlines.

When my father became warden, he discovered his jail had a hole, an eight-by-eight-foot pocket dungeon of despair. It was unfit for rats. No one could recall an inmate ever staying there. No one could find a key to the door.

My father changed all that. The hole was scrubbed, fumigated, painted. A square of wall was bashed in and barred: sunlight! A new bed. New potty. New key.

Baker became the new hole's first resident. A copy of the *Times-Herald* was slipped under the door every day. The guards who brought his meals were instructed to speak to him.

Though my father believed in humane treatment for all prisoners, this was not what drove his actions. He put Baker in solitary simply to keep him alive and healthy. (It's now called protective custody.) So unspeakable was Baker's crime that my father feared the window installer/murderer would never survive a day or two on the cellblock. The solitary, the homey "comforts"—all was done in order to deliver to the courthouse a defendant fit for trial by a jury of his peers. The warden wanted no hunger strikes on his watch.

So Baker had a good life for an inmate—as long as he was inside. But how to get him some fresh air? ("I need some fresh air!" Gonzalez had squawked.) My father sought the answer. Unbeknown to me, he found it shortly before the day Reggie showed up with her picture and ballpoint pen. . . .

As I reached into the kitchen cupboard for the peanut butter, I happened to glance out the back window. If my eyes had had a throat, I would have choked. Reggie was down below, at the chain-link fence. Two guards with rifles stood in the exercise yard. At the far end of the yard, at the Marshall Street wall, a man in denim walked slowly back and forth. I didn't have to be told it was Marvin Edward Baker. This, as I would soon learn, was Baker's one hour per day in the fresh air. High on the wall, Jim was out of the guardhouse, on alert.

I stood at the back-door window, not believing what I saw: a sexy, high school–looking girl in short shorts handing a picture to an armed guard through the space between the gate and fence post . . . the girl with animated shoulders saying things to the guard I could not hear . . . the prisoner at the far wall stopping . . . looking . . . moving toward the fence . . . the second guard stepping forward . . . Jim on the wall raising his rifle . . .

I burst through the door and down the outer steps. I yanked Reggie from the fence. I yelled at the startled guard: "Gimme!" He gave me the picture. I shoved Reggie up the steps, into the kitchen, slammed the door.

"What in the name of God do you think you're doing?"

She gave me her wide-eyed *what's the big deal* look. "Getting an autograph on a picture." She reached for it.

"Not anymore you're not." I tore the picture into a hundred pieces and flung them across the kitchen.

She stared at the floor, blinking those big, beautiful eyes. I thought she might cry, but she surprised me. She smiled. She gave a casual shrug. She wagged the ballpoint pen in front of me and said blithely, "Another half dollar, another picture." She walked out of the kitchen and out of the apartment.

Five minutes later, I had just cleaned up the picture pieces when I heard the stomping of many feet on the stairway, many fists pounding on the door. I knew it was the Jailbirds. When I opened the door, they shouted in unison: "Snowball fight!"

45

On the other side of the creek, up on West Elm Street, was the icehouse. A wooden, green-painted shanty from another time, it had begun selling ice to owners of pre-refrigerator iceboxes and now supplied blocks and cubes for restaurants, caterers and backyard parties—and the hokey-pokey man. Mostly ignored by kids in the winter, the ice-house became fascinating in the summer months because on the back side of the shanty could always be found, even in August, a mound of discarded crushed ice, as if January had left a little bit of itself behind.

Within seconds we were girl-mobbing up Airy Street. Reggie was with us. After she left my place, she had bumped into the gang. She gave no sign that anything unpleasant had passed between us.

At one point the girls veered right. It was the natural way to head for Elm Street. It would also lead us to Oak and Cherry. The Corner. I felt suddenly sour, mushy. I couldn't move. I called, "Hey, no, this way—I wanna go over the bridge." Nobody argued. It was always fun to spit on cars below from the Airy Street bridge. Of course, they knew my mother had been killed by a milk truck when we were all babies. But they didn't know exactly where it had happened. They didn't know about The Corner or my lifelong dread of going near it.

When we reached the icehouse, we were thrilled to discover that the snow pile was undisturbed; we were the first kids to use it that day. We went straight to war: screaming, throwing, ducking, chasing. Mostly screaming. Our hands were soon bright red. We sucked our cold, wet fingers to rewarm them. The icehouse workers ignored us.

The small back lot of the icehouse ended abruptly at a bluff some twenty feet above the train tracks. There was no fence. We stayed well back from the edge.

We were about halfway through the snowball pile when we first heard the rumbling. It was faint, coming from the east. Five years earlier we would have instantly recognized the sound of a steam locomotive. Now it took a second or two to realize that it was the new kind of train engine, a diesel, that was heading our way. Instantly we forgot each other. Frantically we mashed and molded snowballs. We carried armloads to the bluff's edge, just in time to see the flat iron muzzle poke around the curve at Elm and Astor. The earth trembled beneath our feet.

The train was endless. Coal cars. Boxcars. We had to keep returning to the pile to replenish our arsenal. We were merciless. No car went clacking on toward the park without a white splat. The caboose never had a chance.

There's something special about the silence left in the wake of a long train. It seems at once an ending and a beginning—or, more specifically, a waiting, a question. As if the train is calling back: *That was me. Now how about you?*

Maybe that's why I said it. I hadn't planned to. I really hadn't given the whole thing much thought. I hadn't been counting the days. Unlike a lot of kids, I *could* wait to grow up. But there they were, words coming out of my mouth: "Hey, everybody—wanna come to my birthday party?"

Cheers rang from the bluff.

And again I surprised myself: "And a sleepover!"

As they shrieked and pelted me with the last of the snowballs, it came to me that I'd never made people so happy.

46

ON THE LONG WALK HOME THAT DAY, I TRIED TO FIGURE MY-
self out. I had never had a birthday party. Never really wanted
one. My father usually took me to a Phillies game. Now I was
having not only a party but a sleepover, too. (It never occurred to me that my father might not allow it.) Sure, I understood why the Jailbirds liked the idea of sleeping overnight in
a prison. The thrill of it. The cool factor of being friends with
the warden's daughter. But now, quite unexpectedly, I was
tempted to think it wasn't *only* the warden's daughter that
they liked. I was beginning to think it was also me.

My own self.

Cammie O'Reilly.

As I approached the prison, Baker demonstrators were
once again walking their signs back and forth. I noticed a

new one: NEXT STOP—ROCKVIEW. I remembered what Marvin Edward Baker had been overheard to say, as reported by Reggie: "I ain't never goin' to Rockview."

I was halfway through Reception when I was stopped by the voice of Mrs. Butterfield, my father's secretary: "Miss Cammie?" She was holding something. It appeared to be paper, folded many times down to the size of a cigarette lighter. She did not offer it to me. She merely displayed it. I was puzzled. She said, "It's from Evelyn Dunbar." Mrs. Butterfield always used inmates' proper names. Evelyn Dunbar was Boo Boo. "She gave it to Willard"—a cellblock guard—"to give to me. To give"—she smiled; she reached across her desk—"to you."

I took it and headed up the stairs to the apartment. She called after me: "Nobody read it."

This was a reference to the usual practice of reading and censoring all inmate mail that came into and went out of the prison.

The paper I unfolded turned out to be two items: a note and a small envelope. The note was for me. It was penciled in big, blocky letters:

DEER MISS CAMMY
PLEESE PUT THIS ON THE BENCH FOR DELANSY

The envelope was sealed. I could tell there was a note inside. I wondered what it said. Was it something about the place by the water that Delancy was looking for? Or about the wedding? Or just some moony lovey-dovey stuff? I wondered why all the complicated plotting. Couldn't she just say it to him when he came to visit on the weekend? I was too young to understand that leaving a note on a bench was far more romantic than speaking it in the visitors' area of a county prison.

I didn't go to the yard the next day. I assumed the bench in question was the legendary one in the courthouse park. I assumed Delancy still came out and ate his lunch there. I arrived at the bench at eleven-thirty. I taped the note to the seat. I sat there guarding it like a mother hen.

Arching over Main Street in those days was a bridge that carried the P&W high-speed trolley northward out of Two Mills. In the center of the bridge was a huge, ornate clock with Roman numerals—the town's timepiece. I left when the clock said 11:50.

I climbed the marble steps to the courthouse terrace that overlooked the park. I leaned on the balustrade. Below, I could see the trash can, the bench, the white note. I could see the first of the lunchtimers emerging from the building. The brewery whistle blew over the town. More people were coming out . . . and that's when I abruptly turned and walked away. My desire to catch a glimpse of Boo Boo's boyfriend had been canceled by a sense that I was intruding. I had done my job and now I should just get out of there and leave the field to the gods of love.

47

"DID YOU SEE IT?"

A simple question. It was the first thing out of Boo Boo's mouth when I saw her next morning. She dragged me into the Quiet Room. She sat me on the bench, hunkered herself in front of me and said it again: "Did you *see* it?"

I'd expected breathless questions about the envelope plant. This question didn't seem to fit. "See what?" I said.

"The Spootnik." She punctuated the word with a poke to my shoulder that was just a little too hard.

What did the Russian satellite have to do with the note to Delancy? I was befuddled. All I could say was "Huh?"

She squeezed my arm. "I told you to look for it. You can only see it at night. I'm inside. I told you to look up and see it."

For the life of me I could not remember her telling me to do that. My impulse was to say something like *You did?* or *Are you sure?* A second thought advised me to put the blame on myself, not her. "Sorry," I said. "I forgot."

I braced myself for another poke. It never came. Her face changed. She blinked at me, as if she was trying to remember who I was. Her entire body said: *I am hurt.* She went to the wheelbarrow waterfall. She stood there for several minutes, holding her hand under the falling stream. I felt terrible. I wanted to smack myself. She'd asked me to do one simple little thing. And I had blown it. Great friend I was.

I called, "I'll do it tonight. Promise."

She didn't seem to hear me. She stood a while longer before the waterfall, fingering the long green leaves nearby. When she turned back to me, she was Boo Boo again. She pointed. "You ain't shopliftin', are you?"

"No, ma'am," I said, relieved that we were off the "Spootnik" track.

She nodded crisply, mentor to pupil. "Good." She sat beside me. "I don't want you in here."

"No, ma'am."

She laughed. "What would your daddy say?"

We both laughed.

And then she fell silent. We must have sat side by side on that bench for ten minutes and she never said a word. I detected no attitude. She didn't seem upset or angry or, as usual, happy. She wasn't brimming. That was the word. Boo Boo was always *brimming*. There was a sense that things—words, feelings, laughs—were forever brawling inside her to be the first one out. Now, beside me, I sensed . . . emptiness. Emptiness in such a person is not nothing, is not small. It is enormous.

I was lost. Conversationwise, I was used to Boo Boo carrying the ball. I wondered why she was acting this way. Had something bad happened between her and Delancy? Was the note in the envelope not a happy, lovey-dovey note after all? Was it a *Forgive me* note or a *Let's make up* note?

The silence, the tension, became too much for me. I blew it away: "A boy likes me."

Again she didn't seem to hear. Then she turned, just her head. She looked down at me. "A what?" she said.

"A boy likes me." This time the words didn't fly out so easily.

She blinked. She stared. "A boy likes you?"

"Yeah," I said. "Well, I think so anyway. Not that I have a lot of practice with boys liking me." I gave a nervous laugh. She didn't. "Anyway, so, he walked me home from the fireworks on the Fourth of July . . ."

I blabbed on and on about Danny Lapella. I discovered that it excited me to wind my tangled feelings into thoughts and words and belt them out of me, over the walls of myself like stringballs onto Marshall Street. I also blabbed to keep the uncomfortable silence from returning, to keep Boo Boo engaged, locked into here and now, into me.

It wasn't working. Her eyes drifted away from my face and across the room to the waterfall. I kept talking, trying to reel her back. When I ran out of Danny Lapella, I jumped to Reggie and the whole *Bandstand* thing and the fan mail and the snowball fight at the icehouse and my dream of playing for the Phillies. I threw in energetic gestures and laughs. I popped off the bench and demonstrated how I ran over little Benny House at home plate, which I suddenly found funny. I was almost out of material when she turned back to me and—*click!*—once again it was Boo Boo's eyes twinkling at me. I shut up. She slapped her knee and exclaimed, "Scooper Dooper!"

I recalled our plan. "Yeah!" I replied, trying to match her spark. "We're gonna go. Soon as you get out."

She looked at me lovingly. She nodded. "That's right. But you know what?"

"What?" I said.

"I want you to go now."

I wasn't following. "But you're still here," I pointed out.

She looked into my eyes. She took both my hands in hers. "Do you love Boo Boo?"

This was my day for being caught off guard. "Love" was not a word I threw around much. I used it occasionally as applied to Carl's pies or the oil-scented, leathery smell of my baseball glove when I retrieved it from the shoe box every spring—but not to people. Living people.

I swallowed once and swung at a fastball down the middle. "Sure," I said.

My answer made her happy. She was still smiling at me when she said, "You know what a proxy is?"

48

"No," I SAID.

Boo Boo told me that a proxy is someone who is authorized to act on behalf of somebody else. A proxy could take your place and vote for something. Or sign some legal papers for you. It's like a proxy person has permission to play the part of you.

"Sounds like pinch-hitting," I said.

She slapped the bench. "'Zacly! You wanna pinch-hit for Boo Boo?"

"Sure," I said. "What am I doing?"

She told me. She wanted me to go to Scooper Dooper. She wanted me to order a banana split. All three scoops chocolate. Wet walnuts. Hot fudge. Extra whipped cream. Four cherries. One for each scoop, plus one. No pineapple.

Just like we talked about. "And then," she said, and she turned fully to me on the bench and her voice went soft and solemn, "you gonna sit there—in a window table, you got that?"

I nodded. "I got it."

"A window table in front, so's you can see the peoples walkin by . . ." She waited.

"Got it."

"And you're gonna *eat* that banana split. Only"—she poked me softly—"it ain't gonna be *you* eating it. It's gonna be *me*." She could see I was struggling to keep up. "Listen to me, Miss Cammie . . ." She took my hand. She placed it on my chest, then hers. "There's love between you and me. A love bridge."

I squeezed her hand, which seemed big as a baseball glove. I loved the disparity between our fingernails—hers red and long and glamorous; mine stumpy, ragged, dirty. "I like that," I said.

"And that love bridge, that makes us sisters. Y'see?"

I nodded. "I see."

"So you is me and I is you." She frowned. Maybe at the grammar, maybe at the idea. Whichever, she laughed the frown away. "You with me?"

"I'm with you."

"So, when you're up there eatin' the banana split . . ." She paused; she seemed to be getting her thoughts straight. "Eatin' that banana split . . . it's goin' in"—she poked me—"*you*, but the one tastin' it"—she poked herself—"is *me*." She cocked her head. "Still with me?"

"Still with you," I said. Even though I wasn't, not really.

She looked away, into some beyond I could not see. A peacefulness came upon her. "Miss Cammie, as long as you're eatin' that split, I'm gonna be *out* . . . without bein' *out*."

We stared at each other, silenced by the wonderfulness of the notion.

She jabbed a red fingernail at me. "And don't you think you can fool me, girl. If there ain't four cherries gone into that moutha yours, I'll know it."

"Don't worry," I said. "I'll do it right."

She smacked the bench. "It's gonna work. I know it." She leaned into me. "You know why?"

"Why?" I said.

She slumped. "Miss Cammie," she said with exaggerated dismay. "We went over this. It's gonna work *because* . . ."

She waited for me to complete the sentence. I couldn't. I was on summer vacation. The last thing I needed was a pop quiz. "Because . . . ?" I peeped.

She took my face in her hands. She pronounced a syllable: "Luh . . . luh . . ."

I cried: "Love bridge!"

She kissed me on the nose. She swallowed me in a hug. "Only two peoples with a love bridge can do it." She tapped me. "Proxy."

I nodded. "Proxy."

"Sisters."

I looked up at her. I fell into her eyes. "Sisters."

Sisters.

The word occupied the space between us as the brewery whistled lunchtime. We wrapped it up with a flurry of will-yous and yes-I-wills and "Four cherries!" As we left the Quiet Room, I released a thought that had been nipping at me. "Boo Boo," I said, "I know it's really gonna be you eating the banana split, but can I sneak in just one bite for myself?" As I recall, she was laughing too hard to reply.

I was at my backyard gate when a thought flew straight through my brain and out my mouth: "Boo Boo!" I called. "I left the note!"

By then she was heading in for lunch, towering as always above the others. I could only hope that she heard me.

49

I was not going to blow it this time. I had failed to look for Sputnik. I wasn't going to fail with Scooper Dooper.

I didn't even bother to eat the lunch Eloda had put out for me. I grabbed a five-dollar bill from my cigar box savings bank and headed for the West End on my bike.

The day was typical August in the Delaware Valley: hot, humid. I was in such a hurry and so preoccupied with my mission that I failed to notice I was riding west on Oak Street—until I was within half a block of Oak and Cherry. The Corner. Simultaneously I U-turned and mashed the back pedal. My tires flew out. The left pedal raked the asphalt and pinned my ankle to the street. Car brakes screamed. I looked up . . . into the distinctive bullet-nose grille of a Studebaker. I righted myself, flung a "Sorry!" at the horrified driver and hightailed it out of there. Someone in heavy shoes was chasing me . . . thumping . . . No . . . it was my heart.

I didn't slow down till I hit Marshall, then headed west again. Within a block or two, the thumping went away. I took deep breaths. I welcomed the warm smother of the day. I reentered the sanctuary of my mission.

I couldn't pretend to understand all the "proxy" stuff Boo Boo had talked about. She was proving to be much more complex than the jolly giant I had first known in the yard. But the "love bridge"—that was a different story. That I understood. That I believed in.

I parked my bike in front of Scooper Dooper. I pushed open the screen door. The bell tinkled—and things began to change. Yes, it was me walking into the ice cream shop. Me moving toward the long white counter. Me passing between the bright steel-banded Formica tables, some empty, some with customers digging into their treats. Me standing before the squad of topless tubs. Me, yes . . . *but not only me*. Something else, a presence as ethereal as I imagined an angel's to be, was beside me. Was *in* me. Like on a party telephone line, someone else was there—*here*—looking through my eyes, gazing at the frosty mounds, the flavors in all their colors.

"Banana split, please," I said to the man in the white teardrop-shaped paper cap.

I recited the list, slowly, carefully: all three scoops

chocolate . . . wet nuts . . . hot fudge . . . extra whipped cream . . .

"Pineapple?" he said.

"No!" I said. "Cherries. Four."

He gave me a look but he did it. I got the sense that he was about to charge me extra for all the customizing, but as he planted the last cherry in the whipped cream, he stepped back to see what he had done. His admiring smile began at the banana split and shifted over to me. I almost said *It's not for me.* With a show of reverence, or maybe envy, he pushed the masterpiece across the counter. "Eighty cents," he said.

A mother and two little kids were just getting up from a window table. I hustled toward it.

"Miss . . ." The counter man was calling.

I turned.

He was pointing. "Your ankle."

I looked. Blood was seeping through my sock. Bike spill. Studebaker. I grabbed napkins from the dispenser on a vacant table and stuffed them into my sock and practically ran to the table by the window.

I sat. I closed my eyes. I settled myself down. I whispered, "Okay, Boo Boo. Here we go." When I opened my eyes, again I sensed it wasn't just me looking out through them.

I did not plunge in as I would have if I were eating only for myself. I took it slow. I started with a cherry. I held it in my mouth. I closed my eyes. I held it there . . . held it there . . . hoping Boo Boo was tasting, savoring. When my teeth finally crushed that first cherry and the juice exploded in my mouth, I imagined I heard Boo Boo give a quick peep of delight.

Spoonful by spoonful, savor by savor, I received the masterpiece. I may have broken the world record for Slowest Eating of a Banana Split. I spaced out the remaining three cherries, the last one being the last thing of all into my—into *her*—mouth. As I wiped my lips with a napkin, I was not just pretending I could feel Boo Boo smiling. I was believing it. I was sold.

Proxy.

Sisters.

I'm gonna be out!

I raced homeward, my front tire barely skimming the steamy face of Marshall Street. Every muscle in my body was twitching, pulling toward Boo Boo like a dog on a leash. I wanted to crash into her arms, tell her I did my job, ask her if it worked. And then, clattering over the railroad tracks, the problem hit me: I wouldn't be seeing her until ten o'clock next morning.

I couldn't imagine waiting that long. As I pumped up the long town-top hill, I toyed with the idea of visiting her cell. I had never used my privileges so recklessly before, but I doubted the guards would deny the warden's daughter.

A screaming ambulance racing past me brought me to my senses: How long would I be grounded after my father found out? I scotched the idea.

A single demonstrator—BURN BAKER—was braving the heat outside the prison. As I hoisted my bike up the front steps, a flashing squad car went racing down the wall-side alley. I leaned out from the tiny, grassy plateau. Uniforms were dashing across Marshall Street; lights were flashing. What was happening? Had Baker escaped?

Inside, Mrs. Butterfield said nothing, but her face followed me with an expression I could not read. Her glasses were off. A crowd of people, some in uniform, some not, filled my father's office. They all seemed to be talking at once. I could feel urgency. Turmoil. Distress.

As I mounted the stairs to the apartment, solo words rose like bubbles from the boil of voices. But only one stuck to my ear: "hanged." That was all I needed to hear. By the time I hit the top step, Marvin Edward Baker's own words completed the picture: *I ain't never goin' to Rockview.*

I raced back down. I almost veered right and out the door to shout at the demonstrator: *You can go home now!* But I didn't. I ran straight to Mrs. Butterfield, gushing, "He did it, didn't he? He said he would and he did it!"

She blinked. She put her glasses on as if to better see me. She seemed confused. "Who?" she said.

"Marvin Edward Baker!" My stomach pressed into the

238

front edge of her desk. I may have been yelling. "He said, 'I ain't never goin' to Rockview.' And he ain't! He's not! He hanged himself! Right?"

Mrs. Butterfield took her time digesting my information. She removed her glasses. She placed them carefully on her desk. She positioned them precisely in a way that seemed important to her. When her face came back up to me, there was a smile on it, but it wasn't happy.

"It wasn't Mr. Baker," she said. And for the first time ever, the formal Mrs. Butterfield pronounced an inmate's yard name. "It was Boo Boo."

50

Find Delancy.

That's the first sensible thought I can recall. I had to find Delancy. If he didn't know, I had to tell him, find the words I could not even think to myself. If he did know, I had to console him. There would be no wedding. No house by bright water. No ten kids.

I was standing between two massive columns under the entrance to the courthouse.

I found the Recorder of Deeds. Through a square cutout in the wall I could see a woman pecking at a typewriter. Her fingernails were blunt and ugly, more like mine than Boo Boo's. A tortoiseshell comb was sunk into the hair bun in the back of her head. That bothered me. So did her nose. I hated her.

She sat at a right angle to me, pecking. I was sure she could see me in her peripheral vision, but she acted as if she didn't know someone was standing at the window. I wanted to reach in and jam her precious tortoiseshell comb through her bun and into her neck.

"I want to talk to Delancy Worthington," I said.

She pecked some more and finally stopped. She turned her face, nothing else, to me. Direct on, her snout showed nostrils the size of kidney beans. "Excuse me?" she said.

"Delancy Worthington," I repeated. "Can I talk to him, please?"

She blinked. "There's no one here by that name," she said. Her fingertips hovered above the typewriter keys. I swore I would never become a secretary. "Do you have the right department?"

"Recorder of Deeds," I said. I looked up at the sign. "Isn't this it?"

"It is," she said. "But as I say, there's no one here by that name. Not in *this* office."

"Delancy Worthington," I said. It seemed I was in a game that required me to repeat the name a certain number of times.

Her hands fell to her lap. "I'm sorry."

Which struck me as a ridiculous thing to say. "Sorry for what?" I said.

That stumped her. She turned more of herself from the typewriter. "Are you all right?" she said.

I stared at her. I wanted to reach through the window and punch that nose. "Screw you," I said, and walked away, but not before reaping immense satisfaction at the sight of her shocked-wide eyes and kidney-bean nostrils.

I went from sign to sign, window to window. Public Defender . . . Roads and Bridges . . . Voter Registration . . . first floor . . . second floor . . .

No Delancy Worthington anywhere.

Still, the Hancock County courthouse was a big place, with hundreds of people. . . .

Next day at lunchtime I parked myself on the bench in the courthouse park. All trace of the note was gone. Someone came and sat at the other end of the bench, but it was an old lady. I stayed until the P&W clock said two. That's when, finally, I cried.

She had done it with carpet yarn. The same stuff they made stringballs from. She did it from a water fixture in the women's shower room. She must have done it very quickly and very well, they said, perhaps even practiced, because she was alone and unnoticed in the shower room for only a matter of minutes. Equally astonishing was the realization of how much yarn it must have taken to do the job for someone her size. Some speculators said ten balls' worth. Some said fifty.

I have little memory of the faces of others during those days. Dinners with my father were wordless. Same with

Eloda and pigtail time. In fact, I found myself resenting Eloda's hands on my hair. I wanted them to be Boo Boo's. Death changes the angles. Suddenly I beheld a new truth: Boo Boo would have been the perfect mother for me after all.

All the more horrifying, then, to realize that I myself might have driven her to do it. I could not erase from my memory the look of surprise and disappointment on her face when I told her that, no, I had not looked for "the Spootnik" in the sky.

51

I STAGGERED THROUGH A FOG IN THE DAYS THAT FOL-
lowed. I did not aim to do things, go places, say words.
There were simply random moments when the fog lifted
and I found myself in the middle of a doing, a place, a sentence.

Her funeral was at a church called Heaven Help Us in
North Philadelphia, where a surviving sister lived. I didn't
even know I was going until I found myself pedaling in
what I knew to be the general direction of the city.

How did I ever get there? The distance must have been
at least twenty miles. I knew neither the time nor the exact
location of the event. How often did I stop for help? I recall only one face: a grizzled old man, skin so black it was

almost blue, missing front teeth, a crusty fingernail pointing. And, as I rode off, his voice croaking: "You be careful!"

As I drew closer, I began to construct a picture of the funeral and my place in it. I was nagged by a singular problem: How would I see over the crowd of mourners surrounding the grave site? I was a kid from Two Mills, white, not related, not a neighbor. I had no standing, no reason to worm my way to the front ranks or to be welcomed at all. And then a brilliant solution: a tree! The graveyard would have a tree. A climbable tree. Possibly mulberry. Near the open grave. I would look down from there. Best seat in the house!

Spurred by my plan, I pedaled harder. I found the church. A lady in an office said the burial was "across the street, but—"

I raced out the door, across the street. Gravestones poked above the ground, but nothing else conformed to my picture. No trees. No crowd. Unlike the St. John's cemetery next to the prison, there was no grass, as if death were the only crop that would grow. The sky was gray.

Five figures stood in a far corner. As I approached, walking my bike, one of them left the others and came past me: black suit, black skin, white collar, a nod, a smile. The minister. A couple of tire turns closer, I saw that two of the remaining figures stood back from the dark rectangle in the earth, casually postured, shovels to the ground like third legs: the gravediggers. The other two were women, in black, like the minister. One no doubt was the sister. They stood perilously close to the hole.

Warily I walked my bike forward. Obviously I was late. The graveside service had just ended. No one had come to mourn but the two women in black. They did not speak. They did not move. Curiously, to me, they were looking outward, into the city, not down into the dark hole. The soft tick of my bicycle wheels sounded like a clock in an empty house. I stopped. All my chummy hours with Boo Boo in the Quiet Room suddenly seemed to count for nothing. I was intruding. I heard a quick scratch: a gravedigger had struck a match, lit a cigarette.

A sudden breeze on my face. The day was getting darker. A trick of the wind, no doubt, but I thought I caught a whiff of strawberries. As quietly as I could, I turned my bike around and walked back out through the tombstones. I never got close enough to the hole to see the casket.

I pedaled home through a slurry of haunting images: a careening milk truck . . . four cherries half buried in whipped cream . . . Andrew on my bike between my arms . . . Boo Boo's laughter . . . Annamarie Pinto's mother checking out groceries at Fiore's Market . . . my mother's shoe . . . Boo Boo's flashing red fingernails. I must have pedaled forty miles to cover the twenty. By the time I lugged my bike into Reception, Mrs. Butterfield was gone for the day. Al the night guard sat at her desk. Three other guards stood in a group. They all glanced at me, surprised, then toward the apartment. My father stood halfway up the stairs. "Where were you?" he snapped.

I parked my bike behind the brass spittoon. "Boo Boo's funeral," I said.

My father's face softened. I could almost hear his unde-livered lecture whistle from the room.

"It's dark," he said as I approached him on the stairs. He took off my baseball cap. He touched my hair, my shoulder. "You're *soaked*."

This was news to me. Apparently I had pedaled home in rain.

It must have been a Monday, as Carl's weekly pie sat whole and unsliced on the kitchen table. My pie knife and a plate lay beside it.

Eloda was at the gas oven, turning a dial. I wondered what she was doing there. She was usually back in her cell by seven o'clock.

"I'm not hungry," I told her.

She turned and gave me a look. "You're soaked," she said.

"No kidding," I said.

Next thing I knew she was yanking my clothes off in the kitchen, muttering about kids this and kids that. I was an almost-thirteen-year-old girl, but I didn't mind. I was numb to everything. She dried me off with dish towels and swaddled me in my father's chocolate-brown terry-cloth bathrobe.

That's the last thing I remember of what one would normally call *that day*. The partitions of my world had already collapsed. If I had been in a prison of my own before, I was in solitary now. There are no days of the week in solitary, no neat squares on a calendar. There is no dawn. No weather. No window. There is no *that*, no *then*. Only *this*. Only *now*. Only light and dark. And even the light is dark.

I must have gone to bed. I suppose I slept. But all I recall is the terry cloth heaping so cozy about my ears—so unspeakably unlike the brown robe of earth enfolding Boo Boo—and now I am sitting on the high counter stool and Eloda is behind me with comb and rubber band, so it must be another day. I've just polished off a cup of coffee. Nobody, not even my own personal warden, will deny me any request at this time. And now, incited by the caffeine, no doubt, I'm gabbing away, a regular Chatty Cathy.

I'm telling Eloda about the funeral. I'm telling her about my hours with Boo Boo. About Boo Boo's youth in the southern swamplands and her dream of a house by bright water and a life with Delancy and a bunch of kids. About her love of Scooper Dooper banana splits and my appointment as proxy and our sweet-potato-pie deal. And Eloda behind me is combing and listening, and now she is saying, "There's no Delancy."

"Huh?" I say. I'm already floundering, so my bewilderment is merely more of the same.

She repeats: "There's no Delancy, Miss Cammie. I'm sorry. There never was."

I turn so quickly that her hand accidentally yanks my pigstub. "She met him at the park at the courthouse," I tell her. "On the bench by the cannon. He had a sandwich. She said, 'Liverwurst.' And 'onion.' He said, 'What a nose!' He works at Recorder of Deeds but the ugly lady won't admit it." I am strident. I am adamant. I know a thing or two about evidence.

I see the sad, disappointed smile, the smile grown-ups use when they have to tell a happy kid or a know-it-all kid, *Sorry, but you're wrong*. "She made it all up," she says. I gape at her, at the sad smile. I want to punch it.

"You're lying!" I scream, and run from the house.

52

Eloda was right, of course.

As information splashed over me, I was forced to acknowledge that most of what Boo Boo had told me was untrue. There had been no childhood in southern swamplands. No dancer. No roller derby. No circus handler. Contrary to her reports to me, she was not due to get out soon. She had at least ten more years behind bars. Whatever her crime was, it was more than shoplifting.

Delancy was the last to go. I fought for him. I returned again and again to the courthouse. I pestered ugly women at office windows. I questioned county employees leaving work. I sat on the bench by the cannon, waiting, half expecting any moment to catch a whiff of liverwurst and onion, half expecting to turn and see him. The last time

I walked away from the bench, I went to the courthouse terrace overlooking the park. From above I watched that bench, as keenly as any hawk ever eyed a field mouse. He never came. I walked away.

Lies? Dreams? Delusions?

I settled for dreams. I picked them off the floor and wiped them clean with my shirttail and tucked them into the pocket of my jeans. I made a pilgrimage—I walked, not rode—to Scooper Dooper and replayed the proxy, built the love bridge one last time. The last of the four cherries snagged on a sob in my throat at the table by the window. And I knew—I knew with a certainty that made no sense at all—that in some dimension, some universe that mattered only to Boo Boo and me, Delancy *was* real.

53

Solitary.

There is no time. There are no stories. It is where moments go to die. I am flying over the street as the milk truck slams into my mother. . . . The cordite from spent fireworks sweetens the air as I walk the night tracks with Danny Lapella. . . . Stringballs soar over the wall at the end of the world. . . . Snowballs splatter on a caboose. . . . A gravedigger strikes a match. . . . Helen and Tessa squabble at the badminton net. . . . The brewery siren wails both forever and never, for it is both always and never noontime. . . .

Marvin Edward Baker understands. Ask him.

I ride my bike farther and farther from town, keeping an eye peeled for houses by bright water.

I wander the length of Stony Creek, from its feed into

the Schuylkill all the way upstream to the State Hospital grounds.

I prowl the alleyways of Mogins Dip, in particular the one behind the blue-doored house on Mill Street. Though Eloda banished Andrew from the prison, she never forbade me from seeing him elsewhere. But I have not. Why? Do I believe that over-obeying her will earn me some Eloda reward? Have I been afraid of tainting the perfect memory of our bike ride and that day with a new encounter? I don't know. I only know that here I am, parked behind a telephone pole, spying on his mother in her backyard. I see only her head and shoulders behind a white fence. She wears the lemon-yellow wrap. She ducks and disappears for minutes at a time. Maybe she's tending a garden.

There's a yelp—"Mommy!"—and Andrew comes bounding down from the back porch. He's shorter than the fence, so I can only hear him. Excited squeals and jibber-jabber fly until he charges back into the house and the alleyway is quiet once again. I wait some more but he does not return. I pedal off.

I watch the guys play baseball from the park boulevard beyond left field.

I order a foot-long at Ned's. Eat half and throw the rest away.

I gorge on candy. Snickers. Mars bars. Milky Ways. Butterfingers. No Turkish Taffys or Sugar Daddys. They take too long. Candy cigarettes—I don't smoke them; I crush them to powder in my teeth. Signs are beginning to appear on the streets; the planet-conscious sixties are coming: DON'T BE A LITTERBUG! I toss my candy wrappers all over town.

I turn a corner. Danny Lapella is coming. I quick about-face and go the other way.

Red fingernails gash my dreams.

Scrapple scents the air.

Milk bottles rattle.

Children sass.

Did you see the Spootnik?

No.

Did you see the Spootnik?

Yes.

What I'm bringin'?

Carpet yarn to hang you from, my dear.

The Corner . . . The Corner . . .

I reach back. The pigstub . . . is different. My fingers are counting . . . one knot . . . two knots . . . When did it become . . . *two knots?*

I do.

I do not.

I do not visit the yard. I do not look out the kitchen window. I do not climb the Tower of Death to the Salami Room. I do not ride past the house at 428 Swede Street. Light. Dark. Dark. Light. My ankle . . . I have just walked from the kitchen into the living room. I have cut the corner around the kitchen bar too short, brushing my ankle. I'm in bare feet and pedal pushers, forced on me in another life by Reggie. I look down. It's gone: the scab. The scab from my bike spill on Oak Street. It was my last piece of Boo Boo, a reminder of my proxy at Scooper Dooper, our last day. I get down on my hands and knees. I search the carpet. There's pounding at the door. I panic. The scab! Where is it? Pounding. There! I find it. I put it in my pocket. I go to the door. My name is screaming. I gather myself. I push the ponderous iron bar. It grumbles as it exits the iron cuff that binds it to the massive door. Bedlam on the other side. I mash down the iron latch. I'm about to open the door but they beat me to it. They shove the door with such force that I'm knocked to the floor. The Jailbirds scream down at me: "HAPPY BIRTHDAY!"

54

THEY DIDN'T EVEN WAIT FOR ME TO GET UP FROM THE floor. They stampeded over me into the living room. Reggie poured 45s from her *Bandstand* tote while the others ran to my room for the record player. They plunked it onto the coffee table, plugged it in and started rocking to "The Twist." Reggie yanked me to my feet and made me mimic her hip-wiggle moves:

Come on, baby, let's do the twist!

I guess I knew it was my birthday when I woke up that morning. I mean, I *must* have known, right? I was *thirteen!* I must have known they were coming that night at seven. I must have known they were sleeping over. (I had invited them, hadn't I, in that other life before Mrs. Butterfield said, "It was Boo Boo"?) Why else would they have come with bedrolls? Why else would the dining room table be so festively set, with our good silverware and at each place a little gold box with gold string tied in a bow? And a cake in the middle with my name blue-written in the strawberry icing: CAMMIE?

Why else the big red shiny cardboard letters proclaiming YOU'RE A TEENAGER! strung across the dining room wall?

Why else the piñata—*piñata?*—hanging from the living room ceiling?

The evidence was clear, ladies and gentlemen of the jury: a birthday was happening.

I guess Eloda had set the table and put up the sign. I guess Carl had made the cake. I guess I opened presents.

No doubt I (the alleged birthday girl) was first whacker at the piñata. No doubt it gushed candy. No doubt we cheered.

It must have been a night of laughing and dancing and scream-singing and cake and ice cream and thirteen candles and "happy birthday to you!" and cherry cordials (from the little gold boxes) and nonstop nonsense and mirth and on with the pajamas before it was dark and bare-feet fights and pillow fights, and I guess I had fun; I guess I was there.

Or some proxy of me.

The me that *I* was in touch with—the solitaire—the

misbegotten misfit deep in her own black hole—*that* me—looked up from her bottomless *here* and *now* and saw in the unreachable distance the merriment of a birthday party swirling around the funnel top of her funk. And who knows how long it would have gone on that way if the phone had not rung.

55

REGGIE GRABBED IT. "O'REILLY'S SALOON!" SHE LISTENED for a moment, then held out the phone to Glenda. "For you."

There wasn't a peep as we all stared at Glenda Schmoyer and she stared back at us, her eyes listening. Early on in the conversation there were a couple of nos and a slump-shouldered "I'm sorry." Then there was a lot of listening, an "I will," an "I won't," a string of okays accompanied by so much nodding it appeared her neck was stuck at ON, then in solemn procession: "I will. . . . I won't. . . . I promise." And finally: "Good night, Mom."

Glenda was dazed. She couldn't seem to find the cradle for the receiver, so she handed it back to Reggie.

"What happened?" asked a breathless Donna Holloway.

"Is everything okay?" asked Gussie Kornichek.

Glenda sagged. She sighed deeply. For a moment I thought she might cry. "It's my toothbrush," she said.

"What about it?" said Reggie.

"I forgot it," said Glenda.

"That's *all*?" I said.

Another deep sigh. "My mother always packs my stuff when we go away. I asked her to let me do it this time. I"— she swallowed a sob—"I packed everything in my bedroll. I remembered"—she squeaked—"*everything*. Except my toothbrush."

"No big deal," said Reggie. "You can use mine."

"Oh no!" Alarm flared in Glenda's eyes. "I can't use anybody else's. None except my own."

"But your own is in your bathroom at home," Reggie pointed out reasonably.

Glenda sagged even lower. "I know. I guess I just won't brush tonight."

Gussie said, "Well, I'll tell you one thing. *I* ain't sleeping in the same room as somebody with dirty teeth."

Everybody laughed but Glenda, who smiled feebly.

I jumped up. "I'll get you one." In the supply room behind Reception were shower kits, handed out to every incoming inmate. In the kits were toothbrushes. All I had to do was say the word to Al the night guard. I had done it before, when I was little and jealous of the inmates getting kits and not me. I headed for the door.

"No!"

Glenda's shout stopped me. I turned. "No?"

"My mother said. Nobody else's."

My mother.

All night long I had been hearing it:

My mother this . . .

My mother that . . .

Of course, I had heard these words before, all my life, and often felt the sting. But never before had so many my-mothers massed and swarmed on a single occasion.

"Glenda," I said, not kindly, "the toothbrush I'm going to give you is still in its little box. It's brand-new. It's never been used."

Glenda was in pain but held her ground. "My mother *said.*"

I was out of patience. I yelled at her: "I'll *boil* it!"

She winced and the tears came. "I . . . c-can't."

And that was the moment.

56

I KNOW. IT DOESN'T SEEM LIKE MUCH, CERTAINLY NOT A
world mover. But it had been more than twelve years coming. She said, "I . . . c-can't," and all of it, from the birthday
party all the way back to the first rattle of the milk bottles,
all of it tipped and spilled and came crashing into my black
hole, and I tumbled and churned with all the events of
my life and suddenly I was solitary no more. Ha. Anything
but! And I couldn't stand it.

I turned to the door. I removed the iron bar. I opened
the door. I turned back to Glenda. I said, "Go."

Her eyes boggled. "Huh?"

I stepped aside. I pushed the door open more. "Go home."

She still wasn't getting it. She looked at the others,
who in turn didn't know whether to look at her or at me.

She said it again, this time with a faint, disbelieving smile: "*Huh?*"

I snarled, "Go home, Glenda. Get *out* of my house."

She stared at me.

I yelled, "Now! Do you understand English?" I stomped over to an armchair. I grabbed her bedroll. I threw it at her, knocking her over. Rosanna and Donna helped her to her feet. She stood clutching the bedroll to her braless bosom, heaving, sobbing aloud. I pointed at the doorway. "Go! Now! Go home to your *mommy!*"

She suddenly ran, screaming now, down the stairs and out the door. I could still hear her as she fled, wailing, up Airy Street.

I stood at the door, glaring at the rest of the Jailbirds. They glared back, daring me.

I opened the door wider. "Well," I said, "what are you waiting for?"

They snatched their overnight stuff. Reggie lifted the stacked 45s off the spindle and returned them to her *Bandstand* tote. One by one they disengaged themselves from the pull of the party. Gussie made a quick move to snatch her handful of piñata candy from the coffee table, and they dragged themselves out the door. And then Reggie was back, pointing into my face. "You know what you need, *Cammie?*" She spit out my name. "Huh?"

I waited. Nothing happened. Apparently she required a response. "What do I need, *Reggie?*"

Her Passion Pink lip curled in disdain. "*You* . . . need a personality." She spun about smartly and marched down the stairs.

I closed and bolted the door. Eloda's broom was on the floor. It had served as the piñata whacker. I gazed without feeling over the ruins, which already seemed prehistoric: *We believe this was once the site of a birthday party. See here— these are the stubs of candles. Probably arrayed on a festive cake. Thirteen of them. So, perhaps, a teenager.*

57

My mayhem was anything but complicated. (Are you listening, Thomas Browne?) It might be said: She lost it. But to put it that way, as you will see, may be misleading. Say this then: She went bananas.

Those four things I'd always done when I was mad? Piddydibble. Sure, I rode my bike—over people's lawns and flower beds, especially in the rich and pristine North End.

I went down to the Blue Jay, where they served breakfast. I emptied my pockets on the counter and said, "Gimme scrapple." It turned out to be six side orders' worth. I ate it all.

I shoplifted. In honor of Boo Boo. A pack of cigarettes. I wasn't even nervous or very careful. I took them from the counter rack at Morfio's, as Mr. Morfio was looking the other way. They were Salems. Boo Boo's brand.

I returned to the prison, walked into Reception, saluted Mrs. Butterfield, tasted scrapple on the way and threw up in the brass spittoon.

I went upstairs and flopped into my bed until I felt better. Got up. Grabbed my shoplifted Salems. Went looking for Eloda. Found her doing wash. I was all ready to light up when I realized I didn't have a match. I found some in a kitchen drawer. I stood in the doorway of the laundry room. I leaned casually against the door frame. Eloda was bent over a pile of wash, sorting.

"Hi," I said.

"Hi," she said. She didn't look up.

I flashed the green and white cigarette pack and tore open the top and tapped out a Salem as I had seen the women in the yard do. I put the cigarette between my lips and caught myself beginning to suck on it as if it were candy.

It took me several tries to get the match lit. I knew from Reggie that the filter end went into my mouth. I put the flame to the tobacco end and was relieved to see it begin to singe and burn. I had heard about inhaling but decided not to risk it. Besides, to actually smoke the thing wasn't the point. The point was to see the look on Eloda's face. She was still bent over the pile of wash.

Casually, like a movie star, I pinched the Salem between

my first two fingers and drew it from my mouth and held it with great finesse, my hand outward and palm up, as if feeling for rain.

"Whatcha doin'?" I said.

"Cleaning the oven," she said.

I groaned. "E-*loh*-dah. You're supposed to look at people when you speak to them."

She stopped sorting wash. She looked up. She stared straight at me. I could find no reaction in her face. "I'm looking," she said.

"I'm smoking a cigarette!" I screeched.

"Congratulations," she said, and returned to the wash.

"Forget it," I snapped, and stomped out of the apartment, out of the prison.

I was on the sidewalk before I discovered the cigarette still in my hand. It had gone out. A dead butt. I flicked it at a passing car.

I took on the world.

I fought other kids for a stringball home run on Marshall Street—then hurled it back over the wall. I laughed at the obscenities that followed me as I rode away.

I went up the Tower of Death and onto the battlement. I marched back and forth for all the town to see. The telephone switchboard lit up. A guard came to get me. My father scolded me. I did it again next day.

"What's gotten into you?" my father said at dinner.

I said nothing. I gave him the silent treatment. Eloda,

too. Each morning's hair braiding happened without a word, only the whisper of the comb and the snap of the rubber band. I resented that neither my father nor Eloda seemed to be suffering greatly from my treatment. I began to consider something to say, a perfect sentence I would drop on them like a bomb before returning to my silence.

I shoplifted a pack of nail files at Woolworth's. A block away I tossed them onto the sidewalk, in front of a DON'T BE A LITTERBUG! sign.

I harassed crawfish at the creek. Perhaps I was perfectly aware that I was moving down the waterline closer and closer to the Little League field. Sporadic yelps and the *thok* of bat on ball came through the trees. I had just rousted a fat crawfish from under a rock and was poking after him with my stick when I heard the voice: "Hi, Cammie." I looked up and there he was, Danny Lapella, all smiles and cheeriness. He was still smiling when I hit him. Not a girly slap. A full-force slug in the face. He staggered back and down to his knees, the bat clattering on the rocks. When he stood, there was blood on his mouth and a look on his face that haunts me to this day.

Oh Thomas Browne, how bad does the bad time get? The horror of what I had just done might have—should have—snapped me out of my rampage. And yet here lies the measure of my madness: *it did not.*

He retrieved his hat and walked away through the trees,

somehow both destroyed and dignified at the same time. Eons later, it seemed, I found myself standing in creek water halfway to my knees, thread-legged striders skating on the ice-bright surfaces about me.

I saw a mother and her brat. The brat—boy? girl? I don't recall—had just come down the sliding board at the park playground. I saw this as I rode my bike along the boulevard. The brat popped off the bottom of the slide and was dashing for the ladder to do it again when the mother snatched a flying arm. I stopped to watch. "That's enough," she said. "We have to go."

You might have thought she'd stuck the brat's hand in a fire. Screams, flailing. "It's time for dinner," the mother said, maintaining an impossible calm. She kept giving reasons, but the screamer wasn't listening. In that uncontrollable kid I saw them all, a world of brats with the unforgivable luxury of having mothers to abuse. All activity on the swings and seesaw and merry-go-round had stopped. By now I had coasted closer. When the kicking began—the mother yelping as a foot struck her shin—that's when I found myself leaning down from the handlebars into the little, goggle-eyed face with a scream, a lung-emptying roar of my own: "LISTEN TO YOUR MOTHER!" And discovered to my surprise that I had been squeezing and shaking the brat's other arm. I let go. I turned and pedaled up the hill to the boulevard. There were two cries of outrage behind me. I could not tell the difference between mother's and child's.

I returned to the tower battlement. With water balloons. I dropped them on the picketers marching below. Talk about screams and flailing! Not exactly pouring oil on attacking enemies, but the satisfaction was close. I vamoosed before the phone calls started coming in. I went to Breen's candy store and shoplifted a handful of Baby Ruths.

At dinner that night my father said it again: "What's gotten into you?"

I hadn't spoken to him since the last time. But I'd been working on my perfect sentence. I unloaded on him across my plate of spaghetti: "I'm not one of your people!" That my reply bore no relation to his question was beside the point. The point was to hurt him. From the look on his face, I succeeded. To punctuate the moment, I grabbed my slice of pie (Very Cherry), mashed it into my spaghetti and stomped out of the apartment.

I was more out of control than the brat at the sliding board. And loving every minute of it.

58

REGGIE RETURNED.

She acted casual but was clearly distracted, uneasy. I assumed it had to do with the birthday fiasco, but I was wrong. She never mentioned it.

She sat on my bed, chatting me up with empty questions. She held a drawstring bag covered in black and green beads. It was ugly. Probably her mother's.

At last she got down to business. She pulled a piece of paper and a ballpoint pen from the ugly purse. Her voice was shaky. "Cammie," she said, "listen, I know it was dumb about the picture and all. So I was thinking, why don't we just do this. Just his name"—we both knew who *his* meant—"on a piece of paper." She held out the paper and pen. "I even figured out how to do it. Like, *you* don't even have to do *anything*. I can just give it to the guard myself and—"

That's as far as she got.

I smacked the paper and pen from her hands. I grabbed her by the wrist and hauled her out of the apartment and down to Main Street and into Fiore's Market and up to one of the checkout ladies. The lady was pricing a cantaloupe. She was barely taller than me. She had long black hair. On her white uniform dress her name was scripted in lavender thread: *Lillian*.

I barged ahead of the customer. I pushed Reggie until she was face to face with the mother of the murdered girl. "Here," I snapped. "Meet Mrs. Pinto. Her daughter's name was Annamarie. Ring a bell? Tell *her* what you want."

I left them gaping at each other and stormed out of the market.

I headed for Shoplifting Central: Woolworth's. My jeans had four pockets. I stuffed them all. I chose little things because I wanted a great number in homage to Boo Boo. Paper clips. Erasers. Lipsticks. Shoelaces. Safety pins. Baby nipples. As my pockets bulged to capacity, I vowed that next time I would do it Boo Boo's way. I would get fat and wear spacious bloomers and baggy pants and walk off with half the store. But I still had an unused waistband. That's where—front, back, sides—I stuffed a dozen pairs of white socks.

I was through the door, onto the sidewalk, when I felt the hand around my upper arm. "Excuse me, miss." I turned to find myself eyeball to eyeglasses with a man no bigger than myself, smaller than Mrs. Pinto. The noontime sun was glancing off his lenses in a way that erased his eyes and made him seem demonic. But his mouth was smiling and his voice was quite pleasant. "Did you forget something?" he said.

I instantly relaxed. *What a nice man,* I thought, *coming after me like this. I must have dropped something in the store.*

I actually thought about it. "No," I replied. "I don't think so."

"Oh," he said, and he moved so that his eyes came into view, and I saw that he was certainly not a demon at all but a nice, little, bald-headed man whose grip on my arm was beginning to hurt. "*I* think yes," he said. "I think you *did* forget something."

And then he looked beyond me, and suddenly my arm was free and a patrolman was there, looking down at me— way down, for he was much bigger than the little man. It surprised me at first that he did not seem to recognize me. Then I realized I must be known only to prison guards, not Two Mills policemen. His smile seemed as wide as the black bill of his hat and as shiny as the badge above it. "Well, then," he said—and he reached down and, with a daintiness that belied his great size, lifted the hem of my shirt just enough for a peek—"what have we here?"

59

FIVE MINUTES LATER I WAS SITTING IN A CHAIR IN THE little man's office in the back of the store, staring at the pile on his desk. I must say I was surprised at the amount of merchandise that I had shed. It occurred to me that Boo Boo would have been proud.

We talked for a while—the big patrolman, the little store manager and me. What I recall is not so much the words as the tone. It was chatty. Friendly. And then, abruptly, there was silence. The two men were staring at each other, at me, then back at each other. No doubt this was the point at which they realized who I was, probably not long after I told them my name.

I was delivered to the prison in a patrol car. The

patrolman asked Mrs. Butterfield for my father. She told him he was away in Harrisburg. He would not be home till evening. "Is there someone else on the premises, then," said the patrolman, "with authority over the child?" It sounded strange, hearing myself referred to as "the child."

Mrs. Butterfield did not answer at once. Finally she said, "There's a trustee." She pointed. "Upstairs."

We found Eloda having her lunch, a baloney sandwich. I headed for my room while the patrolman stayed behind. I closed my door but not all the way. I listened to the voices in the kitchen, mostly his. I could not make out the words. I didn't have to. I knew what he was saying. She shoplifted. Stole things. Tell her father.

When the patrolman left, I went to the tower. I stayed up there all afternoon. Eloda brought up my dinner: veal cutlet, succotash, milk, and of course my pie. She stopped on the steps, laid the dinner on the floor and retreated, saying nothing.

When my father returned, she did not leave the apartment at once. I stood at the window, staring at Bridgeport in the gray twilight across the river. I tried to picture her telling him. At last I heard the door open. I heard her footsteps as she began the daily return to her cell. I expected my father to call for me. He did not.

It was after dark when I went down. I had hoped my father would be in his room, maybe even already in bed, tuckered out from his trip to Harrisburg. No such luck. He was in the living room, planted in his easy chair, watching *I Love Lucy* on the TV, drinking an iced tea. I walked past.

"Hi," he said.

"Huh?" I said.

"Hi. It's a common greeting. Like good evening." He paused to laugh at Lucy doing something zany. "Did you miss me?"

"Not really," I said, and headed for my room.

I came out twice after that, once to the kitchen, once to the dining room, testing. He never said a word.

In my room, sitting on my bed and staring at the wall, the incredible truth slowly came to me: *She never told him.*

Uncomplicated mayhem, I have found out, is timeless and blind. So the events I am about to report come with questions. Will the order of things be right? (Not sure.) Am I getting day and night right? (Maybe.) Was it all real? (Depends on whether you were me or not—or, as you'll see, *which* me.) Beyond that, I cite my privilege as teller of my own story: I save these things for last simply because it feels right. If they did not in fact happen on the last night and day of the bad time, they should have. In any case, one thing is certain about the end:

I never saw it coming.

60

I AWOKE IN DARKNESS.

I dressed. I slipped out of the apartment and down the stairs to Reception. Al the night guard sat at the desk Mrs. Butterfield occupied during the day. He appeared to be doing a crossword puzzle. He looked up. He was used to seeing me in the summer, when I often came home late. "Hi, Miss Cammie."

"Hi, Al," I said.

"Looking forward to school? Get this dumb vacation over with?" I knew by his grin he was kidding.

"Can't wait," I said.

I got my bike. My glove was looped over the handlebars. I headed for the door. Al cleared his throat. "Uh . . . Miss Cammie . . ."

This he was *not* used to. On the big, round clock behind him the hour hand was on the two. I continued on to the door. I opened it. "I need to go out," I told him. "I just remembered I forgot something at the park today and I have to go get it."

He looked at me without expression. He was stumped. All prison guards were calibrated to protect me from any threat—except myself. I nudged him over the hump. "Just be a minute, Al. I'll be careful."

He fired his last shot. "The park's more than a minute."

I opened the door. I laughed. "Right. *Two* minutes." And I was gone.

I was halfway to the park when I realized I'd forgotten to bring a shovel. A good stick would have to do.

I rode from pool to pool of streetlight, the only sound the tick and whir of my bike wheels. In all the town only I was moving.

I turned left from the boulevard and into the park. Then another left at the Willow Street bridge and onto the path that paralleled the creek. I parked at the Little League field. The moon, high in a cloudless sky, was a perfect half of a Carl's pie. Free of trees and buildings, the field seemed bright enough to play on.

I entered the adjacent woods. Fifteen feet away the creek trickled softly. I heard a plop. Crickets were making their noises, but to me it was not the usual benign soundtrack of a summer's night. Tonight it was summer grinding its teeth.

I found the tool I needed: a two-foot branch, hard, not rotted, one end ragged, sharp enough.

I walked out to shortstop through a winkle of fireflies. I went precisely to the spot where I would have stood, knees bent, hands poised, heels up an inch, ready to go left, ready to go right, eyes on the batter, on the ball, just like Mr. Strong taught me at baseball school, if they'd let me play in Little League. I punched the stick into the glittery sand, which quickly gave way to a darker clay. I dug a good hole maybe two feet deep. I took my glove from the handlebars. I kissed it and dropped it into the hole. I pushed the dug dirt back in with my sneaker and smoothed it over.

Maybe it was finding myself at another burial. I thought of Boo Boo. Of "Spootnik." I looked up through the fireflies. She said it would look just like a star, except it would move slowly across the sky. I stared till my neck got sore. I lay down on my back and stared some more. There were a lot of stars, but not one of them moved. I got up and walked off in defeat, reminded once again that I had failed Boo Boo.

I rode back to the Willow Street bridge. I dismounted. I grabbed the front tube in one hand, the seat post in the other and heaved my bike over the low stone wall into the creek below. I could hear the wheels ticking as I walked off.

I walked back along the tracks. The rails were silver in the moonlight. Somewhere along the way I screamed.

I came off the tracks at Elm Street. A sound: from the

other side of town, by the river. Again. A monster was coughing in the east. I knew at once it was not a diesel. It was a steam locomotive. Maybe the last one ever. I waited.

I saw the beam of light swing around the curve at the old cigar factory, then the monster itself pumping smoke balls into the moonlit sky. I was barely off the tracks but I did not step back. It thundered past, inches from my face. I trembled in my sneakers. As the yellow-eyed snout punched into the park and the freight cars began to click past like a rolling timepiece, I was aware of a tiny pittering all around me. It was the soot, the rain of grit from the coal-fired engine. I could feel the pitter on my forearms. I did not move and the rain of soot did not stop, not when the caboose clattered by, not when the train was a faint mutter in the west. I just stood there and stood there as the soot fell on me and piled around me as if all the nights and all the deaths of the world were raining down on me. The soot was up to my armpits when a dreamy notion rolled by like a second, dawdling caboose: *This is not real.* I took a step forward, out of the soot, out of my unreal self. I could do this, such was my state. I began walking up Elm. When I looked back, the soot pile was up to the streetlight and still rising.

In time I came to my street, Airy. Passing St. John's Church, I was dimly aware of the dark, rounded tombstones, which became the hunched shoulders of the dead, risen to follow me home.

"Well!" said Al as I opened the big door. "That sure was a long two minutes." Despite the mild scolding of the words, his voice was cheery. And relieved.

I may have said "Sorry" or "I know." He may have asked if I found the thing I'd "forgotten." He may have asked about my bike. I may have reached into my pocket and thrown a handful of grit at him. I don't know. I'm picking lint from the sleeve of memory.

And so Al is saying, "That sure was . . . ," and next thing I know I'm in the empty exercise yard. I stand quietly in the shadow of the massive wall. I do not want to alert the guard in the corner tower. I myself become shadow. For a blessed respite, I feel nothing.

Then, despite the warm, humid night, a chill falls over me. I'm puzzled at first. And then I'm not, for I realize I'm in more than one place. This is a lot bigger, of course, but the shape and lifeless void of the women's exercise yard perfectly mimics the open grave at the Heaven Help Us cemetery.

I leave the shadows. I move to the glittering center of the yard. I lie down. I fold my hands over my chest. I close my eyes. I'm perfectly aware of what I'm doing. The moon tonight is only half, but the light it casts is plenty enough to show the tower guard that somebody is lying in the middle of the exercise yard. Any moment I expect a second, more brilliant moon—the tower spotlight—to nail me. I expect to hear a commanding voice—"Halt! Who goes there?"—or something like that. Maybe even the distant snap-cock of a rifle. Sirens! Flashing red lights! Running feet!

I don't care.

But nothing happens, and in time I open my eyes and, behold: the world is gone except for the nighttime sky. Stars! I've heard there are as many stars as there are grains of sand at the beach in Wildwood. I try again to detect movement that might reveal Boo Boo's Spootnik but quickly turn to thoughts of angels. Are they up there? Hiding behind the stars? In the spaces between? Boo Boo's angel?

Thomas Browne's?

My mother's?

I remember my father's lifeless "Sure." How it punctured the balloon of my first try at belief. But that was in a cloistered cellblock. Out here . . . out here a father's skeptical "Sure" has no chance among the grandeur of the night and the stars. Even so, it comes to me to make certain. Perhaps angelhood does not follow death automatically. Perhaps a mother's angel needs to be born, needs the breath of her child. And so I whisper her name, then say it aloud— "Anne O'Reilly!"—and blow it up to the stars.

That's when I hear a metallic clank, and the tower spotlight nails me.

61

No mother is finally buried until her child climbs out of the grave.

Next day, my eyes still closed, I awakened to bright light and wondered if the night before—shouts, hands, commotion—was still going on. Then I heard the brewery hurl its whistle over the town. *Lunchtime!* My eyes shot open. And snapped shut, blinded by the sun streaming into my face.

Past the wake-up annoyance and confusion, I was left with empty. The world, as always, had not changed for the better overnight. In fact, it was worse than yesterday. My bike and my glove were gone.

All my life I had filled up empty with mad. From my pillow I glanced about for a hook to hang my mad on. I found my father, who had caused the blinding sunlight by neglecting to pull down the shade when he put me to bed. Beyond that I found only myself, on top of the sheets, jeans, shirt still on, everything but sneakers.

As usual, my breakfast things were laid out neatly on the counter: bowl, spoon, juice glass, Cocoa Puffs, napkin. I pushed them aside. Who eats breakfast at noon? I knew she was watching from the dining room. I made a grand show of failing to find something suitable for lunch in the fridge. I snatched an apple from the fruit bowl. I attacked it with noisy, goadful bites. I had found my mad. My gorge was rising.

She spoke: "Sorry. You . . . I wasn't sure." The words were okay but not the tone. She didn't sound sorry *enough*.

A sudden thought: *Smoke a cigarette—now!* I went to my underwear drawer. I lifted the stack of underpants, all of them basic cotton whites, to retrieve the pack of Salems I had hidden there. It was gone.

The gorge was in my throat.

I planted myself on my breakfast-and-hair-braiding counter stool. She was in the living room now. "Did you take them?" I said.

She stopped, looked up, the face of innocence. "Take what?"

"You know."

She stared. I stared. "My cigarettes. My Salems. They were under my underwear. You do my wash. You go in my drawer. Where are they?"

"I threw them out," she said. Just like that. Matter-of-fact. No big deal.

Her casual attitude, her quick confession, knocked me off stride for a moment. I glared at her. She was bent over the coffee table, dusting. "*You* don't throw out *my* stuff," I told her.

She kept dusting the same spot. She said something, but I couldn't believe I'd heard right.

"What did you say?" I said.

She stood straight. She faced me. "I said, And you don't smoke cigarettes in here."

I was dumbstruck. "Who do you think you are? *You* don't tell *me* what to do. You're not my father."

"When he's not here, I'm in charge."

The calm and quiet in her voice were infuriating. Where had this sudden entitlement come from? And yet I laughed. "Ha! Yeah—I'll tell you what *you're* in charge of. You're in charge of *dusting*, that's what you're in charge of." I was getting loud.

The dustrag fell to the coffee table. She sat down on the sofa. I couldn't believe it. Except at lunchtimes, I had never seen her sit. She patted the sofa cushion beside her. "Come sit down," she said.

I almost did. Here she was, acting parental, offering me what I'd been aching for for so long—but I was too full of spite and self-pity. I sneered at her. "Don't tell me what to do. It's too late for that. I don't need you."

She folded her hands in her lap. "I know you're going through a bad time, Cammie."

Bad time.

The echo of Thomas Browne's words smacked me like a foul ball to the chin.

I lashed out: "You don't know nothing. And who do you think you are, calling me Cammie. It's *Miss* Cammie to you." I jabbed my finger at her. "*You're* the criminal around here. *I'm* the boss." I picked up the dustrag. "You're a *duster*, for God's sake!" I shook the rag in her face. "You're my *maid*!" I threw the rag at her. "Go dust!" I lunged to the door. I turned. I jabbed at her. "Get off my sofa!"

She never moved. She sat there as calmly as if she were waiting for someone with white gloves to pass her a teacup.

I stormed over to her dry mop, which was leaning at the kitchen entry. With strength from some reserve of fury, I broke the mop stick over my knee. "Sweep!" I screamed. I shook the jagged sticks at her. "Sweep, damn you!"

She was looking at me as she'd never looked at me before, as in my fantasies I'd seen my mother look at me. The sticks fell from my hands. I started to cry.

Through the blur of my tears I saw that she was getting up, coming toward me. I thrust out my hand. "Stop!" She stopped. I blubbered on: "I don't want you anymore! I'm sorry I ever let you in my house. I'm sorry I gave you a birthday present. I'm sorry I ever . . . ever . . ."

She came closer. "No!" I yelled. She stopped again. "Don't you touch me. I want you out of my house. You're not my mother! I'm just a cushy job to you!" I was bawling. I stomped my foot. "Get out! I'm gonna go set a fire!"

She did not move. She did not leave the house. She did not come and wrap me in her arms and smother me with love. She did nothing but speak, in a voice as gentle as milk. "It's time for you to go there, Cammie."

I tried to focus through the blur. "Huh?" I said.

"You must do it now," she said. "You should have done it a long time ago. Don't wait another minute. Please. Do it. Go."

"Do *what?*" I said, or whined, or shouted. "Go *where?*"

She said it in three simple words: "You know where."

Of course I knew *where*. I'd known since she began speaking. But I was preoccupied with a question that was scalding my soul: *How does* she *know?*

I could not speak. I could not move.

"Miss Cammie." Her voice was louder. "Cammie, please . . . trust me. I know you. You *must* . . . you *need* to go. . . . Talk to her . . . *now*."

She was right.

It had been way, way too long.

I bolted for the door. Down the stairs. Voices called as I burst through Reception. The traffic was screaming; the sidewalk was screaming under my feet. By the end of the block I was running. Oh God, she was so right: there was not a moment to lose. I was out of gloves to bury, bikes to heave. I ran down Airy and I ran down Swede and with every step I unwound the days of my life and I ran down Cherry until I came to Oak and finally, finally I found myself at The Corner and I threw myself on the ground, threw myself onto the asphalt, onto the spot—oh, I knew the spot—facedown on the asphalt that was warm and black and finally, finally I cried aloud: "Mommeee!" That's the only word I recall. What the others were or if they made any sense or how long they went on I couldn't say. More than twelve years were gushing out, flooding the street, running down the gutters.

How long did I lie there facedown in the street? I don't know. Did I create a problem for traffic? Neighbors? Probably. I think I remember hands pulling me to my feet, guiding me to the sidewalk. I think I remember walking, walking the sidewalks of town, walking and walking myself to exhaustion until I was on the stairway to my home, staring down at Eloda's black flats, the hem of her denim skirt. I looked up. She had come halfway down the stairs to meet me. Her face was wet with tears.

Inside, she took my hands in hers. My skin was black with asphalt grit. The upper parts of my fingernails were gone. My fingertips were red with crusted blood. She took me to the sink and ran the water to warm and washed my hands. She patted them dry. She kissed every broken fingertip.

She may have made me something to eat. I may have fallen asleep at the table. I only know for sure that eventually I was in bed, and she was pulling off my sneakers, and I think I was already two winks into sleep when I felt a shift in the mattress. I turned. She was sitting on the bed. She was looking down at me with all the motherly love I had ever wanted. I made a deal with sleep: *You can have me, but first give me a minute or two. I am not gonna miss this.* She reached down and touched my face. She caressed my braidless hair. She scratched my back. "Do you like that?" she whispered. I moaned. She scratched some more. I reached back. Our fingers intermingled, a braid of their own. I think I heard her whisper, "Sweet dreams, baby girl. Sweet life." I felt a kiss on my cheek.

62

WHEN I AWOKE NEXT MORNING, I WAS ALONE IN MY BED. My fingers went to my cheek. I could still feel the kiss. Sunlight was streaming through the window.

As always, the smell of scrapple was in the air—but something was different. I sat up. I sniffed. The smell was stronger than usual. Much stronger.

I got out of bed. Went to the door. Opened it. Now the smell was overpowering. And something else: sizzle. I could hear it. Griddle sizzle. Coming from our kitchen. *She was making me scrapple!*

"Eloda!" I cried, and ran to the kitchen. But it wasn't Eloda turning to me from the stovetop. It was my father.

"Where's Eloda?" I said.

"Good morning," he said. "And you're welcome, pig-snout lover."

I said it again: "Where's Eloda?"

"Released," he said.

I gawked at him. *"Released?"* I knew what the word meant, but still it made no sense. "You mean, like, *free?"*

He nodded. "As in time served."

I screeched. "That's impossible! She never said. She would have told me." I still couldn't get it through my head. "She's not in *jail* anymore?"

He was staring at the griddle. "Free as a bird."

I hated the matter-of-fact way he said it. The kitchen was warm with summer and sweet with scrapple cloud, but I was cold as January.

I slammed my fork on the table. "She would never *do* that! She wouldn't not say goodbye." By then I might have been crying.

The spatula was still in his hand. He sagged. When he turned to me, his face was sad. "Cammie, I'm sorry . . ." And then he was saying ridiculous things, things I didn't want to hear, like "The summer is over." And "You're a young lady now." And "You won't be needing a trustee to look after you anymore." Blah blah.

I'd had enough of that bullpoop. I didn't bother to put shoes on. I burst out the door. I was halfway down the stairs when I remembered: my bike wasn't here. It was in the creek, where I'd heaved it.

Shoeless, still wearing yesterday's clothes, I raced down Airy . . . Hector . . . Marshall . . . Swede . . . 428. It looked the same: twin front porch. Except for one thing: the venetian blinds. They were pulled up. The windows stared at me like open, empty eyes. I pounded on the door, punched the bell button. I peered through the front window. Dark. Furniture. I went around back, pounded on the screen door. Rapped on the window. Stood in the side yard and yelled: "Eloda!"

"They went."

A voice from the sidewalk. A kid—eight or ten, maybe—stood at the black iron fence, half a twin Popsicle in his hand. Orange. He wore a New York Yankees cap, so right away I didn't like him.

"What?" I said.

He took a long pull on the Popsicle. "They moved."

It wasn't registering. "They're *gone?*"

"Yeah." He was smiling.

I stepped toward him. He backed off. "What's so funny?"

The smile vanished. "Nothin'."

"Both of them? They went? Moved out of the house?"

"Yeah."

"Furniture's still there."

"They're renters. It's the Puppos. One of them's a criminal. She was in jail. Just got out. They rent from us. We live next door. I heard you." He bit off the top inch of Popsicle.

"It's Pupko," I said. "When?"

Mashed words came through his mouthful of orange slush. "When what?"

"When did they move?" She had spent the night with me.

"Today."

And was gone when I awoke. "This morning?"

"Yeah. The criminal and her sister. They was pulling a U-Haul. I seen it."

The minute she got out. It was all planned. Did she know I'd come looking? "Where did they go?"

The smile was back. "Don't know."

I walked out the gate. He backed up to the curb, watching me. I thought of smacking the Popsicle from his hand. But I didn't.

I was suddenly feeling the sting in my raw fingertips. I began the walk home. I heard him call, laughing, "Hey, you ain't got no shoes on!"

By the time I hit Marshall, I was running. I had remembered something: her birthday gift for me. I had never opened it, or any of the others, for that matter. She had stacked them neatly in a corner of my room.

Hers was on top. I ripped it open and burst out bawling. It was a hair ribbon. Bright green.

The next day I entered seventh grade at Stewart Junior High School.

63

Sports. Clubs. Activities. Studies. I threw myself into school.

Word had gotten around about the birthday party massacre. "Hey, Cannonball," I heard in the hallways, "can I come to your next birthday party?" I laughed it off.

I saw the flinch in schoolmates' eyes when suddenly they found themselves face to face with Cannonball Cammie O'Reilly. And then the surprise in those eyes when I merely walked by—maybe even smiled!—without a punch, a scowl or a nasty word.

Reggie, bless her, was as forgiving as ever. She hugged me on the first day, outside geography class, and gave no hint that she remembered me dragging her off to Fiore's to meet Mrs. Pinto. She never mentioned Marvin Edward Baker again.

In fact, I made peace with all the Jailbirds. I invited them to a pizza-and-pillow sleepover at my place—and everyone came. Even Glenda Schmoyer! I greeted her at the big door with a gift, all wrapped up. She opened it. She howled with laughter. It was a toothbrush.

In those first months of junior high school I seemed to be gaining a new friend every day. By the time the last scab fell from my fingers, nobody was calling me Cannonball.

Of course, I had long since retired from shoplifting, litterbugging and terrorizing little kids and their mothers.

The one sour note was Danny Lapella. He would not speak to me nor even look at me. I didn't blame him. Sometimes I wished he would slug me. That would feel better. But I knew he would never do it.

Something else was bothering me—or maybe I should say *not* bothering me, for it was more an absence than a presence—and it took me a while to figure out what it was.

64

Every night I flopped into bed, exhausted. I had never been so busy in my life. Even weekends were filled with school stuff and friends. My visits to the women's yard now happened only on Saturday mornings.

This is not to say that I was too busy to think about Eloda. On the contrary: I thought of her from the time I got up in the morning till I went to bed. Motherwise, you might say I was worse off than ever: I now had two of them to miss.

Then one Saturday in November, I returned to the apartment from the women's yard. I was sitting on the living room sofa. For once I was doing nothing. I was alone. Just sitting there. And I started to cry.

I had no idea why. I hadn't been thinking or feeling anything in particular. The tears simply came out of nowhere. Not a heavy, blubbery cry. A soft cry. And then after a minute or two it was over, like a sudden summer shower.

I got up from the sofa. I let myself out. I climbed the steps to the Tower of Death, something I had not done since before school began. Gone were the lopped salamis I'd hacked with the Civil War sword. A squad of new ones, wrapped in burlap and twine, hung from the ceiling. The air up there was chilly. Winter was coming.

I stood in the middle of the circular room, slowly turning, sensing I was here for a reason—but why? I beheld the familiar attic trappings of my childhood, my second bedroom: the old wooden file cabinets, the hangman's noose, the tub of yarny rag dolls, the NO SPITTING sign. I touched the wooden drawer that held Thomas Browne's letter. I opened another drawer and took out my mother's shoe. I cradled it. I kissed it and returned it to the drawer. Everything seemed the same as before. I stood still. I closed my eyes. Perhaps if I stopped looking, it would come to me. It did not.

I left the high room. I was halfway down the tower stairs when I heard a voice. It seemed to come from the wall stones that circled me. It was a man's voice, and it spoke the familiar words with such authority that I knew it must be Thomas Browne: *The bad time is over.*

I stopped. I listened for more. I leaned my face against the pale green stones. But the voice was gone, returned to The Letter.

I descended to the apartment. I put on a jacket and went outside. Small, dry white flakes skipped across Airy Street. A brief flurry? Or the first snowfall of the year? Time would tell. This time I did not run. I did not hurry.

Along the way I began to feel so light it seemed I might fly with the flurries. I knew now what I had been looking for and had failed to find. It was, of course, the gloom. The gloom and the anger that had incarcerated me all my life behind walls no one could breach nor stringball fly over. The only home, the only life I had known. Now I understood that when Eloda had sent me to The Corner, she had set me free from my own prison.

At The Corner I did not cry out this time or throw myself down. I stood close by the brick front of 203 West Oak and I felt my mother there and I closed my eyes and I whispered to her: "The bad time is over, Mama. The past is done. I have a future now. I'm okay."

And then I walked home.

65

Months passed.

One day I spotted Danny Lapella in a hallway mob between classes. I thought: *Enough!* I grabbed him. I shook him. "Talk to me," I demanded. "Hit me. Do *something*." We stood like that while the mob surged around us. Then we both cracked up.

Years passed. Junior high. High school.

In ninth grade Danny and I went to the prom together. Double-dated with Reggie and her boyfriend-of-the-month.

In tenth grade we found out we were better at friendship than romance. In fact, we took it a step beyond ordinary friendship. We appointed ourselves honorary brother and sister.

Every August twenty-ninth the Jailbirds celebrated my birthday in my jailhouse apartment. And slept over.

I became captain of the field hockey team. Reggie starred in our high school play, *The Curious Savage*.

Tommy D and Arlene Holtz broke up. Not that the Jailbirds much cared. By then we had stopped watching *Bandstand*.

Somewhere along the line Reggie pronounced me fit to dress myself. I finally applied the Passion Pink lipstick she had bought for me at Woolworth's that summer.

Carl the cook did his time and moved on. No more pie-of-the-week. The new guy tried but it was never the same. On the day Carl left, I pleaded with him to do another crime, just enough to land him back in jail till I went off to college. He laughed, walked out the door and went straight.

One day in tenth grade Reggie held me back as we trotted out of the locker room for gym class. She squeezed my hand. She leaned in and whispered, "Thank you," and gave me a peck on the cheek before running onto the field. By the time gym class was over, I'd made the connection. This was Marvin Edward Baker's execution day. They said he was stoic, made no fuss. They said when the electric-chair switch was flipped, the lights in Rockview flickered. Some said it was the angel of Annamarie Pinto, a shudder in her wings.

I became as comfortable on Mill Street, in Mogins Dip,

as in my own neighborhood. Dinner with the Strongs became a weekly thing. My father even joined us a few times. We laughed endlessly over the day I "kidnapped" Andrew. Missy and I became great friends. Andrew became, and still is, the little brother I never had.

The rattle of a passing milk truck still got my attention, but less and less. And glass bottles were giving way to cardboard.

Most agreeably of all, I discovered Chester T. O'Reilly.

I discovered that he was more than a father and a warden. He was a person. With a history all his own and great stories to tell. He could even be pretty cool sometimes. I discovered that I was not the only one in the family who lost someone irreplaceable when the milk truck came.

I discovered that he was perfectly capable of running the prison himself. So I let him.

I discovered that even as I got older and stayed up later, he was always in the same easy chair in the living room before I went to bed. I discovered that when I said, "Night, Dad," and kissed him on the cheek, I made him the happiest person on earth.

I discovered that it was he, not my mother, who had named me Camille.

I discovered that we could talk to each other. Not bicker. Not argue. Talk. And laugh. Talk and laugh so much that our dinnertimes got longer and longer. I couldn't shut myself up. We never laughed louder than the day I went on and on about the agonies of trying to decide which boy to like. My father finally clamped his hands over his ears and said, "Where's the old silent treatment when I need it?"

I discovered that my father was a great actor. Years went by without my suspecting that he was waiting for the right moment to spring on me the biggest surprise of my life.

66

I WAS SEVENTEEN. ELEVENTH GRADE. JANUARY. WE WERE talking over dinner, as usual. My father was telling me about growing up in Trenton, New Jersey.

"I was a hellion," he said. "I was in the principal's office every other day. I was a teacher's and parent's nightmare." He painted his neighbor's dog. He gave himself a Mohawk when he was eight. We agreed that his misdeeds were all the funnier when you considered what he grew up to be.

Since the spirit of confession seemed to be upon us, I decided to fall in. I told him about the time I let the Jailbirds run loose in the exercise yard. The warden got a kick out of that.

And then I said, "And that same summer, one day I smoked a cigarette in front of Eloda. In the laundry room."

At first his face was a blank. I didn't think he'd heard me. He just stared. In time he put down his fork. He smiled at it. He smiled at me. He said, "I know."

I didn't believe it. "You do *not*," I countered. "You never said a word. She never told you." He just kept smiling. I peeped, "Did she?"

He nodded. "She did. She told me everything."

"But you didn't yell at me. You didn't throw me in the clink."

He reached across the table and took my hand. "I figured you were just trying to get her attention."

Wow. That went straight to the heart. I couldn't speak.

"Sometimes I wondered," he said, "if this day would ever come. How long has she been gone now?" A blink. A flinch. The realization that there were two *shes* in my life. "Eloda," he said.

I didn't have to think. "Over four years. Dad, what are you talking about?"

He pushed back from the table, as if to widen his view. I had the strangest feeling that he was now picturing Eloda at my shoulder. "She said, 'Don't tell Miss Cammie until she cops to the cigarette.'" He gave a chuckle, remembering. "Considering all she did for us, that was a condition I could live with."

"Well, great," I snipped. "I'm so happy you can live with it. Meanwhile I don't even know what we're talking about."

"Hey—" He threw up his hands. "I was just following orders."

"Dad."

"You have to promise me one thing."

"Anything. What? *What?*"

"You won't blame me for waiting so long to tell you? I was just—"

"Following orders. I *promise*. Just *tell* me already."

"I've been working on this for four years. Changing the order around. Practicing."

"*Dad!*"

So he told me.

67

"April twenty-ninth. Nineteen fifty-nine," he said.

I waited for more, but that was all. "Okay," I said. "So?"

"Remember that date."

"April twenty-ninth. Nineteen fifty-nine. Got it."

"Okay. Just hold it. We'll come back to it."

"Okay already."

"So . . . she started working as our trustee housekeeper in January of that year. Remember?"

I chuckled. "The hair. That name. How could I forget?"

"Right. So . . . let's skip ahead. Fire in the bathtub. Ring a bell?"

I gasped. "She told you that, too?"

He put on a look of casual snoot, like, *Of course—I know everything about you.* "So one day she comes to my office. She just walks in and she says two things, right out. She says, 'Miss Cammie set a fire in the bathtub.' And then she says, 'I want to be more than a housekeeper.'"

"What did she mean by that?" I said.

"Exactly what I asked her. Her answer was only three words. I'll never forget them: 'She needs me.'"

She needs me.

A chill went through me. Suddenly I was twelve again. Eloda's words were so real I could see them hover over the kitchen table between me and my father. His hand came through them, touching me. "What could I say? She was right. I was trying my best, but it wasn't enough. It's not just that you were a handful. All kids are. You were . . ." He paused, feeling for the words.

I gave them to him: "Never happy."

He nodded. "Never happy. She saw it, too. She said with the summer vacation coming up, you being home all the time, you'd be needing attention more than ever."

"Smart lady," I said.

"And then some. Yeah. Of course, I had already checked her out before making her trustee. But now . . . I double-checked everything."

Her prison record was clean. She was never in trouble. He asked the women inmates about her. They all said the same thing: she spent a lot of time in the Quiet Room.

I jumped up from my chair. "I heard that from Boo Boo." I clapped. "Dad—it worked!"

"Well, yeah . . ." He seemed suddenly shy. "Be nice to think so."

He went next door to city hall and reread her file. He talked to the patrolman who'd arrested her. From all these sources came the story of a wild child. A Two Mills terror. Smoking. Drinking. Out all hours. Fast crowd.

It all came down to one bad night by the tracks. Eloda was whooping it up with friends in the alley behind River Road. She flicked away a cigarette butt that was still burning. It landed in a heap of oily rags behind Doke's Transmission Repair. Within minutes the garage was blazing, and Eloda, stunned, her face in flame light, was telling a policeman: "I did it."

"You're kidding," I said.

"No," he said. "It's true. The patrolman put it right in his report: 'I did it.' That's when I knew I was onto something."

All I could say was "Wow." We shook our heads and shared a chuckle. Nobody (except Boo Boo) ever said "I did it" in Hancock County Prison. We lived with two hundred people who said "I didn't do it."

Not long after that, young, wild, hell-on-wheels Eloda was a guest of the county. One year. Involuntary arson.

And I remembered:

Number one law.

No more fires.

He went to see her older sister—Roxanne—on Swede Street. "Unpredictable" was the word the sister used.

Roxanne said, yes, Eloda could be wild and foolish, but not in a bad way. She could have gotten out of a lot of trouble just by saying, "I didn't do it." But she didn't seem to know how to lie. As for the garage she burned down, that finally scared her. It was the closest she'd come to actually hurting somebody.

My father told the sister about Eloda's idea to be more than a housekeeper. The sister wasn't surprised. She visited Eloda in prison every week (I never knew), but it was from Eloda's frequent letters that Roxanne learned of her incarcerated sister's concern for me. Which was nice, my father said—but why? Why Cammie?

The fire in the bathtub, Roxanne told him. That really spooked Eloda because it was a fire that had landed her in jail.

And mothers, she said. Neither of them had a mother. The Pupko girls had lost their father in World War II. Killed in action. Their mother died when they were teenagers. Colon cancer. That's when Eloda went off the rails. Never showed up for her high school graduation. Took off for parts unknown. When she came back to Two Mills, she was out of control.

And something Eloda wrote in a letter: *I am afraid for her. She reminds me of me.*

And I remembered: *Cammie . . . trust me. . . . I know you. . . .*

I told my father, "I got worse before I got better."

He nodded. "I know."

"I was a mess. It wasn't just the cigarette thing."

"I know."

"Or the bathtub fire."

"I know!"

We both burst out laughing, the way you do at bad times long past. We clasped hands over the table. We blew on memory's embers.

"My birthday party—oh God—"

"I went to the bathroom in the middle of the night. I thought I'd have to step over sleeping bodies. They were gone!"

"I knocked Reggie to the floor. My best friend!"

"I know. Her mother called me. I know about the shoplifting, too."

My heart sank. "I've always believed she didn't tell you."

"She didn't. The police chief did."

"Oh, Dad—how could you *stand* me? Dad, I trampled a little kid in a baseball game at the park. You should have heard what I said to other little kids. I *slugged* my friend Danny Lapella. I *buried* my baseball glove."

"I wondered where it went. And your bike?"

"Into the creek! Dad"—and suddenly I wasn't laughing anymore; I was sobbing—"Daddy, I was hell on wheels. I was a basket case."

He kissed my hand. He wiped the tears from my face. He smiled, "You were perfect."

What a curious thing to say. I blew my nose into a napkin. I sniffed, "What do you mean?"

"I've been thinking about it for four years," he said. "Maybe you were just what she needed. Maybe you were a package deal. Fixing you was her way of fixing herself."

"More than fixing, Dad," I said. "She saved me."

He nodded. "Amen."

He went to the fridge for the ice cream. He scooped out two dishes. Chocolate for me, butter pecan for him.

"Dad," I said, "why so long? Four years. Why didn't you tell me all this sooner?"

"As I said, following orders. 'Wait till she cops to the cigarette.'"

"Fine," I said. "But why? *Why* wait?"

He considered the question. "I think she wanted to put some distance between you and her and that summer."

Distance.

I thought of her moving silently about the apartment. No laughter. No chitchat. Cool. Cold. With those few precious exceptions.

"You know, don't you?" I said. "That's why I was puffing away in the laundry room. I wanted to provoke her. Show me some emotion. Holler at me. And she acted like she barely noticed. Or cared."

"A big bluff. She noticed. She cared."

"'Call me Cammie,' I used to tell her. I hated the *Miss*."

He took a spoonful. "Even I told her it was okay to show

her feelings more. But she wouldn't hear of it. She knew you were broken. She wanted to leave you better than when she found you. But not interfere. Not come between you and your mother. She did *not* want you to think of her as your mother."

Ha! I thought. *You sure botched that, Eloda.*

"So, not too chummy," I said.

"Not too chummy," he said.

An unwelcome question came creeping. I thought I knew the answer, but I needed to hear someone else say it out loud. "So . . . Dad . . . you said package deal. Fix us both up. At the end of it all, is that what I was? A way to help her fix herself? A project?"

His smile was small and private. "See if you still think that way when I tell you the last part."

"There's more?"

"Hey, I told you I've been rehearsing. Save the best part till last. That's what a good story-writer does, right?"

"Yeah, Dad," I said. "The climax."

"Only one problem," he said.

"What's that?"

"You're not going to believe it."

68

HE PUT HIS SPOON DOWN. HE LEANED FORWARD. HE looked me in the eyes. "Okay," he said. "Remember, I told you she came to my office?"

"Yes, Dad," I told him. "It was only ten minutes ago. She said she wanted to be more than a housekeeper. You asked why. She said, 'She needs me.'"

He nodded. "Very good. One more question. The date I asked you to remember?"

"April twenty-ninth," I said. "Nineteen fifty-nine." For a silly moment I felt all proud, like a first grader.

"Very good. A-plus."

"Thank you," I said, playing along. "And someday are you going to tell me why I'm memorizing this date?"

"Because . . . ," he said, clearly savoring the last taste

of this information he'd waited over four years to release. "That's when her time was up."

In my memory the following silence lasts for hours. Of course it was really only seconds. But packed into that time were my frantic efforts to make sense of what my father had just said. This was information that needed fitting into my world, but there was no place for it. So I rejected it. And asked a dumb question: "What time?"

"Jail time," he said. "Time served. She was free. That's the part I didn't tell you before. When she came to my office in April and said she wanted to be more than a housekeeper, she was due to get out in a couple of weeks."

"Dad—no." He *had* to be wrong. "She was here all summer." I rapped the tabletop. "*Here*. I saw her go back to her cell each day. After she did our dinner dishes."

He nodded. Agreeable. Encouraging. Letting me work it out.

"I woke up that morning—that *September* morning—and she was gone. I asked you where she was. You said 'released.' You said 'as in time served.'"

Nod.

"And now you're saying she didn't *have* to be here that summer? Because way back in April she could have gone home? Free as a bird?"

Nod.

"You're saying an inmate asked to stay in jail four months *longer* than her *sentence*?"

Nod.

"Well, you're right," I said. "I don't believe it."

He gave a sniffy laugh of self-congratulation. Then all expression left his face, all trace of levity. He locked me in his eyes. He said in a voice that left no way out: "Believe it."

I had to get up. I had to move. Something massive was shifting beneath me. I went to the living room. Lapped the sofa. Came back.

"I never *knew*."

"You weren't supposed to."

"But people don't *do* that."

"This one did."

"Dad, she lived on Swede Street. Just blocks away. She could have walked home each night."

"That's what I told her," he said. "All she said was she wanted to stay. It seemed important to her to share that summer with you as totally as possible. To be under the same roof with you. Fixing you. Fixing herself."

I reached for another objection, for common sense, but nothing was there. My defenses were gone. I felt myself tilting. I grabbed the table sides to keep from falling. "So she stayed in jail . . ."

I was kneeling on my chair.

". . . gave up her freedom . . ."

"Say it, Cammie."

". . . for *me*."

He closed his eyes. A great burden seemed to fall from him. He said: "Bingo."

For me.

Eloda Pupko, an ex-convict, an orange-haired angel, had stayed in jail so she could take care of me.

I sat, stunned. Silenced. Staggered by the wonder of it.

My ice cream was chocolate soup.

When I finally found my voice, I said to my father, "Since you know everything, I guess you know she stayed with me that last night. She scratched my back. Held my hand." I was losing it. "Kissed me."

The look on his face told me he hadn't known. "No," he said. "But I'm glad she did." And added: "At least one time she was not so distant, huh?"

I felt the spot where her lips had touched my cheek. "She never said goodbye."

"Well now . . . ," he said. He stood. "Maybe she did. Sort of." He left the kitchen. He returned in a minute with something in his hand. Red. Gold.

I snapped to attention. "Her diary! I gave it to her for her birthday. I assumed she threw it away."

"I know," he said. He placed it in front of me.

"But what are you doing with it?"

"She sent it to me. She said I could read it, but I never have. 'Give it to her when the time is right,' she said."

The red cover looked brand-new. I traced the gold letters—MY DIARY—with a fingertip. I stared at the tiny gold key. Curious as I was, I felt like an intruder. As I had at Boo Boo's funeral.

My father sensed my discomfort. "It's yours. She wanted you to read it. Keep it."

I tried the cover. It wasn't locked. With trembling fingers I turned to the first page.

ELODA

1959

June 24

Miss Cammie O'Reilly gave me this Diary for my birthday last week. I never had a diary. I do not know what to write in it. But she wants me to.

June 25

I braid Miss O'Reilly's hair each morning. She is a tomboy. Her hair is so short I can not even make one full knot.

June 27

I still cringe when I think of her making the fire in the bathtub. That's when I went to her father and told him I wanted to stay. She has no mother. I have no mother. Her father does his best but he can not be up there all the time.

She needs somebody. I think of myself and what I have done. How can somebody like me be that somebody? But I want to.

June 28

I found cigarette butts in her room. She wants me to think she smokes. She wants my attention. I did not understand that at first, so now I must be careful. I remind myself that my job is not to make her like me but to help her be strong and not so sad and angry all the time. I wish somebody could tell me how. I let her think I did not tell her father about the cigarette butts.

June 29

My time was up on April 29th. I have been free for two months now. But except for my sister and the warden the world thinks I am an inmate. The other day after dinner when I came down from the apartment I almost went out the front door instead of back to my cell. I guess I am starting to believe in my freedom.

June 30

When my sister visited me today, I told her my time here will be over on September 7th. That will be the last day of Miss Cammie's summer vacation. I must finish my job by then. I told Roxanne to get everything packed. Be ready to go. She thinks I am crazy.

July 3

Miss Cammie's best friend Reggie went to *Bandstand* today. The living room was full of giggling girls. It is good to see her laugh.

July 4

I am missing the fireworks at the park. I could be there. I could be free. This is one of my hardest nights in the jail.

July 10

When Roxanne visited me today, she told me Mr. O'Reilly came to see her back in April. He could hardly believe I was serious that I wanted to stay in jail and help his daughter. She told him I am not perfect but I do not lie.

July 14

A little boy came to the apartment today. He is cute. I am glad they like each other. But I had to scold her. A child that young should not think jail is fun.

July 17

She touches my heart. This is what I did not want to happen. Or did I? She wants me to call her Cammie. Just that. But I must be careful. I can not allow her to become too attached to me. She does not know that at the end of the summer I must leave.

July 19

She never mentions her mother.

July 24

Up in the tower for hours what does she do? Does she cry? Does she say her mother's name? Often she is grouchy. I almost like her grouchy because the other way is worse. When she is nothing. When her eyes are empty. Her father told me they go to the cemetery, but she never goes to the place where the accident happened.

July 25

She talks about Boo Boo Dunbar a lot. She seems to like Boo Boo best of all the inmates.

July 26

Miss Cammie has been staying overnight with her friend Reggie this week. They are reading Reggie's fan mail. I am alone all day in the apartment. I think about her. She wants me to be like a mother to her. She tries to trick me into it. One day she pretended to cry so I would comfort her. She is such a bad actress. I said to myself do NOT laugh.

July 27

I think I was wrong about her eyes. I think they are not empty. I think they are looking. Searching. For her mother.

They search for her mother in me. I want to tell her she is looking in the wrong place.

July 28

I know why she wants me to braid her hair. It is her excuse to talk to me. I go as slow as I can. I am surprised how long I can make one knot last.

July 29

Miss Cammie's birthday is one month from today. She tells me she will have a party. She has invited the Jailbirds. That is what her friends call themselves. I will speak to Carl about a cake. I want to make her day special. People with picket signs outside today. They hate our most famous inmate Marvin Edward Baker. He murdered the Pinto girl.

August 1

Sometimes I sit here in my cell at night and I stare at the wall and ask myself why am I doing this? Is it because she has no mother, like me?

August 3

I wish her hair was as long as that girl in the tower in the story. I could make our talk time last for hours.

August 4

How do you look for somebody you never knew?

August 7

As I braided Miss Cammie's hair today—it is still too short to take a ribbon—she asked me about sputter something. It flies in the sky but it is not an airplane. It goes around the earth like the moon but much smaller. The Russians put it there. Boo Boo Dunbar told her about this.

August 9

How do you find somebody you cannot remember?

August 10

She was leaving this morning after the braiding. I was making her bed. Before she left, she called I am going out! I stood at her bed with her pillow in my hands and I cried. It was such a small moment. I am going out! It is something that happens in families. It is something that children call out to parents.

August 11

Miss Cammie stood up for me today! Her friend was smoking a cigarette and I told her to put it out and she said it's not your house and Miss Cammie said yes it is. I wanted to hug her. They got into a fight because her friend tried to get Marvin Edward Baker to sign his name on a picture.

August 13

Today was a terrible day. But it began so nice. Miss Cammie went to the ice cream shop for a banana split. I am sure she was happy. She did not know what happened until she came back. Boo Boo Dunbar hanged herself in the shower. The cellblock is in shock.

August 14

She keeps talking about somebody called Delancy. She says Delancy was going to marry Boo Boo. She says she must find him and tell him what happened to Boo Boo. I am afraid to tell her there is no Delancy.

August 15

For the birthday party I want to have one of those bags that hang from the ceiling and the kids are blindfolded and hit it with a stick and candy comes out. Will she be happy that day?

August 16

She was in the tower all day. I am torn in half. I want to hold her in my lap and rock her to sleep. But I dare not get too close.

August 17

She went to Boo Boo's funeral in the city. She rode her bike. She came home in the rain all wet. I took off her wet clothes in the kitchen. I dried her off with dish towels. She was in a daze. I was thankful for the rain so I could take care of her.

August 18
She was in the tower all day.

August 20
I think I did a bad thing. She has been so sad and silent. I wanted to hear her talk again. I wanted to give her a little life. So I gave her coffee before I braided her hair this morning. It worked. She talked. She told me everything that Boo Boo told her. It was hard to listen to. I believe she must face life as it really is. That is the only way. Even so I could not bear to tell her everything so I just told her one thing. I told her there is no Delancy. She screamed at me and ran out of the house. I am afraid she hates me.

August 21
In the cellblock they are saying look how strong our yarn is to hang somebody so big. They do not mean this as a joke. They are just very proud of their rugs. I asked Mrs. Butterfield if she would get a birthday party decoration downtown for me. I said I will pay but she would not take my money.

August 22

Mrs. Butterfield gave me a wonderful decoration from Woolworth's. It is a banner that will stretch across the whole room. It says YOU'RE A TEENAGER! I am having so much fun doing this. I do not have to pretend. I do not have to bite my tongue. I am doing this for Cammie.

August 23

She spends her days in the tower or riding her bicycle. Her father is worried. I am worried. She sits for her braiding every morning but she does not speak. Her braid is two knots long now. I do not know how to tell her that by the time she gets to three knots I will be gone.

August 25

Her birthday is in four days. Everything is ready except for one thing. I cannot decide what to give her. I have been thinking of this for weeks. I want to give her something special but it can not be expensive and I can not go shopping for it on Main Street. Except for my sister Roxanne and the warden the whole world thinks I am an inmate. A real inmate.

August 27

I know what to give her!!! I told Roxanne to bring me one of her scarfs from home. A green one. She will not miss it. She has so many. I will get a box. And scissors from the kitchen drawer. And wrapping paper from her father. You lucky Diary. Your writer is so clever! I am not even going to tell you what it is.

August 28

Her birthday is tomorrow. Maybe it will come just in time. Maybe the Jailbirds will bring her back to life. She sits on the morning stool and she rides her bicycle and she climbs into her tower. She is a lost little girl. I am sad along with her but for another reason. I have not been able to help her. In my mind I keep seeing her thrown by her mother flying through the air, landing on the sidewalk on Oak Street.

August 29

I gave her the gift this morning. She looked surprised. She said thank you but did not open it. I put it on the coffee table. I worked all day getting her party ready. She is still in her fog. She walked under the YOU'RE A TEENAGER! sign and did not seem to notice it. As I was leaving for the day, the Jailbirds were running up the stairs.

August 30

I am confused. When I arrived this morning, I expected to see girls sleeping all over the place. There was no one. Even Miss Cammie was gone. But the hanging bag was smashed—candy pieces everywhere. When Miss Cammie came back later, she smoked a cigarette in front of me. I pretended not to care.

September 1

She is different. The fog is gone. Now there is a wildness in her eyes. She does not talk. I braid her hair and then she is gone for the day. The birthday gifts are still on the coffee table. They are not opened.

September 3

I am afraid for her. I have failed her.

September 4

A police officer brought her home today as I was having lunch. She was caught shoplifting at the Woolworth store. He said they will not press charges because of who her father is. Her father wants me to tell him everything but I just can not tell him this. She is worse than ever.

September 5

I know what she needs. She needs to go there. Talk to her mother. I was not a baby. She was. I have a memory. A connection. She does not. The cemetery is not enough.

On my last day I found her sleeping with her clothes on. The tower guard saw her in the yard at three o'clock in the morning. Her father carried her to her bed. When she woke up at noon, she picked a fight with me. She called me her maid. I thought she was going to hit me. She did not know our time would be over the next day. As she was screaming and crying, I told her to go to the place where it happened. To her mother. To her self. She was gone for a long time. When she returned, I took care of her. I stopped pretending. I put her to bed. I scratched her back. She liked it. She held my hand. She would not let go. I stayed all night. In the morning I moved the birthday gifts to her room. Then I left the apartment. I will not go back. I am gone. Gone from prison. Gone from her. Roxanne is driving the moving truck. We are two hundred miles from Two Mills. I already wish I was back in jail with her, but we must both move on. I pray we are ready. O Diary I will never see her again. Cammie. Cammie. No Miss. Just like you wanted.

CAMMIE

2017

SHE'S TWELVE. ELLIE, MY GRANDDAUGHTER. THIS IS THE moment I've been planning for fifty years. Since before I met her grandfather.

We stand on the Airy Street sidewalk, the ancient castle front looming before us. Her reaction is everything I've hoped for. Her eyes are wide, her mouth agape. She is staggered.

When she finds her voice, it is stumbling with wonder: "Ganny . . . I . . . I was afraid you made it all up. Like a bedtime story." Her hand fumbles for mine, squeezes. "Is that the Tower of Death?"

"That's it," I tell her.

"The Salami Room?"

"At the top. Behind the skinny windows."

She huddles into me. "Ganny." She might be crying. But it's over quickly and now she's pulling me. "C'mon!"

We hurry up the walk and through the great door, under the sign that says TWO MILLS AVIARY AND NATURE CENTER.

She races through Reception—it's a gift shop now— and up the stairs and into the old apartment. The massive bar-lock door is gone.

I huff up the stairs after her. The living room is now an office. A young man sits at a computer, ignoring us. Ellie races from room to room, calling, "What was this?"

Only the bathroom is still a bathroom. My voice certifies the past: *Yes, they existed.* "Kitchen! . . . Great-grandpa's room! . . . My room!"

And now she's bounding up the tower stairway. She yells back down: "It's empty! The hangman's noose is gone!"

I hear her bouncing about, squeaking, pretending to pour boiling tar over invading enemies.

"Ganny—I think I can see Camarillo!"

"Could be," I call. "If you're looking west."

We've come from California. I haven't been back here in half a century. The memories are flooding.

She flies back to me, red-faced and breathless. Until ten minutes ago it never occurred to me that she might not have believed every word I've said all these years.

Her eyes get wider, if that's possible. They sweep the

room. It's hit her. She knows exactly where she is. She points: "The big sign—the banner—was it there?"

"YOU'RE A TEENAGER!"

She's hopping in front of me. "And Ganny! Ganny! *Puh-leeeze*"—her hands are steepled in prayer—"tell me you *really* did it. You really *did* kick the Jailbirds out of your birthday party."

I nod. "Every one of them."

Her yip of joy draws a disapproving head turn from the young man at the computer. Of all my jailhouse stories, this has always been her favorite. She climbs onto a folding chair, which instantly becomes a stage. She jabs her finger at the door. She scowls. She growls. "Out! You! You! You! Out! All of you! Out!"

We crack up. My granddaughter is funny and popular and sweet-tempered. Every day I'm thankful she is not like I was.

She's leading the way back downstairs when she suddenly stops, turns and blurts: "Pig snouts!"

She's been hearing about scrapple all her life.

"It's a breakfast thing," I remind her. "Tomorrow morning."

Then we'll fly back to Camarillo. She's got a Little League game the next day. She plays for the Blue Sox. Shortstop.

She tugs at the green ribbon tied around my wrist. "And then you'll tell me about this."

I've never told her about Eloda, at least not directly, not by name. I wanted her to be as old as I was at the time. She knows I've been saving something. She knows it has to do with the faded green ribbon I've worn since we left for the airport.

I nod. "All will be revealed."

She claps—"Yay!"—and bounds down the stairs.

I lead her through the women's cellblock, which is now a show-and-tell theater for school groups, and on to the larger men's cellblock. Ellie flits from one feature to another—*Mimic a Bird Whistle, Pennsylvania Songbirds*, three rescued, flightless eagles—but I am somewhere, somewhen else . . . more than sixty years ago and the guard is unlocking the door and I am racing down the cellblock to tell my father of my momentous discovery that my mother might still be alive as an angel in a place called Heaven . . . and I don't understand why my elation has made my father so sad and makes him utter the devastating words that don't at all mean what they say: "Sure, Cammie." I am nine and many more years will pass and he will be gone before I find countering words of my own: *Oh yes, Daddy, there are angels, and I do believe, because it was an angel who stayed with me that summer, an angel who saved my life a second time.*

My granddaughter comes at me whistling, exactly like a meadowlark, she claims, and runs off. *Ellie.* And again I am so happy that my daughter, Anne, gave me naming rights to her only child.

When Ellie returns, she is wide-eyed and bursting and pulling my arm. "Ganny—you gotta come! You *gotta!*"

You gotta

Her words fall into my heart.

You gotta

You must

Thomas Browne's final words. The unfinished sentence. The mysterious, tantalizing incompletion.

I am barely aware of Ellie dragging me through a warren of exhibits and out of the old cellblock, and now I hear the noise. Voices. Children. Happy.

We turn a corner and the noise is louder. Another corner and . . . butterflies! Butterflies fluttering and little kids squealing as butterflies land on arms and heads and fingers.

"It's the Butterfly House!" Ellie announces triumphantly.

"It's the old Quiet Room," I say.

She boggles. "Where you sat with Boo Boo!"

I nod. It's getting hard to speak. The bench we sat on, it's still here, bolted to the concrete floor. The sky a second ceiling beyond the glass. Water still falls from a wheelbarrow. I smile at the shrieking kids. It's anything *but* a Quiet Room now.

Some kids are quick learners. They stand still as statues

and the butterflies come. Others run, chase. *Stop!* I want to tell them. *Be still. They'll come to you.*

I am struck by the exuberance and wonder in this happy room. The butterflies, the children—everything is so . . . *here*. There is no five minutes ago. No yesterday. No tomorrow. Only, gloriously, *now*, and I see at last that I have wondered too long.

You must

Now

You must

I am doing as you say, Thomas Browne. I am leaving the memories to you, leaving them to you and leaping joyfully into the end of your sentence, which was never as empty as it seemed. For I know now what you were about to say: *Mind the butterflies.* That was it, wasn't it, Thomas Browne? *Be still and mind the butterflies.*

Ellie is smiling at me, and I'm aware that there is something extra in the smile, and her eyes are shifting from my face . . . ah . . . a butterfly, a big one, half the span of my hand, has landed on my shoulder. I crane my neck to see. Its color is the prettiest blue, with black trim and yellow dots.

"Ganny—" she whispers.

I hush her: "Shh."

Time spins a Quiet Room around us: me, the butterfly, Ellie's wonder-struck face.

Another blue beauty appears, a copy of the one on my

340

shoulder. It flutters above us. Ellie, focused on me, doesn't see it. I shift my eyes. "Look . . ."

She looks. She sees. "Oh, Ganny—"

"Shh. Be still."

She can't help herself. "Please . . . please . . . ," she squeaks. She moves her shoulder, as if to prepare, to invite.

"Be still . . . still . . . ," I whisper. "It will come to you."

And it does.

THANK YOU

Ellen Adams entered my life as a reader. She became my friend. And then my inspiration. Like the narrator of this story, Ellen Adams did time in a prison: she was a real warden's daughter. I'm afraid you won't recognize much of your life in these pages, Ellen, but the simple fact is this: Without you, there would be no Cammie O'Reilly, no story. Soon we will meet again in Norristown and celebrate our book over zeps (hot peppers for me).

Others have earned heartfelt thank-yous as well: Rinky Batson, Becky Gilbert, Bob Hopple, Jeff James, Katie James, Leah James, Dottie Lieb, Kaye Lindauer, Pete Pennock, Glenn Ritter, Dave Wetzel; my wonderful literary agent, Bill Reiss; my copy editors, Karen Sherman, Marianne Cohen, and Artie Bennett; my story-whisperers, Nancy Hinkel and Nancy Siscoe; and my wife, first reader, and first friend, Eileen.

A MODERN CLASSIC FROM
NEWBERY MEDALIST
JERRY SPINELLI

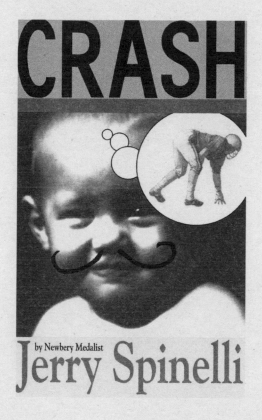

CRASH

by Newbery Medalist
Jerry Spinelli

★ "Readers will devour this humorous glimpse of what
jocks are made of." —*School Library Journal*, Starred

1
MY NAME

My real name is John. John Coogan. But everybody calls me Crash, even my parents.

It started way back when I got my first football helmet for Christmas. I don't really remember this happening, but they say that when my uncle Herm's family came over to see our presents, as they were coming through the front door I got down into a four-point stance, growled, "Hut! Hut! Hut!" and charged ahead with my brand-new helmet. Seems I knocked my cousin Bridget clear back out the doorway and onto her butt into a foot of snow. They say she bawled bloody murder and refused to come into the house, so Uncle Herm finally had to drag his whole family away before they even had a chance to take their coats off.

Like I said, personally I don't remember the whole thing, but looking back at what I do remember about myself, I'd have to say the story is probably true. As far as I can tell, I've always been crashing—into people, into things, you name it, with or without a helmet.

Actually, I lied a minute ago. Not everybody calls me

Crash. There's one person who doesn't. It's just one of a million things that have bugged me for years about this kid.

I can still remember the first time I saw him. The summer before first grade, seven years ago.

THEN

It was a sunny summer day. I was in the front yard digging a hole with my little red shovel. I heard something like whistling. I looked up. It *was* whistling. It was coming from a funny-looking dorky little runt walking up the sidewalk. Only he wasn't just walking regular. He was walking like he owned the place, both hands in his pockets, sort of swaying lah-dee-dah with each step. *Strollllll*-ing. Strolling and gawking at the houses and whistling a happy little dorky tune like some Sneezy or Snoozy or whatever their names are.

And he wore a button, a big one. It covered about half his chest. Which wasn't that hard since his chest was so scrawny.

So here he comes strolling, whistling, gawking, buttoning, dorking up the sidewalk, onto *my* sidewalk, *my* property, and all of a sudden I knew what I had to do, like there was a big announcement coming down from the sky: *Don't let him pass.*

So I jump up from my hole and plant myself right in front of the kid. And what's he do? He gives me this big grin and says, "Good morning. I'm your new neighbor. My name is Penn Webb. What's yours?" And he sticks his hand out to shake.

I ignored his question and his hand. "Penn?" I said. "What kind of name is that?"

"I was named after the Penn Relays," he said.

"Huh?" I said.

"It's a famous track meet. When I was born, my parents let my great-grandfather name me, and that's the name he picked. He won a race at the Penn Relays in the year 1919. Thirty thousand people cheered him on. He lives in North Dakota. I lived in North Dakota too until yesterday. Then I moved here to Pennsylvania with my mother and father. My mother had me when she was forty years old. I was a late baby."

You're gonna be a flat-nosed baby if you don't shut up, I'm thinking. "What does your button say?" I asked him.

He stuck out his scrawny chest. "It says, 'Hi, I'm a Flickertail.' "

"What's a flickertail?"

"A flickertail is a squirrel. There are lots of them in North Dakota. That's why it's called the Flickertail State. What is Pennsylvania called?"

"The Poop State."

He didn't crack a smile, didn't even know it was a joke. He got all frowny and thought about it and nodded and said, "Oh." Then his motormouth took off again. "North Dakota is real flat. Where we lived, anyway. And there's prairies. My dad says when the wind blows over the prairie, it looks wavy, like the ocean. I never saw a real ocean yet, but my dad says we're going to see the Atlantic Ocean soon. My dad's an artist. He makes birds out of glass and ceramics and wood and metal. He can make any kind of bird you can name, but he's the best in the world at prairie chickens."

I cut him off. "My father is starting a new business. He works seventy hours a week. Sometimes more."

"My mother works at home, like my father. She makes greeting cards and buttons like this."

"My mother works *and* goes to school. Both."

"I like dogs, but I *love* turtles. Would you like to see my turtle?"

"No. I have a grandfather named Scooter. He was a cook in the U.S. Navy."

"I'm an only child."

"I'm starting first grade this year."

"Me too," he said, and for the second time he asked me my name.

"Mergatroid," I said.

He didn't even blink. He just stuck out his hand and said, "Nice to meet you, Mergatroid."

Instead of my hand, I stuck out my shovel. He shook it. He laughed. He thought it was the funniest thing since Bugs Bunny.

For some reason, that laughing was the last straw. I plucked the silly button off his shirt, dumped it in the hole I was digging, and covered it over with dirt. I stomped and flattened the dirt with my foot.

The kid froze in midlaugh. His eyes took up his whole face. Then he turned and walked down the block. He wasn't whistling now.

I figured that was the last time I'd ever see that hambone.

2

The next day I was out digging again. This time I brought my dump truck along. I shoveled dirt into the dump truck; then I drove the truck over to the flower bed and dumped dirt onto a purple pansy until I buried it.

In the meantime my little sister Abby was picking worms out of my shovelfuls of dirt. She was having worm races. It surprised me to see a girl not afraid to pick up worms. But she was only four then, so I figured she was too young to know better. I figured in a little while she would become a regular girl and scream if she ever touched anything slimy or crawly.

Anyway, as I was busy burying pansies I kept looking down the street. Maybe it was more than looking. Maybe I was hoping to see the new kid, Penn Webb, hoping to do something else to him. But I wasn't seeing him, so after I buried the last pansy I hopped onto my bicycle and headed down the sidewalk.

I had no idea where he lived. I wasn't supposed to cross streets at that age, but I did. Pretty soon the houses and the yards were smaller. I made a U-turn. I was heading back when I heard his voice: "Mergatroid!"

He was running toward me. He wore a new button. He seemed all happy to see me, which made no sense.

"My name's not Mergatroid," I told him.

He gawked at me. "No?"

"No. It's Humphrey."

He grinned. "Ah, you were tricking me, huh?"

"Yeah," I said, "I'm a real tricker. But I'm not tricking you now. My name really is Humphrey."

He nodded and snapped his hand out. "Okay, nice to meet you, Humphrey. I'm still Penn Webb."

I stuck out my hand, but when he went to shake it, I snatched it away. I poked his forehead with my finger. "Ha-ha, tricked ya again."

He laughed. "Want to see my turtle?"

"No," I said. I pointed at the new button. I could tell it only had one word. "What's it say?"

"Peace," he said.

"Peace?" I snickered. "What kind of junk is that to say on a button?"

I pretended to reach for the button. His hand shot up to cover it. "Hah!" I laughed. "Tricked ya." His hand went away. He stepped closer to me. Crazy as it sounds, I got the feeling that he was inviting me to snatch this second button if I wanted.

So I did. I plucked it off his shirt. But there was no hole this time to dump it in. I thought of pinning it on myself, but what did I want with a button that said PEACE? So I gave it back to him.

"Where's your house?" I said.

He pointed right behind him. "There."

I couldn't believe it. "Who're you tricking?" I said. "That's no house. That's a garage."

He looked at the place, looked at me. "No, I'm not tricking you. We live there. We moved in two days ago. Honest."

I still couldn't believe it. It was no bigger than a garage. In fact, I found out since then that it really was a garage once, until somebody changed it into the world's dinkiest house.

An old man came out of the place. He waved at us, called, "Hello, boys," and went around back.

"Your grandfather lives with you?" I said.

The kid giggled. "That's my father."

"Your father? That guy has white hair."

"Sure. He's fifty-one years old. He's five years older than my mother. I was a late baby."

"I know, I know."

"I was a happy little surprise, too."

"Huh?"

"I was. My mother and father thought they could never have any babies. And then all of a sudden, *poof!*"—he threw his hands in the air—"I came along. They called me their happy little surprise."

I was ready to give him a two-finger surprise up his nose if he didn't cut out all this baby doodle.

Seeing the white-haired old guy, father or whatever, made me remember something from the day before. "Who did you say you got your name from?"

"My great-grandfather. He named me after the Penn Relays. Not many children have a great-grandfather. My dad says I'm really lucky. Want to see my turtle now?"

"No," I said. "I'm lucky, too."

"Really? Do you have a great-grandfather?"

"No . . . I have a great-*great*-grandfather."

His eyes rolled, his head wobbled. "Wow! You *are* lucky!"

"He's a hundred and fifteen years old."

His head almost wobbled off. "Yikes!" He staggered backward across his front yard, which was the size of a bathroom mat, and flopped onto his back. "One hundred and *fifteen!*"

I could tell this moron anything. "Okay," I said, "I'll see the turtle now."

He jumped up and ran into the house. He came back with a turtle. The shell was yellow and brown.

"It's a box turtle," he said. He turned it over. "See, here's his name." THOMAS was carved into the bottom shell. "Want to hold him?"

He handed me the turtle, and I took off on my bike. "Hey!" he yelled. I steered with one hand and pedaled like a demon up the sidewalk. Then I quick-stopped, put the turtle on its back in the middle of the sidewalk, and called, "Ha-ha, tricked ya!" I took off. I stopped again as he was picking up the turtle. "My name's not Humphrey, either!" I rode on.

By the time I got home, a question was really bugging me. I felt silly asking my four-year-old sister, but there was no one else around.

She was collecting those bugs that roll themselves up into little gray balls. She had them all lined up. She was being real quiet so the bugs would think it was okay to open up. As soon as one of them did, she touched it with the tip of her finger and it balled right up again and sent her into giggles.

"Do we have a great-grandfather?" I said.

She went, *"Shhh!"* and gave me a dirty look. She whispered, "I don't know. Ask Mommy."

Well, it turned out that we didn't have one, but I didn't learn it from my mother. I was staying out of her way for a while. Because when she came outside that day you could hear her all over town: *"Where are my PANSIES?"*

3

Next time I heard him he was calling, "Hey, John! Hey, John!"

He was running up the street. I was busy peeling bark off a tree in the yard.

I glared at him. "Who says my name's John?"

He came up to me, huffing, button going in and out. "Your sister. She said your nickname is Crash, but your real name is John Patrick Coogan."

I didn't know whether to be mad at him or her. "What were you doing talking to her?"

"Yesterday. I was looking for you. I saw her out front here. She didn't know where you were."

"I was out on business," I said. He never seemed to turn off the goofy grin. It was starting to bug me more than the button. "You want to know my name," I told him, "you check with me."

"Okay," he said, still grinning. "Can I call you Crash?"

Any other time, to any other person, I would have said yes. But even that felt like too much to give him, so I said, "No."

He blinked. "No?"

"That's what I said."

He shrugged. "So what can I call you?"

"Call me horsemeat."

He blinked some more. I was almost starting to enjoy this kid, like I was the cat and he was my mouse. He started to say something. I poked him in the chest. "You call me that and I'll cut your hair off." I held up the kitchen knife that I was peeling the tree with. I had him so bamboozled he didn't know which way was up. I was practically choking trying not to laugh.

"So," I said, "why were you looking for me?"

His old beaming face came back. "I wanted to ask you if you would like to come to dinner at my house."

The only word I could think of was "Why?"

"Because you're my first friend in Pennsylvania. We do that all the time in North Dakota, have our friends over for dinner. Don't you do that here?"

"We do what we want," I said. I was stalling for time. The last thing I needed was to have dinner with this family of hambones. And I didn't like him calling me friend. On the other hand, I was kind of curious to get an inside look at the boss dorks and the garage that thought it was a house. But if I did go, I had to make him pay for it.

"Maybe I'll come," I said, "but only if you beat me to the draw."

"Draw?" he said.

"Yeah. Water pistols. Wait here."

I ran to my room. I got two water guns, loaded them at the

bathroom sink, and brought them out. I gave him one. "Here's yours. Stick it in your pocket like this. We stand five steps apart. At the count of three, draw and fire. Got it?"

He didn't say anything for a long time. The grin was gone. He just stared at the green plastic gun in his hand. He wasn't even holding it right. He was biting his lip. Finally he looked up at me. "I can't."

I gawked at him. "You *can't?*"

He shook his head.

"Why not?"

He looked me dead in the eye. "I'm a Quaker."

DON'T MISS
STARGIRL,
ABOUT ANOTHER GIRL
WHO DEFIES EXPECTATIONS

JERRY SPINELLI

A New York Times Bestseller

★ "A magical and heartbreaking tale."
—*Kirkus Reviews*, Starred

IN HOKEY POKEY GROWN-UPS ARE NOWHERE TO BE FOUND....

★ "Masterful." —*Kirkus Reviews*, Starred

JERRY SPINELLI
PENS HIS AUTOBIOGRAPHY IN

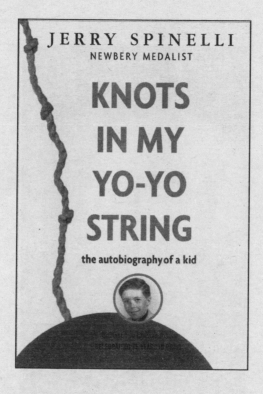

JERRY SPINELLI
NEWBERY MEDALIST

KNOTS
IN MY
YO-YO
STRING

the autobiography of a kid

"A master of those embarrassing, gloppy, painful, and suddenly wonderful things that happen on the razor's edge between childhood and full-fledged adolescence."

—*The Washington Post*

THE STORY OF A BOY NAMED
STOPTHIEF

"Jerry Spinelli has fashioned a novel of beauty out of
the ugliness of the Holocaust." —BookPage